Hanging On

SISTERS IN A SMALL TOWN

HOLLY KERR

THREE BIRDS PRESS

Hanging On

For my aunts—
Donna, Della, Joan, Jane, Lorna, and Lois
And for my lady cousins who meet up at Cheryl's.
Thanks for thinking I'm cool enough to sit at the big kids' table!

Chapter One

As Maggie unclenched her hand and the fistful of dirt sprinkled onto the casket, she pictured herself taking a running leap into the grave, black dress flying up like bat wings, tired granny panties visible to all.

The image caused a giggle to bubble up her throat, bypassing the lump that for the last twenty-four hours, had made eating difficult. She pushed it down.

One should never laugh at one's husband's funeral.

But what if she did it? Jump right into the grave, landing on the coffin as it lay snug in its new home? If she jumped on it, would she break through the wood and the pillowed satin lining, landing right on the body? Would Mike appreciate that? One last show of affection?

What if she jumped *over* the grave and just kept running?

Her shoulders hunched as the laugh escaped.

"Maggie?" Brenna whispered.

Maggie glanced down at their clasped hands. Only the tips of her sister's pink-painted nails were visible as Brenna squeezed tighter. She remembered the time Brenna had helped Maggie's six-year-old daughter, Clare, paint Mike's nails a vivid blue, both fingers, and toes. He'd worn the polish proudly for over six weeks; to work, to baseball, to play darts with his friends, accepting the ridicule from his friends with good grace.

Maggie mashed her lips and swallowed the next outburst.

Cat glanced over. She was the youngest of Maggie's four sisters. The tears streaking down Cat's face seemed to melt her tough persona and Maggie looked away before she could drown in the pity of her sister's gaze.

Everyone looked at her like that—with pity, with sympathy, with regret. Poor Maggie, with Mike gone. How would she manage now?

At least she wouldn't have to de-polish her husband's toenails, stained blue because he didn't know what to use to take it off.

Another laugh/sob bubbled up and Maggie covered it with a cough. Her five daughters, with their tear-streaked faces and mascara smudges, stood huddled together, red hair flaming in the sunlight. They were flanked by their Aunt Cat on one side and Aunt Kayleigh on the other, protected and supported, the way they'd been their entire lives.

There was a lot of estrogen standing at the grave site.

Mike had handled the giggles, requests for fancy ponytails, and lack of bathroom space like a champ. He'd loved his daughters with all of his big, bleeding heart, even as he hoped and prayed for a son.

"Would you just give me a penis?" he had jokingly complained after their third daughter, Kady, was born. "Just one?"

They'd tried for a boy two more times, with two more girls as a result. Sometimes the excessive estrogen even got to Maggie.

"You okay?" Cat rubbed Maggie's shoulders, and Maggie choked on another swell of laughter.

"He always smelled of mushrooms." Tears streamed down her face, but she was smiling, thinking of the bottles of fancy body washes and shampoos still cluttering the shower in Mike's never-ending attempts to conquer the faint aroma of dirt and manure that clung to him, a side effect from his job at the mushroom farm.

"Mushrooms don't smell," Brenna whispered, glancing over her shoulder to where Reverend MacLeod was standing with the last of the mourners. Maggie covered her mouth with her hand. The townsfolk would think that she was as loony as her mother if she couldn't control herself.

"They do. I can't describe it—he said they smelled like cheese," Maggie said from under her hand, biting her thumb in an attempt to gain control.

"He smelled like dirt," Clare interjected. "But it was okay, Momma."

"It was more of a faint almond smell," Evie added. She was the peacemaker in the family, the one daughter who had never been on the outs with the others. Maggie could never admit to having a favourite, but everyone who knew her realized Evie was special. "But not bad."

"No, he smelled like bad fish. That's what bad mushrooms smell like," eldest daughter Addison argued.

"When they get all slimy in the fridge." That was it. Maggie couldn't stop it, didn't know what was so funny, but the giggle burst out, causing her girls and her sisters to look at her with horror. Their expressions, Kayleigh's mouth open with astonishment, Brenna's eyes widening with dismay, only made it worse.

The giggle became a hiss, then a chuckle; the chuckle morphed into a laugh, a real, deep belly laugh, the kind that made Maggie's cheeks hurt and wish for a washroom.

If she didn't laugh, she was going to cry, and then she wouldn't be able to stop. Maggie pulled her hand out of Brenna's grip and covered her face. She couldn't do this in front of the girls. They had just buried their father and they couldn't handle their mother breaking down in front of them too.

"I hate mushrooms, but Mike would always bring them home so we had so many." The words hiccoughed out, Maggie's shoulders shaking with the effort to stop laughing.

"How can you hate mushrooms?" Cat wondered. "They're so good with garlic and butter."

"I like when you cook them with wine and make that mushroom sauce for pasta," Brenna said.

"Or if you dip them in that ranch stuff you make," Kayleigh added.

"Is anyone else hungry?" Cat asked, a hint of a smile creasing her face.

Maggie closed her eyes, breathing in and out. She'd get through this with her sisters, this horrible, gut-wrenching pain that threatened to wipe her out like a car taking out a squirrel darting across the road.

"Why are we talking about mushrooms?" Clare asked.

The group broke into laughter, leaving little Clare staring at them with confusion.

Three weeks later, Maggie finally gave in to Brenna's suggestion to start going through Mike's papers. She kept trying to ignore the task, but Brenna, her beautiful, brilliant, and now slightly bullying younger sister, had insisted they do it ASAP in case there were legal documents that needed to be dealt with. In the two years since Brenna had moved back home to Forest Hills, Maggie had realized it was better not to argue with her sister about anything that had to do with business, financial or legal matters. She'd soon discovered Bee knew what she was talking about.

Maggie took an afternoon, her shift at FoodMart ending with enough time to go through the boxes in Mike's closet. Brenna sat gingerly on her bed with her, an ancient shoebox between them.

"These are great." Brenna sifted through the homemade Father's Day cards she'd pulled out of the box. Maggie refused to look at the colourful paper, the years of Father's Day celebrations blending together in a merge of presents and Mike's favourite cake, games of catch, beer, and family gathered for barbeques.

What was she supposed to do with them? She couldn't throw them out, but it seemed silly to keep them. Maggie picked up last year's card from Clare, the white paper cut in the shape of a ball, with holes punched and red yarn threaded through and did her best to blink back the tears.

"What's this?" Brenna held up folded papers, yellowed with age. "It looks like a contract." Her eyes widened. Maggie knew what the papers said—offering Mike a one-year contract to play professional baseball. "I've never seen this."

Maggie closed her eyes. "San Diego Padres wanted to sign him," she said stiffly. "One of the farm teams, but still. Thought he had great potential. They really liked him."

"And he turned them down." It wasn't a question. The whole town knew the story of how Mike Monroe gave up his chance to play professional baseball for his family.

Maggie smiled ruefully, the long-forgotten guilt swelling up. "He really liked me."

Brenna tucked the contract back into the box. "He made the right decision."

"Did he?" This is why she hadn't wanted to go through Mike's things. It led to remembering both the good and bad stuff, and then because Brenna was here, having to talk about it. "The Padres sent this scout all the way here to see him play. He came to the house." Maggie choked on a laugh. "I remember answering the door. Addison was five months old and refusing to nurse. She was crying and my boobs were so big." She touched her chest, still recalling the sensation of breasts painfully swollen with milk. "Cat was there, chasing after me because Mom—Carly—was having one of her *spells* and wouldn't come out of her room. I'm not sure where you were. I had just turned eighteen."

Eighteen, with a new baby and the responsibility of her sisters heaped onto her. Kayleigh at sixteen had been a help, but Dory, Cat, and Brenna—Maggie had raised her younger sisters along with her own daughters. Their father had left when Maggie was thirteen, left his five children to fend for themselves because he was too selfish and too weak to deal with his wife's emotional issues.

Back when Maggie was growing up, Carly was considered crazy, but things were a little more politically correct these days. If it was today, Carly Skatt would have been diagnosed as bipolar.

It had been after Roger had left that Maggie had learned that Carly Skatt wasn't even her biological mother.

"Mike stayed with you. To help," Brenna recalled. "He was like a father to us."

"I told him to go," Maggie said, her voice breaking slightly. She steadied it, reached down deep to grab control. "I broke up with him twice, trying to get him to leave. He deserved his chance and only stayed because I had the baby. Because I had gotten pregnant."

"He loved you."

"He could have loved me and still played ball. It's what he always wanted to do, and he couldn't because of me."

"Maggie, that's not true. He made his decision and he accepted it."

"How do you know? You were too young to remember and then you were gone for all those years. You didn't even know him." Brenna's face fell, and Maggie instantly regretted her sharp words.

Maggie threw the cards back into the box, a rainbow of construction paper that made the meticulous Brenna shiver. Maggie was hanging on to control by fingertips that were slowly giving way. Each day was worse than the one before. Last week was dealing with the lawyers, the day before the insurance. Clare had refused to sleep in her own bed since Mike died. McKenna was becoming more and more withdrawn every day and Kady had thrown herself in with her friends, desperate for any type of distraction.

Kady was sixteen, and Maggie was afraid of what the distractions would lead to. If there was one thing she'd tried to drill into her girls, it was that, in certain situations, it was better *not* to be like mother, like daughter.

Mike would have known what to do.

But Mike was gone, and Maggie was on her own, save for her Brenna sitting beside her on the bed, sniffling slightly. It was easier for Maggie to focus on Brenna's sadness, rather than deal with her own.

"I'm sorry," she said. "I shouldn't have said that."

Brenna slowly rifling through the box of papers. "You're right," she said slowly, pulling out a yellow sticky note. "There's so much I didn't know about him. Like, I had no idea he made so many notes." She motioned to a pile of yellow sticky notes on the floor, most illegible.

Maggie smiled sadly. "He had a horrible memory. He'd forget his own name if he didn't write it down. He made notes about everything." She picked up one of the squares of yellow paper. "Look—Paula and Will; that's Adam's parents. He made a note the first time we met them, just before Adam proposed to Addison. He was so afraid he would forget their names and embarrass Addison." Maggie picked out another. "Thundercloud—that was the shade of blue that he painted one of the rooms at the house. He was the only one who wanted to use a dark colour and he argued with Cat..." Maggie swallowed the lump in her throat.

"And it turned out to be the best room in the place." Brenna smiled, her green eyes sparkling with tears. "What about this one—talk to mom, Fiona re: Maggie." Brenna wore a confused expression on her face, one that mirrored Maggie's own.

"I have no idea." Maggie took the scrap of paper from Brenna, stared at it. She didn't remember any conversation that had to do with her, Mike's mom, and family friend Fiona Todd. "He must have forgotten about it. I guess the notes didn't always work." She put the notes back in the box. "I think we're done here."

"I miss him," Brenna whispered, clutching the lid of the box. The unshed tears darkened Brenna's eyes into a muddy green. Mike at twenty had been more of a father to Brenna than her own had been. He had given up his dreams of playing professional baseball to stay in Forest Hills, taking on Maggie's four fatherless sisters as well as his own daughter. He'd done it without a word of complaint, never showing a hint of regret.

Had any of them ever thanked him?

Maggie pressed Brenna's hand. "He loved you. He was so proud of you. Even when you were gone, you were still one of his girls."

Brenna had choked back a sob. "He had enough of us. Your five girls; us five...well, maybe not Dory."

Maggie shook her head, still bitterly disappointed at how middle sister, Dory, hadn't bothered to come home for the funeral. She still hadn't heard from her. "Even Dory. Mike had enough love for all of you, but Dory just couldn't accept it."

"I thought she'd come back for the funeral." Brenna had always been close to Dory, able to forgive more than the rest of them. More than Maggie.

"Dory isn't ready to be our sister, part of this family. She never has been. Until that happens, maybe it's best she stay away." Her voice was cool and concise. Maggie had learned a lot about dealing with their sister—how easy it was for Dory to hurt them.

"You don't mean that," Brenna whispered.

Maggie shrugged and stood up. "I think we're good here."

It had been as if the mention of their sister had shaken Brenna enough to grab control of her emotions. She took a deep breath, reached for the card still in Maggie's hand to place it gently back in the box. "Cat was telling me she had a...moment...with Mom. The day of the funeral. She was in Mom's room."

"She's always had a connection to the room," Maggie said drily, calmer now that Brenna had put the lid back on the box. "I still don't get it how people sleep there."

Brenna stood up to put the box back where they found it in the closet. "She said the room got cold, and she could feel a presence. Same as always."

"You live with a ghost," Maggie pointed out. "What do you expect? Carly hid out in that room when she was alive and nothing changed when she died."

For years Maggie had refused to acknowledge the possibility of a ghost in the family home, mainly because she couldn't deal with Cat living with one. But Cat seemed to like the company if a paranormal spirit could be considered company.

Two years ago, when Brenna had come home, Maggie had finally experienced what her sisters had talked about—the ghost of Carly Skatt inhabiting the family home.

"I wonder..." Brenna began, "if Mom...What about Mike?"

Maggie narrowed her eyes. "What about him?"

"If Mom is still there, maybe Mike is too. Or can be. Maybe you could talk to him."

Had Brenna lost it? If logical, rational, *lawyer* Brenna was telling her to go talk to a ghost... "What are you talking about?"

"When we opened the B & B, I did some research. It was one thing for Mom to be there, but what if there were more?"

"More—ghosts? Are you nuts? Isn't one enough?"

"Actually, in this case, more would be better. I found out there used to be a little cemetery in the woods behind the house. And I heard stories about years ago, how people saw floating things in the woods around the house, and strange lights. In all of this town, the house is the only place any of this happened. Maybe it means something."

"It means you're as crazy as Carly was."

"I don't think so. We started telling people we have *ghosts*—not just one."

"Is that like a lawyer thing to do? Lying to people?"

"What if it's not a lie? How can we tell who or what is actually haunting the house?" Brenna's voice rose with her excitement. "We assume it's Mom, but what if there's more? What if Mike's there too? Or could be? Maybe there's something like a portal–?"

Maggie stared at Brenna, refusing to acknowledge the hope surging inside of her.

Later that night, Maggie let herself into the huge Victorian house. Earlier that day, she'd heard Cat complaining about the lack of guests. The couple who had booked a room for their honeymoon cancelled at the last minute. Maybe they had reconsidered sharing their wedding night with a ghostly observer since Bee & Cee's B & B catered to those who didn't mind a little paranormal in their overnight stay.

It wasn't Maggie's idea of romance either.

She lingered by the front door for long minutes, playing with Cat's dogs until she got enough nerve to head up the stairs. Then she went straight to the room that used to be Carly's, now the most reserved room in the inn.

Turned out quite a lot of people wanted to spend the night in a room that was supposedly haunted.

Cat had painted the room herself, a calming blue, several shades lighter than Mike's Thundercloud. It was no longer the musty, dusty pit of memories, but clean and fresh, with no evidence of the supernatural.

"What the hell am I even doing here," Maggie scoffed as she let herself into the room. She sat on the bed for some time, alone with her thoughts, the only sound the tapping of the lilac branch against the window. The smell was so gradual that Maggie didn't notice it until the goose bumps rose on her arms.

Lilac. Carly's favourite flower.

"So you *are* here," Maggie said aloud rubbing her arms against the chill. "I know it's you, not Mike." There was no answer, not that she thought there would be one. "What am I supposed to do here? Just talk? No offense, but I don't really want to talk to you."

The room grew colder, and as crazy as it seemed, Maggie was sure someone was sitting beside her on the bed. She fought the urge to run.

"What?" she demanded, refusing to back down. "You don't think you had enough chances? Didn't have enough time to talk to me when you were alive? Because you did. Lots of time. Lots of chances." She took a deep breath and tried to banish the bitterness out of her voice. She was here for Mike, not to fight with ghost Carly. "You can be offended if you want. I don't really care."

The room grew colder, the smell of lilacs stronger. "This is a little freaky," Maggie admitted. Maybe her sisters were used to sitting around with a ghost, but she sure wasn't.

"I want to talk to Mike." Maggie's voice sounded loud in the room. "Or—is he here? Mike?" Sudden tears pooled in her eyes. She blinked furiously. "Mike? Are you here? Please? I thought maybe... You lived here for a while. This was your home too."

Maggie pushed away the images of her and Mike living here with their baby, so young and unsure and overwhelmed, but happy. So happy.

"You looked after all of us, and you didn't have to," Maggie said. "We found the contract that scout brought you. Remember that? I was so mad at you. You should have signed it, played baseball like you always wanted to. You could have left." She paused, anger growing. "I don't know why you didn't. Why didn't you *leave* when you had the chance?" The sudden shout hung unanswered in the room. "It's my fault. You stayed for me, and I told you not to! If I hadn't gotten pregnant, you would have left, and you wouldn't have died. If you'd left, you'd still be alive."

She swiped at her cheeks. "I'm sorry."

And then she let herself cry, the first time since they told her Mike was dead.

Chapter Two

EIGHT MONTHS LATER

THE HOUSE LOOMED BEFORE Maggie as she pulled up into the newly paved parking pad. As the bed and breakfast had finally turned into the black, Brenna and Cat had spent the last few months sprucing up the outside gardens and yard of the house. A new sign by the road welcomed visitors to Bee and Cee's B & B.

There were no guests that night. For the last eight months, Cat had taken the opportunity of an empty house to insist Maggie and her girls join her and Brenna for a family dinner. In the beginning, Maggie knew her sisters had been worried about how she was coping with Mike's death and wanted to do what they could to help her, even if it only meant feeding the girls. Now, Maggie suspected Cat and Brenna both wanted Maggie to act as a buffer when they were forced into each other's company.

Age and maturity had solved many of Brenna and Cat's arguments, but it couldn't do everything. Her sisters still sometimes fought like the Cat and Brenna of their younger years and looked to Maggie to referee.

The late afternoon sun bathed the house in a special glow, almost as if the white paint was shimmering. As Clare tumbled out of the car, followed by fourteen-year-old McKenna, still with her nose in a book, Maggie pulled her cell phone out of her bag and snapped a picture of her family home. She still wasn't one for social media but had to admit Instagram was the best way to keep in touch with her daughter Evie while she was at school in Toronto.

Maggie posted the picture to Evie with the caption *Missing You.* Evie was coming home for good on Wednesday, and Maggie was counting the hours until she had her girl home. It had been a long four years with only visits at Christmas and a short time in the summer. Evie had spent the breaks from school working in Toronto, but now she was coming home to stay.

No one knew how long Evie would be home, because Maggie hadn't asked. She didn't want to start thinking about her girl leaving again.

Evie must have been online because she liked and responded to Maggie's post right away. *Hugs! See you soon!! xoxo* She had a smile on her face as she headed into the house, following the sounds of Clare's chatter to the kitchen.

Her nine-year-old was a bundle of nonstop energy, so different from her four sisters. All of her girls had their own personalities and quirks, but none exhausted her as much as Clare.

Maybe she was getting old.

Clare was already talking Kayleigh's ear off as she sat at the scrubbed kitchen table, a glass of wine before her and Joss Ryan, at her side. Joss and Brenna had been an item since she came back into town, and he was a good man for her sister.

But from the expression on Joss' face, Maggie could tell he was still overwhelmed by Clare's exuberance.

Maggie bypassed the table to head to the counter, where Brenna was waiting with an expectant smile. "Heading upstairs?" Brenna asked.

"I thought— maybe." It had been eight months since Maggie had first gone to Carly's room. Now her visits had become a routine. At least once a week, more in the early days, Maggie stopped by the house to chat. Some people kept vigils at the grave site; Mike's grave was always kept neat with weekly flowers dropped off by the girls, but Maggie felt his presence more here, in the house.

At least she thought she did. *Something* was there with her, whether it was Mike, Carly, or some random ghost who felt like haunting the place, but it had given her a measure of peace in the months since his death.

Whoever it was felt like an old friend to Maggie by now. Each week she arrived equipped with stories about the girls, little anecdotes about things little Clare had said and done, how seventeen-year-old, boy-crazy Kady was driving her nuts. She would apologize for McKenna's grades slipping, made promises to help more with her homework, even though ninth-grade math confused Maggie as much as it did McKenna. She heaped praise on Evie, exclaiming how well she was doing at university and shared her worries about Addison's marriage.

Just talking out loud helped.

"I got you something to take up." Brenna turned to the refrigerator and pulled out a bottle, showing it to Maggie. "You told me once… I thought maybe…" she trailed off, eyes wide and apologetic.

Maggie mashed her lips together, blinking quickly so as to not let the sudden flood of memories force out the tears. Brenna held out a bottle of Asti Spumante that Mike had loved.

Every year for their anniversary, she and Mike used to drink a bottle of the sweet wine, trying to keep their giggles quiet as they cuddled on the couch, the girls banished to their rooms.

"It is your anniversary," Brenna finished in a whisper.

Maggie stared at the bottle. Twenty-seven years ago, she had married Mike Monroe. She'd been seventeen, her pregnancy was already showing, but Mike hadn't wanted to wait until after the baby was born. He'd married her, standing tall and proud at the front of the church as she had made her way down the aisle, alone.

But now, technically, she was unmarried. A widow.

It was a horrible word.

"Thank you," Maggie said stiffly. She forced a smile and after a moment, it became a real one. "You remembered he liked it."

"He loved the horrible stuff." Cat joined them at the counter. She took the chilled bottle out of Brenna's hand and made a face. "I remember one year he made me go buy a bottle for you."

"That was the first alcohol I ever drank," Brenna confessed. "You'd left some in the bottle once, and I drank it. It was warm and…" She grimaced. "Never again."

"You'll have to drink it yourself," Cat warned, getting her a champagne flute from the cupboard. The glasses were a recent addition, due to the influx of honeymooners who had begun to frequent the B & B. Brenna now kept a stock of champagne on hand, a much better quality than the Asti Spumante.

But Mike had loved the cheap stuff.

"I'll start with a glass," Maggie said as Brenna nudged the cork out of the bottle with her thumbs. The *pop* of the escaping gases drew the attention of those at the table.

"Ooh, anniversary wine," Clare called, looking up from the cards she was dealing to Kayleigh and Joss. "Is it...?" Her face suddenly fell. "It's..."

Kayleigh covered Clare's hand.

"I'm going upstairs for a few minutes," Maggie said to her girls after swallowing the lump in her throat. "Do either of you want to come with me?"

Clare glanced at McKenna, who sat folded on the window seat with her book, warmed from the sun as well the cat curled up beside her. McKenna met Maggie's gaze with a firm shake of her head. McKenna was her quiet and studious daughter, the one who worried her with her refusal to talk, to cry.

Maggie worried, but she wasn't sure what needed to be done for McKenna. Clare and Kady were more demanding with their needs.

"Clare?" Maggie asked, watching Brenna pour the wine, the bubbles quickly rising.

"Daddy's not there," Clare said, her attention drawn back to the cards. "So there's no point in me going up and talking to him."

"You don't know that," Brenna corrected.

"I do." Clare glanced at Maggie. "But it's okay. You go." She picked up her cards, ending the discussion.

"She doesn't know," Brenna whispered, handing the glass to Maggie.

Cat raised her eyebrows. "She might."

Maggie took a sip of the sweet wine, one that quickly became a mouthful. She soon drained the glass. "Maybe I'll have a top-up?"

Brenna refilled it without a word. Brenna and Cat always took the lead from Maggie when they talked about Mike; if Maggie seemed relaxed and open, they would talk about him. If she was closed-mouthed and sad, they would change the subject.

Unlike Kayleigh, who often forced Maggie to talk about things she didn't want to.

Maggie didn't know how she would have gotten through the last eight months without her sisters.

Maggie sat in the cold room, the smell of lilacs surrounding her and raised her refilled glass of sparkling wine. "Happy anniversary."

Why did it have to be so damned cold? The room was downright freezing every time Carly showed up. Or whoever was in the room with her. Maggie resisted the urge to pull the quilt off the bed. Cat accepted that Maggie needed the room for her personal séances, but she wouldn't appreciate having to remake the bed every time Maggie sat on it.

A few mouthfuls and Maggie finished the glass. Her appreciation for wine had definitely changed since Brenna had come home to Forest Hills three years ago. Most of the time she spent with her sisters now involved alcohol. It helped make the constant bickering between Cat and Brenna bearable, almost funny at times. And it definitely made it easier coming to talk to her dead husband with a full glass of wine in hand.

Maggie held up her empty glass. "I'm done."

It had been a long and painful eight months, but Maggie had gotten through it. Things had gotten easier with time, which was better to hear than some of the other adages her well-meaning friends and family peppered her with.

"He did what he came here to do, and it was his time to go."

"He'll always be in your heart."

"He's gone to a better place."

That one was complete bullshit to Maggie. There was no better place for Mike than here with her and the girls. She had bit her tongue so hard the last time Reverend MacLeod had said that to her and hadn't been back to church since.

There would never be a day when Maggie wouldn't miss her husband, but life had gone on. Unbelievable as it had seemed at first, she found she was able to exist in a world that Mike didn't inhabit.

She had to.

There were her girls and her sisters; people depended on Maggie. She couldn't crawl under the bed and stay there, as much as she wanted to.

Maggie put the glass on the nightstand beside the bed, careful not to leave a ring. Carly's room was booked for the next day.

Months of sitting in a cold room had to come to an end.

"I think I'm going to stop coming to talk to you." Maggie heaved a sigh. Her eyes began to prickle, usually a prelude to tears. She gritted her teeth, refusing to give in to the sadness. "I think it's time. I'm okay now... It's our anniversary. It's not the best day to stop this, but you know, I think it's time. I'm okay."

"I'm okay."

"I'm fine."

"Things are good."

The phrases had become her mantra over the past eight months, so much so that she almost believed herself when she replied to the countless questions.

"I'll always love you," Maggie sniffled, wiping her nose with the back of her hand, the same move that grossed her out when Clare did it. "Same with the girls. We'll always miss you—"

Maggie choked on the sob that threatened. Her daughters had no father now.

She'd tried to say goodbye when she'd kissed his dead body at the hospital, and again when the dirt had covered his casket. Mike was gone, and she couldn't pretend he was here with her, but she hadn't been able to say that final goodbye.

Maybe she could now.

A deep breath, and then another one. She could get through this. Only another minute or so. The others were waiting on her for supper.

"If you're here, great," she said aloud. "If not, could someone get him a message? Mike Monroe, recently departed. I'm not sure if it's recent for you...if time moves the same. If you have time..."

Maggie shook her head. This was like a bloody science fiction movie. Or a silly rom-com where the girl moons over a ghost. She wasn't mooning. She was talking. Explaining things.

"I'll always love you," Maggie continued. "And we'll always miss you. I'm sorry about what happened to you. I'm sure it was horrible, but I can't do this anymore." She stared at her wedding ring. "It's...hard...and I need to be there more for the girls...I love you, but I won't be coming back to talk."

Before she could reconsider, Maggie got up from the bed and slipped out of the room.

Chapter Three

MAGGIE CAME DOWN THE stairs to find two of her sisters clustered in the kitchen. Her heart lifted. Their presence was as warm and welcoming as cozying with a blanket in front of a fire.

"I told you to take it out ten minutes ago!" Cat shouted.

"And I did, saw that it wasn't cooked, so I put it back in! I *can* cook, you know, Cat," Brenna retorted.

Maggie paused at the bottom of the stairs, out of sight from the kitchen.

Maybe cozying with an old blanket full of holes in front of a fire that hadn't been lit.

"Not as good as me," Cat muttered loudly. The tantalizing smell of bacon-wrapped pork made its way around the corner to where Maggie lingered.

"How do you know? You never let me near the stove!"

"Because I like this house and don't want to lose it!"

"That was *one* time! There were no flames, just the smoke detector going off. Jesus!" Maggie peeked into the kitchen just in time to see Brenna throw up her hands with disgust. Cat did guard the cooking duties a little too zealously, but Maggie had tasted some of Brenna's attempts and thought maybe it was better that way.

But she knew better than to take sides. Even though her two youngest sisters got along much better than they had during the battles royale of their childhood, Maggie was still amazed that the two had decided to run the B & B together.

Maggie had only been upstairs for a half hour and already they were at each other's throats. Time to play referee. Or mediator. Or be a wall between the two to stop things from getting physical. It'd been a while since Brenna and Cat had had one of their knock-down, drag-em-out fights, but Maggie didn't want her girls to have to witness it.

Even though Clare would have cheered them on. Maggie's youngest was as bloodthirsty as they come.

"I'm glad you don't have any guests." Maggie stepped into the kitchen. "I would have been able to hear you yelling all the way to my place if I'd been there."

Both heads whipped around quicker than the ceiling fan. Maggie knew they were searching for evidence of tears, of anger, of any emotion they could help her deal with.

This was the part of Mike's death Maggie hated the most. Everyone wanted to help her deal. Well, she could deal fine on her own. If she needed something, she'd yell.

The third sister, Kayleigh, was seated at the end of the big wooden table on the other side of the room, plates and cutlery pushed aside, playing UNO with nine-year-old Clara and Brenna's boyfriend, Joss.

"I need to teach you how to play poker," Joss grumbled as he folded his cards. "At least I can win at that."

"Clare, can you help put the table back in order," Brenna called from the counter where she was pouring glasses of milk. "Mags, is Kady coming?"

Maggie snorted as she grabbed the wine glasses to set on the table. "She's seventeen with a boyfriend. I barely see her at home, let alone here."

"They broke up," McKenna said without lifting her head from her book.

"When?"

"Last night," Clare said helpfully. "She was crying and crying when she came home."

"What happened?" Maggie was confused. "Where was I?"

"She didn't want to bother you." Clare cleared away the cards. "Said you're too sad to hear any more bad news."

Maggie's insides lurched at Clare's words, and she dropped her head. Her baby girl needed her, and she was too caught up in her own grief to notice.

"How are...things?" Brenna asked in a low voice, wiping her hands on her apron before taking the milk glasses to the table. "Upstairs."

"As good as can be." Maggie helped herself to a handful of potato chips as she cleared the bowl off the table and followed Brenna back to the counter. "I had a nice chat. But that's it. No more."

"Are you sure?" Brenna gazed at her, green eyes searching. When Brenna had come home, Maggie had been surprised at Brenna's resemblance to Carly. Same heart-shaped face with the furrow beginning to be etched between her eyebrows, same wide smile that was slow to start, but transformed her face from merely pretty to stunning when it fully bloomed.

As different as they were, it was easy to tell Brenna and Cat were sisters, both with the thick, rich auburn hair and green eyes. Kayleigh had similar features but not as delicate, and the red of her hair had begun to fade. None of the sisters got Maggie's freckles and bright red waves that led to so many nicknames growing up.

Maggie had always sympathized with Anne of Green Gables being called carrot.

"She's sure." Cat dumped the potatoes into a bowl and pushed it toward Brenna to take to the table. "It's not going to bring him back. When Alex died—"

"We're not talking about Alex," Brenna said.

Maggie flicked Brenna a grateful look. Cat's third marriage to Alex had been sweet, but short-lived and couldn't compare to the decades-long partnership she and Mike had shared.

Twenty-seven years today.

"If it helps her…" Brenna continued but Maggie stopped her.

"That's just it. I don't know if it helps. I sit there and talk to a cold room. I have no idea if there's a ghost or a spirit, or it's just the air conditioning whacked out." She took another handful of chips. "It's not like I tell him anything anyway. Just stuff about the girls. Nothing that would worry him."

"What would worry him?" Brenna asked immediately.

Cat rolled her eyes. "He's *dead*. Nothing would worry him."

Brenna whirled on her. "You believe in the ghosts as much as I do."

"I believe there's something hanging around here, but I don't know if it's Mike. And why would Mom give up her spot for him? It's not like she's the unselfish-give-everything-up-for-her-kids type, right?"

No one argued.

"And even if it is Mike, what can he do for Maggie now?" Cat finished.

Maggie wasn't the only one bitter about Mike's death. It was odd, the varying ways each of her sisters had dealt with his passing. Brenna still got weepy and filled with regret, probably because she had wasted fourteen years in Vancouver with her no-good husband and missed all the years with Mike. Kayleigh was as stoic as ever, saving her tears for behind closed doors and being the rock that Maggie would always be grateful for. But Cat was angry—angry on behalf of Maggie and the girls, bitter that they were denied a father and prone to rages because she missed her beloved brother-in-law.

"It doesn't matter now." Maggie took the potatoes to the table. "Let's eat so I can find out the gossip because my daughter doesn't tell me anything."

"She's seventeen." Cat was always Kady's biggest defender. "What did you tell Mom when you were seventeen?"

"I told her I was pregnant." Maggie raised an eyebrow in Cat's direction. "Can you see why I might worry?"

Her sisters joined her and her daughters, the table big enough to sit the eight of them with room left over. The aroma of roasted pork wafted enticingly through the room, joining the sweet smell of the cake that Cat had made earlier in the day.

The rest of the evening was spent without tantrums, although Maggie felt the kick on her shin from Cat that had been invariably meant for Brenna. Soon-to-be-brothers-in-law Seamus Todd and Joss Ryan were both at the table, which usually meant better behaviour from her sisters.

Cat had finally accepted Seamus' ring but was holding off picking a date. It would be her fourth wedding, and she wasn't looking forward to being Forest Hills most married resident.

Maggie couldn't think of anyone else who had been married three times, so maybe Cat already held that honour. But she wasn't about to point that out to her sister. Cat never did anything she didn't want to.

Seamus had moved into the house with Cat, the two of them taking over the biggest bedroom on the third floor, the farthest away from the guest rooms. He helped out as much as he could when he wasn't at Woody's, the bar his family had owned for years.

Joss had taken over the unofficial role of handyman but hadn't yet moved in. Brenna spent half her time at his place when she wasn't on duty.

Either Cat or Brenna was always at the house when they had guests; Cat did most of the cooking. Brenna looked after the books, and they divided the cleaning and laundry between them. Somehow they made it work without bringing the house down around them over one of their fights.

The town still talked about the last big one, with both of them landing on the ground outside, covered in flour.

Maggie waited until the end of the meal, and McKenna and Clare had vanished into the living room. "I heard back from the insurance people," she said without preamble.

"Less than a year. That's not bad," Joss mused.

"They paid?" Brenna asked in a sharp voice.

"They paid." Maggie's voice sounded hollow in her ears. "They paid a lot."

Almost a million dollars, but Maggie wasn't one to gossip about money, even to her own sisters. They would never know how difficult it had been, the lean times, the canned spaghetti years, as Mike used to call them. One of the few times Maggie had broken down after his death was when she realized she was the sole financial support of her girls. She'd barely gotten Evie through school, asking her paternal grandfather for help. There was a nest egg from the sale of her grandfather's farm, but that had been shared seven ways, and she'd already dipped into it to help Addison with a down payment for her little house.

The insurance money would help her sleep more soundly at night.

"They should," Seamus said, the bitterness in his voice mirroring Cat's.

"I'd rather not spread the news." Maggie frowned. "It's going to be impossible to keep it quiet after I walk into the bank with the cheque tomorrow, but I'd like to keep the details between us."

"Easy to do when even we don't know the details," Cat pointed out.

Maggie was about to tell them when she heard the front door bang open. "Mom? Are you here?"

Maggie was on her feet as soon as she recognized her eldest's voice. "Addison? We're in the kitchen."

"You missed dinner," Cat called. "I can fix you a plate." She stood as Addison entered the room, her belly stretching her black T-shirt.

Addison was six months pregnant. That was something Maggie hadn't shared during her conversations in the chilly room upstairs. Mike would have loved being a grandparent.

Maggie wasn't sure she was that keen on the idea.

"What's wrong?" The sight of her daughter's face, tearstains marring the perfect makeup, her red hair caught up in a messy bun, had Maggie running to her. Then she noticed the bag Addison was carrying.

"Adam kicked me out," Addison said bitterly.

"What?" Chairs scraped as they were pushed back.

"Where is he?" Seamus demanded, jumping into protective mode.

"What happened?" Brenna demanded.

Addison gave a wave of her hand and dropped into the chair Maggie had vacated, her bag falling to the floor beside her. "He heard...things..."

"What things?" Cat asked carefully.

Maggie studied Addison's face. She loved her daughter more than life itself, but she wasn't the type of mother who ignored her child's imperfections. Addison was wonderful in so many ways, but she wasn't without her faults.

Lack of remorse was one of them. And a streak of selfishness.

"What did you do?" Maggie demanded, taking a deep breath. "Or—who did you do?"

"Mom!" Addison admonished.

"Maggie!" Kayleigh exclaimed. "How can you say that? She's married and pregnant."

"Addison." Maggie locked gazes with her daughter, her heart sinking. Here she was celebrating her twenty-seventh year of marriage and Addison couldn't even manage three. "Who was it? You might as well tell me because I'm sure someone else is going to as soon as I step outside this house."

Addison dropped her eyes first. "Adam found out about Brady."

"You've got to be kidding me." Seamus groaned. Brady was his nephew, and notorious around Forest Hills for the string of broken hearts he left behind.

"Brady Todd?" Brenna gasped, her face draining of colour.

"I had no idea you and Brady…" Maggie said carefully, unable to resist glancing at her sister. When Brenna had first come home, Maggie had been furious to discover that she and Brady—

Maggie hated thinking about it, but it was difficult not to since Brady had told everyone he could about his latest conquest.

And now Addison…

Maggie grabbed the edge of the table. "When did this happen?"

"It's been going on a while," Addison said sullenly. "Me and Brady."

Maggie closed her eyes. "Please tell me the baby—"

"Is Brady's." There wasn't a trace of remorse in Addison's voice. "Brady Todd is finally going to be a father."

Chapter Four

S UNDAY NIGHT DINNER ENDED quickly after that

"You're having Brady Todd's *baby*?" McKenna demanded. She'd been quiet the entire evening, barely saying two words at the house, but obviously listening to everything going on. As soon as Maggie had unlocked the door, McKenna had burst in the house with as little restraint as the dogs desperate to go out. Maggie held open the door for the pair of Labradors, which had been Mike's main love after his family.

"That's so gross!" McKenna continued. "Brady's practically family. He is family. Seamus is his uncle."

"That doesn't make him family," Addison corrected. "Cat isn't even married to Seamus."

"Yet. What about the fact that Evie used to be in love with him, and Aunt Brenna and Brady..." McKenna trailed off. Both she and Addison glanced at Maggie, waiting for her reaction.

For a kid who always had her nose stuck in a book, McKenna had certainly pulled it out tonight. Maggie wondered what else her normally quiet daughter had picked up on.

"You had sex with more than one boy?" Clare asked before the conversation could take a dangerous turn into Brenna-and-Brady territory. The image of the two of them together in Maggie's own kitchen had been seared into her brain when their little interlude had happened. "*That's* gross! I don't want to have sex with any-one."

"That's good to know," Maggie said tiredly. How was she supposed to deal with this? Adam had found out about Addison and Brady, which, from what Maggie had garnered, hadn't been a one-time thing.

"It's Sunday night, and you both have school tomorrow." Maggie turned to Clare and McKenna. "Start getting ready for bed." She wanted nothing more than to collapse into her own bed, but she had to deal with the girls first. The girls always came first.

"What about me?" Addison asked in a sad voice, just as the door opened again.

Maggie heaved a sigh. "You can stay in your old room with Kady tonight and we'll talk more tomorrow." She glanced up to see seventeen-year-old Kady, her face tearstained and looking remarkably like her older sister with her sadness.

"She can't stay here!" Kady cried shrilly.

"Kady, what—?"

"She's the reason Matt broke up with me! Because she had sex with his brother! And he doesn't want to have sex with me if Brady had sex with Addison! It's not fair!"

"I'm sorry—what?"

"She can't stay here! Addie has her own house. Make her go back there!" Kady burst into noisy tears.

"I'm not making anyone go anywhere unless it's you all going to bed." Maggie held onto her patience with an iron grip. "I don't understand why *you're* so upset, Kady."

"Didn't you hear what I just said? I can't have sex with Matt because she—" Kady pointed to Addison. "—had sex with Brady, who is Matt's brother."

Maggie stared at her daughter. Kady was always the dramatic one. "Okay. Forgive me if I'm not too broken up about that."

"How can you say that? I love him!"

Maggie patted Kady's shoulder. "I'm sure you do, but one crisis a night, okay, hon? Let's deal with your sister's collapsing marriage first."

"Why is that so important?" Kady screeched the question, causing Clare to pop her head out of the bathroom.

"What's all the racket?" Clare called over the sound of running water.

"Addison is ruining my life!" Kady wailed.

"It has nothing to do with you," Addison shouted. "This is my life. I don't know what you're getting so upset about, anyway. Brady said that Matt's planning on breaking up with you at the end of the summer, so you're better off not having sex with him anyway."

"He is *not* going to break up with me!"

Maggie thought Kady's shriek had the capacity to shatter the wine glasses in the old china cabinet.

"But I thought you said he broke up with you because you can't have sex with him?" Not wanting to miss the moment of a fight, Clare danced out of the bathroom, naked as a jaybird.

Maggie's shoulders slumped with exhaustion at the sight of Clare.

She couldn't do this anymore. Not tonight, not after saying goodbye to Mike.

She turned away from her daughters before they could see the sudden tears welling up in her eyes. "Get back in the bath," Maggie said to Clare. "Kady, Addison is staying here tonight, so no more arguments. And no screaming." She rubbed her temples. "It's late; everyone's upset, so go to bed. Addie, you can stay in McKenna's room."

"She can stay in my room," Clare offered. "You can have Mr. Woody to sleep with so you don't miss Adam. Do you miss Adam?"

"I don't know," Addison admitted in a low voice. "I love him, Mom."

"I know, sweetie." Maggie put her arm around Addison's shoulder, noticing the extra weight Addison had gained in the last few months. The pregnancy weight didn't seem to be contained in her belly, but all over her body. Just like each of Maggie's pregnancies.

"I'm sure you can work it out with Adam," Maggie continued.

"But I love Brady," Addison said piteously.

Thank god Mike wasn't around for this. It would have broken his heart to learn that Addison—his precious firstborn—had dismissed her marital vows so easily.

It was a struggle, but ensuring the dogs were back and Clare and McKenna off to bed, Maggie eventually escaped to her room.

Addison was still awake, watching television and Kady's light was on, but two out of four was pretty good for that night.

As exhausted as she was, Maggie's eyes wouldn't close. She lay in her bed, staring at the ceiling. Moonlight shone through the thin curtains, creating shadows in the corner of the room.

It looked like a hand reaching for her.

If Mike was a ghost, why wouldn't he come here instead of hanging at the house? Then she wouldn't have had to spend each week in Carly's bedroom.

Growing up, she'd made a point to avoid that area of the house. Since Mike's death, Maggie had spent more time in the room than she had in the eighteen years she'd spent in the house.

Carly wasn't her biological mother.

She didn't remember exactly when she'd found out, only that it had been some time after her father had left; abandoned five daughters to the care of a woman with severe mental health issues.

Maggie had been picking up Brenna's Barbie doll collection that Cat had dumped in the hallway after Brenna had accused her younger sister of ripping the head off of the Ken doll.

It had been just before the Christmas when she was fifteen, Maggie recalled suddenly. Brenna and Cat had been six and five, Kayleigh, thirteen, and Dory already a moody and truculent eleven. Maggie had been acting as both father and mother.

Fiona had been there. Carly had locked herself in her room two days previously. Maggie, with her hands full of dolls, had drifted closer to the room down the hall as she heard Fiona's voice rise as she pleaded with Carly to come out.

"Christmas is in a week," Fiona had said. "The girls need you. Maggie does so much, but she's not their mother. Come out and let me make you something to eat."

"I can't."

Maggie recalled how her shoulders had sagged when she'd heard Carly's voice. It hadn't been the words, but the tone. The sound of it, so flat and lost and empty. Carly had once been so full of life. Maggie, being older had remembered the sound of her laughter, of her singing to the younger ones.

I can't had been the words of a stranger, and Maggie knew she would never have her mother back the way she was.

"You can. You're their mother," Fiona had said angrily. Fiona would always come regularly to check on the girls, as often as she could get away from the boys but it had become difficult. Her husband had been an alcoholic, and Maggie knew things weren't good. Knowing this, she had made a point of thanking Fiona for everything she did for Maggie and her sisters, including begging with Carly to come out.

"I'm not their mother!" Carly had suddenly shouted.

"Carly, stop."

"I'm not! Maggie's not mine. And she's more of a mother to the others than I ever was. She can have them if that's what she wants."

"Maggie is *fifteen*," Fiona said urgently. "She's a child. This is not what she wants."

Wasn't it, though? Didn't Maggie get a sense of satisfaction when Brenna ran to her, rather than Carly? When Cat curled up in her lap for a story? As difficult as it could be at times, Maggie loved her sisters more than anything. If she wasn't their sister, then who would look after them? Would they be taken away from her, because Carly wasn't her mother, and therefore, she had no claim to them?

Maggie had backed down the hall, her feet silent on the worn carpet, numb with the realization that there was a reason why she'd never felt close to her mother.

To Carly. Not her mother.

As Maggie tucked the dolls away in Brenna's room, she vowed that no one could ever find out that she wasn't Carly Skatt's daughter. Because what would happen to her sisters, then? If Maggie didn't have a claim on them, then who would look after them?

Maggie rolled over. She never liked thinking about Carly. It served no purpose other than filling her with rage that a woman's selfishness had robbed her of her childhood.

It hadn't been selfishness. Maggie knew that now. But deep down, there was still a fifteen-year-old's anger and fear and confusion that she had been left in charge of her family, and no matter how Maggie pushed them away, the emotions lurked, waiting, hungry to be fed.

She pushed them away and tried to clear her thoughts.

Despite having the entire bed to herself, she stuck to her side. Often, she'd wake up in the morning to find Mike's side of the bed still neatly made.

Mike's side of the bed. His bedside table was still as he'd left it—the latest John Grisham with the bookmark Clare had made for him, a stack of Post-it Notes with a now-dried-out pen.

He'd never finish the book. And he'd never leave Maggie another note.

She didn't want to think about Mike tonight. It had been hard enough telling him she wasn't coming back to visit. If he had even been in the room.

After tonight, there was no point in going back, because there was no way Maggie could sit in that room and not tell him about what was going on with Addison.

She didn't want to think about Addison either. It wasn't pleasant being disappointed in one's daughter. She didn't like the feeling.

What had Addison been thinking? She'd only been married for two years. And Adam was so nice, albeit a bit boring. Maybe that was the problem. She was young, still immature. She wanted excitement.

Brady Todd had provided the excitement.

Hadn't he done enough to this family? Evie had been in love with him for years, her infatuation coming to a screeching halt when Brenna had come home. Maggie still didn't know exactly what had gone on between Brenna and Brady, only that her kitchen was now tainted and would be forever.

She'd gotten Mike to repaint the room last year, but he'd drawn the line at new countertops. But now Brady would be around and a constant reminder.

Had Fiona known Maggie's mother?

The thought popped unbidden into Maggie's mind, a welcome respite from the cringeworthy thoughts of Brenna and Brady.

Someone had to know. Maggie had never delved into the circumstances of her birth, just assumed she was the result of one her father's affairs, that her biological mother had given Maggie to him.

Maybe she didn't want her, couldn't look after her. Maybe she had died.

Fiona must have known, Maggie decided. Other people must have known. Forest Hills was a tiny town, full of well-meaning gossips who liked to tell tales. Roger Ebans showing up with a newborn baby would have been fodder for months. It had been the best-kept secret in Forest Hills, possibly the only secret about the Skatt family.

Why had no one told her the story?

Chapter Five

IT TOOK MAGGIE A long time to fall asleep that night, and once she did, she dreamed about the one thing she could never tell anyone about.

She dreamed about Joss Ryan.

The X-rated sort of dreams.

At least it wasn't Seamus.

It wasn't that she had a crush on her sister's boyfriend per se, but the man was Jason Momoa hunky with his big, broad shoulders and a twinkle in his eye. It wasn't that Maggie would ever act on her sort-of crush but Joss had made more than a few appearances in her dreams.

The residue of the dream, as well as the dull ache deep inside her, was the reminder of how long it had been since she'd been with a man.

Weak, early morning sun pushed into the room, the thin curtains doing nothing to keep out the brightness. Mike had been a morning person and had liked nothing more than to wake up Maggie with a hand on her breast and a hungry gleam in his eyes.

"Why did you have to die?" Maggie said aloud.

The morning that had started off on a bad note, grew steadily worse. Maggie had arranged for a later start at her job at FoodMart that morning to give herself time to deposit the insurance cheque in the bank, but that meant she was around for the early morning drama at home. There had been more tears and shouting from Kady and Addison, with little Clare listening avidly, no matter how much Maggie tried to shoo her out the door to the bus.

"Why did it have to be Brady Todd?" Maggie muttered to herself as she finally parked behind the store. The trip to the bank had taken longer than expected, due to the pointed questions about the money from the manager.

Maggie had snapped that she had too much on her plate to think about how she was going to invest the money, or what room she had in her RRSPs.

As she hurried into FoodMart, using the main entrance rather than the bakery door at the back of the building, the store manager looked pointedly at his watch. "Oh, give it a rest, Paul. You're bloody lucky I even made it in this morning," Maggie grumbled as she hurried past him.

The smell of fresh bread and the sweetness of icing invited her to the back of the store. Maggie had been managing FoodMart bakery for almost ten years now and preferred it to the cashier role she had before that.

Thinking about how long she'd worked at the FoodMart only deepened her bad mood.

Leila, her closest friend since grade school, spied her arrival from the deli and came running with a knowing grin. "Things a little crazy this morning at the old homestead?"

Maggie stashed her purse under the counter. There was no use trying to hide things from Leila, who always had her ear to the ground for all things gossip related in Forest Hills. "What did you hear?"

"Only that Adam asked Addison to leave, due to the fact she's having Brady Todd's baby, rather than his." Leila's long hair was pulled back into the mandatory braid, and her dark eyes, under the triple coat of mascara, shone with excitement. Maggie knew when it came down to it, Leila would be sympathetic to everything Maggie was going through, but there was no denying how her friend was enjoying relating the gossip. "Apparently there's a bit of a question whether the baby is Brady's or rather, Billy Sams'—"

"You've got to be kidding me!" Maggie kicked the cupboard shut with enough force to leave a black footprint on the door. "No one told me about Billy. Or that there was even something to tell about him. What kind of daughter did I raise?" As Leila raised her eyebrows, Maggie pointed a finger at her. "Do not say a word. You know very well, Mike was the only man I ever slept with. We just started a little early."

A soft cough snapped her mouth closed. Maggie looked up to see elderly Mr. Harrison in front of the counter with his loaf of dark rye, and a shamed expression on his sweet, wrinkled face that told her the man had heard every word. "Would you like me to slice that for you?"

As she took the loaf from Mr. Harrison, who was suddenly unable to meet her eyes, she hissed at Leila. "I need to know *everything*. Come find me on your break."

The morning moved fast for Maggie. Her head still on Addison, Brady and unfortunately some of the more enjoyable aspects of her dream, she worked on autopilot, helping customers, making up the new schedule, phoning around trying to cover a shift for the next day.

She was setting up a cake order at the side of the counter with a customer when the crash of a shopping cart hitting a shelf made her look up. Boxes fell and a muffled curse was heard.

Maggie's customer, Mrs. Fields, one of the town's curmudgeons, jumped as if she was shot, startling her ancient toy poodles that lay panting at her feet.

A man, dressed in a battered concert shirt and baggy cargo shorts stared at her as a fellow customer scooped up the boxes of crackers that had fallen off the endcap he'd hit.

"Maggie Monroe," Mrs. Fields hissed. "Stop staring at him. You're a *widow* for god's sake. Now, write everything down that I'm telling you."

Maggie blinked in surprise. "I think I've got it, Mrs. Fields."

"*Extra*-large flowers, not like those piddly things you passed off last time. And don't skimp on the filling. The last cake had layers practically touching each other. We like our sweet stuff, my boys do."

It was difficult keeping a straight face since Maggie was well aware that the cake Mrs. Fields ordered was to share with her pets—three dogs and at least half a dozen cats. She glanced up again at the shopping cart commotion and found the man still staring at her. She frowned at the niggle of recognition he caused. There was something about the dark curls, and the hazel eyes, that smile...

"Maggie?" he asked with more than a hint of embarrassment.

And still, it took her another moment to fully recognize him. "Ben? Ben Higgins?" Her face broke into her first smile of the day.

"Hey, Maggie." Ben pushed his cart up to the bakery counter with the same wide smile and dimple that had won Maggie's heart when she was twelve. He smiled warmly at Mrs. Fields, who harrumphed and turned her back to him.

"I heard you were back." Maggie glanced between Ben and Mrs. Fields. "Give me a minute here?"

"I think you'll need more than a minute, Maggie Monroe," Mrs. Fields said irritably. "I swear with the skimping of the middle and the bad service, I'm about to take my business to your sister if she wasn't living in sin at that brothel you all call a motel."

"Cat and Brenna run a bed and breakfast, Mrs. Fields." Years of practise with all kinds of customers kept Maggie's voice calm and even. "Last time I checked, Forest Hills didn't have a brothel."

Mrs. Fields lips disappeared as she sucked in her breath.

"Now, I think we're just about finished here. Your cake will be ready on Friday, first thing in the morning. I hope you have a good party." One of the dogs barked in response, and Mrs. Fields bent down, cooing a response.

The cake was for Mr. Biggles' eleventh birthday.

Without another word to Maggie, Mrs. Fields shuffled off, wearing house slippers covered in animal fur. As Maggie watched, one of the dogs, scruffy and ill-kept, lifted a leg as he passed the shelf Ben had run into.

A puddle formed before Mrs. Fields jerked the dog's leash. Maggie sighed.

"Did that dog just pee in the store?" Ben asked, his voice a mix of delight and disgust.

"It's not the first time." Maggie made a mental note to call for a cleanup, but as she turned to Ben, the thought vanished.

On first glance, it was like the last twenty-seven years had never happened. She had known Ben Higgins her whole life, from kindergarten to their fleeting pre-teen love affair, drawing closer when Ben had tutored her in math in high school. But Ben had been like Brenna, chomping at the bit to get out of town, moving away soon after graduation, leaving his parents and younger brother to run the family hardware store. And despite their friendship, Maggie had been occupied with Mike and their new baby and hadn't made an effort to keep in touch with Ben after he left. She had thought of him now and then, though. And asked his parents about him, whenever she ran into them.

"Hi," she said. To smile, or to shake hands? Or hug—Maggie had always been a hugger, so she hugged him.

"Hi." Ben's smile widened as she back away. "It's good to see you."

"You, too. I heard you were back." Maggie had heard the talk of his return to Forest Hills a few weeks ago—of his wife's short fight with ovarian cancer that left Ben a widow and his three children motherless.

"I thought it was time to figure out how to run the store," Ben said ruefully. "You heard about Dad's stroke? He's agreed to retire, but neither he nor Mom want to let the store go, so it's up to the dutiful son to step in."

"Hardware not Brett's thing?" Maggie asked, referring to his younger brother who now ran the summer camp that used to be Ebans' Riding Stables, Maggie's grandfather's place on the top of the hill.

"Not really. Look, Maggie..."

Maggie took a deep breath. Here it came, the awkward condolences, after which Ben would push his cart away, never to be seen again.

"I'm sorry about Mike," he said, looking her straight in the eye. "I heard about what happened. I wanted to come to talk to you, but there hasn't been a good time for it."

"There really isn't ever a good time for it."

"I haven't seen you in years, so I'm not about to push myself forward, offering support, but I wanted to let you know if you ever wanted to talk, that I've been through it. It sucks, but I've been there." He shrugged, giving her another smile, his hazel eyes searching her face. "I've been told I have strong shoulders."

"Thanks," Maggie said, averting her eyes from Ben's shoulders, which did seem strong and muscular. Maybe not Joss Ryan's width, but much broader since their high school days. She was used to the gradual aging of her old schoolmates, watching the slow spread of tight tushies, and envious abs became muffin tops and beer bellies.

Ben seemed to be the exception. The man seemed taller than the eighteen-year-old she remembered, or maybe it was the confidant saunter, rather the scurrying walk he'd been prone to as he hurried from class to class. And while his dark curls had thinned and his waist had thickened, Ben somehow looked better now than when Maggie had last seen him on graduation day.

His graduation, not hers. She had taken an extra year to graduate, going part-time to classes as well as working at the store. Mike's mother had been a godsend then, looking after baby Addison during the day.

"I'm good," she added. "It's been getting easier."

"Really?" There was the Ben she remembered, the one who wouldn't let her blow off her math homework when she wanted to party with Mike, the one who helped her with every last question. Ben was the reason she'd been able to get her high school diploma.

Maggie shook her head with a rueful grin. "No. But I heard it does with time."

"Whoever you heard that from is full of shit."

Maggie laughed, and Ben's face lit up. "Good to know," she said.

Out of the corner of her eye, Maggie noticed Mr. Purdue glance at her, followed by Leanne Sams, who didn't bother to hide her interest at the sight of her standing at the counter with Ben. She knew the gossip mill would be cranking out the stories before Ben even left the store.

"It's really good to see you. I've wanted to, but you know." Ben shrugged. "Moving back...there hasn't been a lot of time. Getting the kids settled..."

"I know what that's like. Not getting them settled, but the kid thing."

"I guess. Five daughters. Wow."

Maggie thought of the wailing that morning before she left for work and didn't say anything.

"Now that I know where to find you—" Ben continued.

Maggie spread her arms. "I'm always here. Or at home, dealing with the five girls."

"Maybe we can grab a friendly drink sometime."

"I'd like that."

Now that would really set the tongues wagging.

Maggie noted the use of the word "friendly". Of course it would be nothing more than friendly. Even if she was so inclined, Maggie knew there was no one in Forest Hills who saw her as a datable prospect. Five daughters and a family full of notorious stories starring her sisters erased some of the eligibility of a person.

"It's the least I could do. You did get me through grade-eleven math," Maggie added.

"It's a wonder why after you broke my heart."

"We went out for *two weeks* in grade six." She laughed aloud, wondering when the last time she had laughed had been. A real belly laugh, rather than a polite chuckle, and not the hysterical laughter of the funeral, eight months ago. "I'm not that memorable."

"You'd be surprised. Look, I'll let you get back to work. But—I'll see you?"

Maggie nodded, ignoring the looming reservations by telling herself Ben's invitation was him being polite. "That'd be nice."

She watched him push his cart over to the snack aisle and was rewarded when he glanced back. It had been a long time since she had let herself look at a man, but looking at Ben felt safe because they were friends.

It would be nice to have him as a friend again.

Was she allowed to think her friend had a nice ass?

"Maggie?"

Maggie sent a last smile in Ben's direction before turning her attention to the next customer. The smile vanished from her face as quickly as if it was slapped off.

"Heather."

"Can I talk to you?" Heather Vreeland was another one who had changed since high school days. Back then, she had been the queen bee of the school, reigning over her hive of wanna-bees. Her father was the principal of the school and Heather set herself as the monarch of the school. She'd acted as though she was untouchable, and she was. Her taunts and teasing and nastiness going unpunished for the time she was there.

And she was still a bitch, dressed to the nines for a morning at the grocery store, looking down her narrow nose at everyone she came across.

"About what?" It was a strain to keep her voice light and carefree.

"Dylan."

Maggie felt her face heat up, as though the slap had been real. Not now, not today.

"I know you've been through so much," Heather began, her voice suddenly syrupy sweet. "But Maggie, he's been arrested again."

"Why is that any business of mine?" Maggie snapped.

Heather took a step back and a pleading tone replaced the sweetness. "Hank won't give me the money to bail him out. I know you got the cheque from the insurance company today."

"How the holy hell did you find out that?" Maggie clicked her tongue against her teeth as the realization set in. "Ah. Your sister works at the bank. Why don't you ask *her* for the money to bail him out?"

"Maggie, you're family," Heather reminded her, the sweetness in her voice returning and giving Maggie a toothache. If she could only focus on how irritating Heather had always been, how offensive she was now, it might be okay. "Mike would have—"

"Mike wouldn't have done anything because Mike is dead." Maggie took a breath through her nostrils to calm herself down before she said something she'd regret.

Nope. She wasn't going to regret this, not one little bit.

Maggie stepped out from behind the bakery counter. She stood eye to eye with Heather in her high-heeled sandals, ones that cost more than Maggie's entire collection of sneakers.

"Do you know why Mike is dead?" Maggie asked in a quiet voice. Too quiet. Her girls would have run for the hills if they heard her speak like that. "He's dead, Heather, because of your boy, the one who is now in jail. Mike may have been a cousin to Hank, but I'm not. I want nothing to do with your family because your son and his reckless, infantile behaviour at work—doing a job *Mike* got him—caused my husband's death."

The scene was still so vivid in her mind. Mike catching Dylan Vreeland and Conner, the owner's son, taking the forklift for a joyride. Conner, at the wheel of the forklift, with music blasting from his phone, laughing hysterically, still high from the joint the boys had smoked during their break.

And Mike...Mike arguing with Dylan as the out-of-control forklift barrelled toward them, pushing Dylan out of the way at the last minute...

He didn't have time to get clear before the forklift, with its load of pallets, had hit, sending him flying into the wall, the pallets and the forklift crashing down on him.

They had said he had died instantly but in Maggie's nightmares, Mike had been alive under the debris, calling for her.

Heather clutched her chest. "Dylan is so, so very sorry…"

"Is he? Is he really? Is he sorry that he was high? I doubt it if he's still wasting his miserable life on drugs. That's what he's been arrested for, right? He's dealing now, isn't he? You'd think he'd learn his lesson, wasted on the job. If he hadn't been stoned, Mike would still be alive." Maggie stepped closer and Heather took a step back.

"Why are you here, Heather, on the very day that I cashed the insurance cheque? The money I wouldn't even have if Mike was alive. But he's dead, and he's dead because he tried saving your son's worthless ass. So tell me again, why do you want the money?"

"I thought…maybe…" Heather whispered.

"You thought what? What did you think, Heather?"

"Maybe you could…lend…"

Maggie laughed without humour.

Then Maggie shoved Heather with all her might, sending the woman and her high-heeled sandals back into a bakery table stacked high with plastic clamshells of cookies and muffins.

Gasps sounded from the crowd that had gathered, wide-eyed and ready to report every word to friends and family about how Maggie Monroe took on Heather Vreeland at FoodMart. Maggie didn't hear anything but the furious racing of her heart.

She loomed over Heather, caught up in the destruction of the table, but still trying her best to crab walk away from Maggie.

Maggie kicked at one of her shoes. "You've got to be fucking kidding me. You wear shoes like this in here, to come to beg me for money."

"Maggie?"

She heard the voice from a distance, along with shouts to stop. But she wasn't listening. The rage that she'd felt in the months since Mike's death welled up in her like a pot filled with spaghetti ready to boil over, sending a wave of starchy water over the stove.

Maggie leaned down, grabbing a fistful of Heather's expensive jacket. "Let me say it again for you. Your son is an obnoxious asshole. Mike. Died. Saving. His. Life. And now you want me to save it again?"

Her hand balled into a fist. "No fucking way."

Chapter Six

"I DON'T REMEMBER THE last time you lost your temper," Cat marvelled. "I know it's still there, but it's been a while since it's come out to play." She uncorked the bottle of wine balanced between her legs. Maggie held the glasses for her as she poured.

"I couldn't help it." Maggie sighed, setting the glasses on the little table by the railing before pulling it closer to the line of Muskoka chairs.

Word of the fight in FoodMart had spread through town quicker than wildfire. By the time it was over and Maggie had been sent home for the day, she already received three texts from Cat and two from Brenna insisting that she come to the house. Kayleigh was already on the porch waiting for her when she drove in.

There had been no need for Maggie to tell her side of the story; Cat and Brenna had already heard the various versions, most of which portrayed Maggie as the victor. But Maggie couldn't believe she'd lost control that way.

It was beyond embarrassing.

"What did Paul say?" Brenna asked, stepping out of the house onto the porch with a bag of chips and a plate of brownies. They all knew Paul Boyd, who had been the manager of FoodMart for over twenty years, and who had been in a perpetual bad mood for even longer.

"What could he say?" Kayleigh cried. "She runs the place. Plus, after everything that happened with Mike..." The rest of Kayleigh's thought trailed off as she flicked her lighter and lit the joint caught between her lips. Taking a long pull, she passed it to Cat beside her before she exhaled. "Everyone loves Maggie. No one is going to say anything about this."

A thought popped into Maggie's mind as she waited her turn—how long would she be given a pass for bad behaviour? If she was forgiven for public brawling because her husband died, what else could she do?

No. Maggie was the responsible one, the dependable sister, the loyal friend. The reliable worker, the mother to all. Being a mother to all meant she couldn't go around punching the Heather Vreelands of the world whenever she felt like it.

It sure had felt good, though.

Maggie shook her head. "Paul didn't say much, just told me to go home and we'd talk about it tomorrow. I don't think he knew what to say. I can't believe I did that."

"I can't believe you didn't do it sooner. Heather Vreeland is nothing but a leech. She actually asked you to bail her kid out of jail?" Cat winced, passing Maggie the joint.

The sweet-smelling smoke invaded her lungs, and Maggie could feel herself relax. Responsible or not, this was exactly what she needed.

"I honestly couldn't see straight," Maggie confessed, passing to Brenna before snagging the bag of chips from beside her sister. Some people thought tea cured all ailments. Brenna believed wine could solve all problems. Maggie thought it was potato chips. Luckily, the two went together nicely. "I don't remember the last time I was that mad."

"You never get mad," Kayleigh said loyally.

Maggie shook her head. Kayleigh had no idea that Maggie had been angry every day since Mike died. Being the main maternal figure for most of their lives, there were certain things Maggie didn't share with her sisters.

"You got pretty mad at me when I moved back home a couple of years ago," Brenna said, joint in one hand, wine glass in the other. "I'm still sorry about that."

"Do you blame me? You don't come home for fourteen years, and when you do, you act up like a teenager. Passing out at Woody's, that *thing* with Brady..." Maggie shook her head to send the image skittering out her ear. "Fighting with Cat in front of the whole town."

Cat laughed. "You were really pissed at her."

"You don't have to be so happy about it," Brenna snapped at her sister. "If you remember, I wasn't fighting by myself."

Kayleigh waved a hand between the two. "That wasn't anything. The best was when Maggie decked that girl in Woody's when she came on to Mike." Kayleigh's laughter woke up Cat's dog, curled up beside Maggie's chair. She reached down and stroked his brindled head. "Best thing ever—Maggie was eight months pregnant with Evie, and Mike was playing darts with the boys. Someone calls her, tells her this girl is all over Mike–"

"Leila called me," Maggie supplied.

"Of course she did. So Maggie carries in a sleeping Addison, who's about four, gives her to one of the boys at the bar and wad-dled over to where this girl had her hands all over Mike. Then big sis here pulls back and plows her in the face." Kayleigh continued to laugh at the memory, even with the joint back in her mouth.

"It wasn't my finest moment," Maggie admitted, shamefaced, digging into the bag of chips.

"I would have paid money to see that," Cat crowed. "I can't believe I wasn't there that night."

"I hope you wouldn't have been there," Brenna said scornfully. "You'd have been twelve."

"I was in Woody's when I was twelve," Cat protested. "I just had to make sure Fiona didn't catch me."

Maggie rolled her eyes at Kayleigh. "We were such good parental figures, weren't we?"

"You were awesome," Brenna said softly.

The roar of the engine of a transport truck broke the quiet as it laboured up the hill. Forest Hills was exactly as the name suggest-ed—forested hills. Two massive hills bordered the town with most of the village tucked into the valley between. In the last five years, builders had begun to develop subdivisions in the valley, and now the expanse of trees was dotted with streetlights and new homes.

Maggie knew the new residents were good for the town, but she missed the days of wandering the woods for hours without coming across another person. Now there were roads crossing the footpaths of her youth and the sounds of construction interrupting the chirping of the birds.

Maggie leaned back in the wooden Muskoka chair. The June sun peeked over the porch to warm her ankles stretched before her. As awful as Heather had been, she couldn't help but be glad the incident had gotten her an afternoon off work. "I can't believe she wants me to bail him out," she mused.

"That woman's got a steel set of balls on her." Cat let out a witchlike cackle. "You've got to give her credit for that."

"Don't have to give her credit for anything," Kayleigh announced. "I've never liked Heather Vreeland."

"Tell me about who broke it up?" Brenna gave Maggie a sideways glance. "That part of the story wasn't exactly clear, at least the version I heard."

"I pushed her into a table," Maggie recounted. "Then I don't remember much until Ben pulled me off her." Her face flushed as she remembered how Ben had wrapped his arms around her waist and literally pulled her away from Heather, sprawled on top of the baked goods.

They had ended up in the condiment aisle, with Maggie pulling against his restraining arms to get back to Heather. During the struggle, she must have pushed him against the shelves, knocking over a few jars of mayonnaise.

"Maggie. Stop it. It's not worth it. She's not worth it," Ben had repeated over and over while she fought against him, seeing only Dylan's face the day after the accident.

"He killed Mike. He *killed* him!"

"I know. I know." Ben had pulled her closer, her back nestled against his strong chest as he held her. "But she's not worth this."

It wasn't until Maggie's breathing calmed and her fists loosened that Ben had relaxed his grip. "You okay now? Maggie?"

"I'm fine," Maggie had snapped and stalked away, leaving him standing amid the mess on the floor.

"Ben Higgins?" Kayleigh asked, pulling Maggie back into the present. "I forgot he was back in town. The two of you were friends, weren't you? He's gotten a lot cuter." Brenna and Cat both glanced at Kayleigh. "What? I'm gay, not blind! I always liked him. So did Maggie."

"He's a nice guy." Maggie felt the heat of her sisters' gazes but kept her eyes straight forward. "We were friends. Only friends. He used to tutor me."

"I think he wanted to tutor you in other ways. I remember the way he used to look at you when you had your head in a book."

"That's not creepy at all," Cat muttered.

"I don't remember any of this," Brenna announced.

"Because you were five," Maggie said. "You forget, Mike came along when I was seventeen, and then Addison. All my exciting teenage adventures happened between the ages of fourteen and sixteen."

She rarely thought of her high school years; for her, life began when Mike Monroe's tight white baseball pants had caught her eye while he played second base. He had been in Forest Hills for a tournament the summer she had turned seventeen, and Maggie and Leila had haunted the park, cheering loudly on the bleachers for Mike's team. By the end of the first game, Mike had her number; by the end of the game on Saturday, they had been making out in the park.

It had been love at first sight for Maggie, and she never looked back. Luckily, Mike lived in the nearby town of Spanish, had his own car, and was willing to spend money on gas to visit.

By the end of the summer, she had been pregnant.

Cat reached for the wine bottle, topping up her glass before adding some to Maggie's. She tilted her head back and wished the sun would warm her face instead of her feet. "What a shitty morning."

"Sounds like last night wasn't too good either." Brenna raised an eyebrow as she glanced over.

"Not really. With Addison's little bombshell..." Maggie sighed. "Thanks for taking her last night, Kay. I never would have gotten any sleep with Addison and Kady going at it."

"What's Kady upset about?" Brenna asked.

"Other than the fact her sister is the talk of the town? Apparently, Matt broke up with her because he doesn't want to sleep with the sister of someone his brother has had sex with."

Brenna frowned as she tried to work out the logic. Then she glanced over at Cat, a hint of a smile on her face. "Guess we didn't have that problem."

"I had sex with him first," Cat said automatically.

"Because you got him drunk. Even though he liked me."

"He liked me more!"

"No more! I thought you guys had gotten past fighting over Seamus." Maggie groaned.

Brenna and Cat had been fighting over Seamus Todd since they had first played doctor with Seamus and his brothers at a young age. At only a year older than Brenna, Seamus had been paired up with her his whole life, only to have teenage Cat swoop in to steal him from her sister.

Seamus had bounced back to Brenna, the two becoming high school sweethearts until Brenna left him for school in British Columbia. And then he and Cat had paced around each other for years, waiting through several marriages and relationships until the timing had been right for them.

Maggie, along with the rest of the town, was convinced this time it would work out for Cat and Seamus, if only Cat would stop being so stubborn about not wanting to be married again. With three marriages under her belt, Cat was proving to be gun-shy for a fourth.

"With the current living arrangement, either they've gotten over fighting about him, or something *very* kinky's going on in the house." Kayleigh gave a laugh that morphed into a cough as she exhaled.

"There's nothing kinky going on," Brenna muttered.

Cat gave a cackle that echoed Kayleigh's. "Speak for yourself!" She tapped her wine glass against Brenna's. "More."

"We have guests checking in at four o'clock," Brenna reminded her as she topped up the glass. "But it's still early, so I'm going to get another bottle."

"I can't sit around drinking all day," Maggie protested, accepting the joint.

"Well, right now, you're smoking." Kayleigh laughed. "Isn't it great that it's legal?"

"I'm good until at least three," Cat said.

"Don't you have a game tonight?" Brenna asked Maggie as she was about to duck into the house.

Heather Vreeland had gotten under her skin so much that Maggie had forgotten about Clare's softball game that night.

"Not for a while," Maggie said heavily. Coaching Clare's baseball team was another weight on her shoulders. She would have enjoyed it if Mike has been beside her in the dugout, but without him...

She remembered when she registered Clare for the team, at her sudden breakdown.

"Daddy was supposed to coach my team this year!" Clare had sobbed like her heart was broken, sitting amid a pile of stuffed animals, her brand new ball glove in her lap. "I worked in my glove like he told me, and he promised I could try shortstop. No one else will let me play shortstop!"

"Anyone will let you play shortstop," Maggie had assured her, blinking back her own tears. "You're so good. The best on the team."

"But Daddy was supposed to coach me! It was my turn this year."

Mike had coached one of the girls' teams each year. It was to be Clare's turn that year. As Clare cried, Maggie ran through a list of names of potential coaches, people she knew and who would give Clare the attention she deserved.

"I'll coach you," she said in a decided tone.

"You don't know how to play." Clare's sobs quickly abated as she peered up at Maggie.

"I lived with your father for twenty-six years. I think I know a few things about baseball," Maggie had said.

How could she not step up to take Mike's place? Maggie enjoyed the sport from the safe distance away on the bleachers, but Clare's disappointment had put another crack in her broken heart.

Cat topped up her glass. "Relax. If you're worried, stop smoking. Everything will wear off before the game."

Chapter Seven

T HE MORNING BLED INTO the afternoon, and still, they sat on the porch together.

Kayleigh left for a half hour to check on her store, The Hills of Christmas. Being late June, a store focusing on the holiday season wasn't too busy. And being a small town, Kayleigh was able to lock the door with a sign pointing the way to the house and her cell number should any customers arrive.

Brenna opened another bottle of wine, and Cat made them sandwiches. Kayleigh shared another joint, leaving Maggie relaxed and no longer wanting to push Heather Vreeland through Food-Mart by her face.

But soon, Kayleigh began to fret about having to fill some of her online orders, and Brenna mentioned some paperwork for her law practice that she needed to finish. Only Cat was content to sit with Maggie, but Maggie soon realized that was because Cat had drunk most of the second bottle of wine by herself.

"Go back to work," Maggie told her sisters, pulling herself up from the chair. Her foot had pins and needles, she was tired from being in the sun, and her thoughts were fuzzy like they were covered by a thick layer of lint.

Kayleigh headed to the store as Maggie lingered on the porch, waiting for Cat to finish her glass of wine. How on earth was Cat going to prepare a meal for paying guests? Maggie was leaving her car at the house until she was able to drive, but Cat shouldn't be allowed anywhere near the kitchen until she sobered up.

The mother in her opened her mouth to worry her thoughts to Cat, but the sister/friend shut it. Cat was a big girl. She knew what she was doing.

Plus, if she'd been hanging out at Woody's since she was twelve, she might have a bit more tolerance for alcohol than Maggie suspected.

"You okay?" Cat asked, squinting into the sun to look up at Maggie.

What if she said no? What if Maggie said, no she really wasn't okay and didn't think she'd ever be again?

"I'm good," she said instead. "Thanks for this. It was nice."

"Who'd have thought we could hang out like this without you and Kay having to pull Brenna and me apart." Cat chuckled.

"I'm glad you're getting along so well. I was a bit worried when she moved in, not to mention when the two of you started the B & B." And that was why Maggie couldn't tell her sisters that she really wasn't fine—they all had their own problems and they always turned to Maggie to fix them. Brenna had once called Maggie the sun they revolved around, the most important thing in their lives.

Maggie disagreed. She wasn't the most important, but without her, her sisters' lives might not have run so smoothly.

With a wave, Maggie stepped off the porch, fighting the urge to look back at the house. She had been there for hours, and not once did she steal away to Carly's room, as tempted as she might have been.

But what could she have said to him?

If Mike knew Dylan Vreeland was in jail, there was no doubt in Maggie's mind that Mike would have helped bail him out without even being asked.

"But she can't ask him," Maggie muttered as she headed down the drive. "And I'm saying a big fat no."

At the end of the drive, she waited for three cars to pass, engines pushing to make it the rest of the way up the hill. At the top of the hill was the mushroom farm; Maggie had to face it as she walked part way up to her own house.

She should be working; the afternoon off was a rare thing and she'd wasted most of it drinking with Brenna and Cat. There were things she should be doing at home—tackling the mountain of laundry that had appeared in Addison's room, finish going through Mike's clothes to see what was suitable to give to the church, organize the outside shed...

Maggie turned and walked down the hill, straight to Woody's Bar and Grill.

Seamus was behind the bar as she pushed open the door. "Hey, Maggie. Everything okay?"

"Does something have to be wrong? Can't I pay a visit to my favourite almost brother-in-law?" She blinked, her eyes slow to adjust from the bright sunlight to the dimness inside and smiled fondly at Seamus.

She'd met Seamus the day he came home from the hospital, two days after he was born. His mother, Fiona Todd had stopped by the house to show her best friend, Carly, her brand-new baby. Carly had been in one of her locked-in-the-bedroom moods and ignored eleven-year-old Maggie's repeated pleas to come out and see the baby.

"Would you like to hold him?" Fiona had asked Maggie instead and settled her on the couch, showing her how to support Seamus' head.

Maggie had gazed in wonder as Seamus' fist clamped onto her finger, had felt a swell of love in her heart.

"I've never had a brother," she had said.

"Maybe someday. But Seamus can be your almost brother." Fiona had smoothed the red hair off Maggie's forehead and smiled. Carly and Fiona had been friends since childhood, and Fiona's two older boys ran wild with the girls in the woods around the house.

Fiona might have wished for Seamus to become Maggie's brother, but no one had any idea the drama that would occur on the path for him to get there.

"I'm your *only* almost brother-in-law," Seamus reminded her as he wiped the bar in front of Maggie and set down a coaster. "Stressing the only, since Joss and Brenna seem to be avoiding any talk about the future."

"I think I'd like another wedding," Maggie said with a smile.

"Talk to your sister. So what can I get you? Coffee?" he asked hopefully.

"When have you known me to drink coffee in the middle of the afternoon?"

"Well, since I've never known you to spend the afternoon on the porch with your sisters..." Seamus trailed off at the sight of Maggie's frown.

"Why does everyone know what I'm doing before I do? I suppose you heard about what happened at the store too."

"It's a small town, Maggie." He set a glass on the counter before her. "I assume Brenna had the wine out?"

"I'd like a beer instead," she said pertly. "I haven't had one in a very long time."

"You're the boss." Seamus tipped the tap, and the two of them watched the foam rise in the glass. "But I'm stopping you at one."

Woody's was practically empty this time of the day. The day shift at the mushroom plant ended at four so things would pick up then, but only old Herb Buttar sat on the other side of the bar, nursing his drink, and a group of town busybodies held court by the window, the remains of the late, mostly liquid lunch, still on the table before them. Maggie did her best to avoid making eye contact but could still hear their whispers.

"I'm sorry about Brady," Seamus apologized as he placed her beer on the coaster.

Would Addison's drama never end? "What, that you never taught him to keep it in his pants?"

Seamus flinched at her words.

Was she drunk? She felt something but wasn't sure what it was. Whatever it was, it was nicer than feeling numb all the time. Or angry.

"You're only his uncle. I don't think that one is on you," she added quickly. "Brady's been like this since he was ten. I'm only surprised he hasn't got caught sooner."

"You mean caught by a husband? How is Adam?"

"I meant caught like getting someone pregnant. And of course, it had to be someone in my family." Maggie snorted into her beer, another signal that she'd drank too much. "Addison didn't say much about Adam. I think she was more worried about *I love Brady*." She mimicked Addison's heartbroken whine. "Nothing about *I love my husband and I feel really bad*."

"Addie's always been a bit..." Seamus trailed off.

"Selfish? Self-absorbed? I'd say spoiled but I don't think she is. None of the other girls are."

"If there's one thing your girls are not, it's spoiled," Seamus reassured her. "They're good girls. Even Addison. Brady just has a way about him."

"You're telling me," she muttered into her glass before rearing her head up. "Not that I have—never me. Only that stuff with Brenna and Evie and..."

Seamus didn't bother to hide his smile. "I never thought he was your type."

"Young, buff, and beautiful? No, that's *definitely* not my type." She realized Seamus looked faintly ill at her talk. "Sorry. That's the beer talking. Or maybe the wine."

"Can I get you something other than beer or wine? Like some of our new sweet-potato fries?"

Maggie grinned with delight. "So you did listen to Brenna about putting them on the menu!"

"When she started nagging, I thought it best to."

Maggie cocked her head. "And what did Cat think of that taking Brenna's side?"

Seamus gave a sheepish grin before ducking into the kitchen to place her order. Maggie looked around.

Woody's had gotten a bit of a facelift in the last year with new tables and chairs, as well as the removal of several of the neon beer signs that had been flashing since Maggie had had her first legal drink. Another one of Brenna's suggestions.

Brenna had gone through a transformation since she'd moved back, but there were a lot of changes in Forest Hills people and places that could be attributed to her as well.

Maggie lifted her glass. Like her newfound appreciation for alcohol was definitely Brenna's doing.

Seamus served her the sweet potato fries and stayed to keep her company, which meant he ate almost as many as she did. Conscious of his disapproval, Maggie didn't order a second beer, as much as she would have liked to. Customers were beginning to trickle in, and a drunken Maggie Monroe at the bar would start tongues wagging even worse than her actions this morning.

The thought of Heather's request still made her blood boil.

She pushed the last few fries toward Seamus. "You finish them. I should go."

"Did you walk? I should drive you home." Seamus frowned at the barstools, now peppered with bodies enjoying their happy-hour pints. Maggie knew he was the only one working until four-thirty.

"I'm fine stumbling home," Maggie assured him. "You stay and look after other drunk people. But I'm not drunk, so don't worry."

"Of course," he agreed. If Maggie hadn't been looking at him, she wouldn't have caught the quick change of expression on his face.

"Who's there?" Maggie turned just in time to catch sight of Seamus' handsome devil of a nephew, the father of her soon-to-be-grandchild before he ducked back outside.

Every head in the place swiveled in her direction as her voice rang out in a deadly explosion. "Brady Todd! You wait one minute."

Chapter Eight

"MAGGIE, WAIT!"

Maggie didn't have the time or the patience with Seamus' peacekeeper attempts. She had her finger out, wagging it at Brady before she'd gotten halfway across the room.

"Do you want to do this inside or out?" She poked him in the chest twice.

"Not at all?" Brady suggested.

"Yeah. No." Another poke, and Brady turned with a last beseeching expression directed at his uncle.

Maggie led him across the parking lot, under one of the trees bordering the river, conscious that all of those inside Woody's were trying to get a window seat. "What were you thinking?" she hissed. "No, don't tell me, because it was obvious you weren't thinking with this head." She smacked him lightly on the side of the head, wishing she could hit him with as much force as she'd used with Heather.

But she'd never hit her children, and Brady was family.

About to be an even closer family.

"Maggie, I'm sorry," Brady pleaded. "I didn't mean for this to happen."

"You slept with a married woman—my married daughter! Can I ask what you *thought* might happen? No, don't tell me—you wanted a night of fun. Or a day, since I know you get up to no good in the daytime too. Do you remember Brenna? That was in the daytime. Do you remember how Evie was so crazy about you? Do you remember how Kady is going out with your *brother*? Could you not leave my family alone for once?"

"I love her," Brady said in a small voice.

"You love her. You *love* Addison. Why do I not believe that's possible?"

"What's not possible?"

Maggie was so intent on Brady that she didn't notice Fiona Todd approach until she spoke. "Maggie, why are you browbeating my grandson?"

"Because I'm sure you've heard that he's about to give you a great-grandchild. Him and my married daughter."

Fiona winced. "Not one of his better moments, true."

"But I love her," Brady bleated.

Maggie resisted the urge to hit him again. "You don't know what love is."

"I do. It's the real thing." Brady stared at her with his big brown eyes. "I mean it, Maggie."

Fiona touched her arm. "Why don't you let me give you a ride home? This isn't going to fix anything and you know that."

Maggie sighed. "I'm not sure what's going to fix this."

"I—"

Maggie thrust her hand in Brady's face to stop him from talking.

"Enough, Brady." Fiona sighed. "Why don't you go inside and settle up Maggie's tab. I'll give her a ride home." Obviously happy to be rescued, Brady ducked back into the safety of Woody's, and Fiona was gently ushering her into her car.

"What a mess," Fiona said cheerfully as she started the car.

"I can't believe my own daughter would do something so stupid. With Brady Todd, of all people."

"Maybe something good will come out of it. I hate the thought of the marriage being over, and poor Adam, but maybe they do love each other."

"They're both too selfish to know what love is and you know it." Maggie stared out the window as Fiona pulled out onto the road, speeding up to make the run up the hill. "I don't trust him. He's been through most of the single women of this town and a lot of the married ones. Including my own sister!" Maggie shook her head to block the image of a just-divorced Brenna and a much-younger Brady taking root in her mind. "And Evie. She was in love with him for two years. Everyone knew it."

"Except Brady, since he's somewhat clueless. Maggie, I certainly don't condone my grandson's behaviour but maybe all Brady needs is the love of a good woman to settle him down. Maybe Addison is that woman."

Fiona didn't seem old enough to be a grandmother, let alone great-grandmother-to-be. These days, Fiona's youthful demeanor ensured she remained a friend to Maggie and her sisters, as well as motherly figure.

Maggie herself was going to be a grandmother. The thought heightened her anger. "And maybe she's just another notch on his belt!"

"Does your bad mood have anything to do with your little outburst this morning?" Fiona asked bluntly.

Maggie craned her head to look as they passed the inn. Neither Brenna nor Cat were on the porch or Maggie would have told Fiona to stop.

"You gave Heather Vreeland quite the scare."

"Do you blame me?"

"Not at all. It was rude and callous to ask that of you. But she loves her boy, just like you love your girls. Can I point out that you love them so much that you went after Brady not three minutes ago?"

Maggie's face creased in almost a smile. "That's different."

"Not really. I'm a mother too. I understand." Fiona took her hand off the steering wheel and reached over to squeeze Maggie's knee.

"Being a mother sucks."

"You don't mean that."

"I don't mean that." She sighed again. "It's just hard sometimes."

"Especially without Mike." Fiona pulled into Maggie's drive, the front yard littered with bikes and the kid-size picnic table, still laid out with Clare's mud pie concoctions. Maggie hadn't had time to bring the garbage bin in yesterday, and it now lay on its side on the shoulder of the road. "It gets easier."

"Please don't say that." Maggie fought to contain the waver in her voice.

The car idled as Fiona wordlessly pressed her hand into Maggie's. Maggie couldn't handle another well-meaning *it'll be okay* comment. Because it wasn't going to be okay. It would never be okay again.

"What can I do?" Fiona asked in a low voice. "I'm here for anything, Maggie, even if it's just to talk."

Talk... Suddenly the Post-it Note Maggie had found with Mike's things popped into her mind. "I'm fine," Maggie said automatically. "But there's something I wanted to ask you. Did you ever talk to Mike or his mom about my mother? My real mother—not Carly?"

"Your mother? Why would I talk to Mike about that?" Fiona stared straight ahead, not meeting Maggie's gaze. "Or Mike's mother, Patrica? I haven't spoken to her in years."

"Bren and I found a note months ago when we were going through his things. It said something like talk to Mom and Fiona about Maggie...maybe something about my mom? I don't remember the wording of it." Maggie rubbed her temples. There were so many little things that she found difficult to remember those days.

"I don't recall ever having a conversation like that. I'm sure the note meant something entirely different."

"Probably." Maggie didn't want to get out of the car. She was content to sit there with Fiona. But as she felt herself relax, a yellow school bus stopped at the side of the road.

"Uh oh." Fiona grinned. "Clare."

Maggie shook her head. "McKenna and Kady get home first." They watched as McKenna stepped off the bus, slim in jeans, her red hair caught up in a ponytail, a book in her hand. Her elder daughter followed with a scowl on her pretty face. "Poor Kady.

She hates the bus. Matthew used to drive her home, but looks like that's done now."

"Brady didn't mean to upset everyone," Fiona murmured.

"No, but that's just what he does." She put a hand on the door handle. "Thanks for the ride, Fiona."

"I mean it, Maggie. If you need anything…" She looked at Maggie, blue eyes imploring. "Your mother was my dearest friend—"

"Carly was. Not my mother. I have no idea who my real mother was."

Fiona took a deep breath. "Maybe that's for the best. Some things are best left undisturbed. Carly *was* your mom, Maggie. She loved you in every way that mattered. Maybe she wouldn't have won an award for it, but she did her best."

Maggie pushed open the car door. "And that's a discussion for another day. Or never. Thanks for the ride."

She paused at the door to wave as Fiona drove away. As she honked, Maggie was hit with a wave of guilt for her sharp words. It wasn't Fiona's fault that Carly hadn't been much of a mother. And if that had been her best attempt at mothering, Maggie would have hated to see the worst.

The conversation was yanked out of her mind as Addison met her at the door.

"What did you say to Brady?"

Maggie stepped back instinctively, mouth dropping open at the sight of her eldest daughter, red-faced and shouting.

"You leave him alone! It's none of your business."

Maggie drew herself up. "You're my daughter, and I paid for your wedding, so I think it is my business about how your marriage fell apart," she said coolly.

"You have no right to be so mean to him!"

Maggie choked back a laugh. "Is that what Brady said? That I was *mean*?"

"No, but—"

Her anger softened as she realized Addison was close to tears. She pushed her way past Addison into the living room, with Addison waddling after her. "I wasn't mean to him at all. I am upset with all of this, but it's because I'm worried you'll get hurt."

"Brady won't hurt me," Addison insisted, sounding more like a teenager in the thrall of a serious infatuation than that of a twenty-six-year-old married woman.

Maggie sighed as she cupped Addison's cheek, feeling the soft skin under her hand. "Baby, he already has. And he has a history with this family. You can't get angry with me for being concerned."

"But this is about *me*, and our baby, not about the rest of the family."

"It's always about family." She was interrupted by Clare bursting through the door, red ponytail flying.

"You're home already! What's for dinner? Can we go to the game early to practise? I got one less than a hundred on my math test, and Piper and Ashleigh were so jealous they wouldn't sit with me at lunch. I sat with Brandon and shared my cookies with him. That's okay, isn't it? But now everyone will think we're going out, but we're not." Clare's running commentary continued as she bounced through the living room, dropping bags and books in her wake.

And then she was gone, disappearing into her room. Maggie drew a deep breath.

"She's a freak," Addison exclaimed.

"So were you, at one time." She patted Addison's cheek. "Can we talk later, when it's quieter? Just to clear the air?"

"Do you promise not to be mean to him?"

"I'm not going to be mean to anyone. But Addison—" Maggie paused to pat the protruding belly—"one day you'll understand."

Chapter Nine

MAGGIE'S MELLOW MOOD OF the afternoon wore off in the chaos of getting a quick dinner on the table. Today hadn't been a good day. In fact, it had been downright awful. If she could be thankful for anything under the circumstances, it was that she'd had enough awful days lately to know how to deal with them.

Push it away. Push it down. Don't dwell. Everything looked better in the morning.

After a quick meal of fish sticks and fried potatoes, Maggie bundled an excited Clare into the car. "McKenna?" she called just as she was out the door. "Sure you don't want to come to Clare's game?"

"I have homework," McKenna's laconic voice drifted out of her room.

"Addison? Can you help her if she needs it?"

Addison's mouth made a perfect O before she burst out laughing. "You're asking *me* to help *McKenna*?"

Maggie stopped with bewilderment. "Why wouldn't you help your sister?"

"Because it'd be like Clare helping Evie! McKenna's the brain of the family, after Evie. I'm just a receptionist at the vet's. I can't help her," Addison said scornfully.

"That's not true."

Addison rolled her eyes. "When did you ever see me do homework? My own, let alone help anyone?"

Maggie stared at her eldest, seeing her fresh, young beauty marred by the tired eyes of her pregnancy. For the life of her, Maggie couldn't remember once seeing Addison camped out at the kitchen table, spread with books and papers like Evie, Kady, and McKenna were prone to do.

She heard Clare calling to her from outside.

"We'll talk about this later," Maggie said impatiently. "Just be here if she needs you. And try not to fight with Kady." The last request was thrown over her shoulder, even as she knew neither of the girls would heed it.

Maggie was going to have to deal with the two of them, but not tonight. She heard Clare call her again. "I'm coming!" she shouted angrily.

"Mom!" Addison hissed from behind her. "There's a cop at the door."

Maggie whirled around to see the uniformed officer raise his hand to knock at the screen door. Her heart caught in her throat at the memory. The police had been at the door just like this when Mike... When they came to tell her...

She gave herself a visible shake, taking a moment to recognize Caleb Todd in his OPP uniform. "Caleb. What's wrong? Who's hurt?" The questions shot like bullets from a gun.

"Sorry to scare you, Maggie," Caleb said, his sheepish smile making him look like his younger brother, Seamus, as he stepped into the house. "Everyone's fine."

Maggie heard Addison's exhale of relief.

"Why are you here?" Maggie demanded. "Not that it's not good to see you."

Caleb nodded in Addison's direction and cast a quick glance at her belly. "Addison."

"Is this about Brady?" Addison asked warily.

"No, although I did have a talk with my nephew," Caleb said, his expression cop hard. Addison flushed in response. "I'm here about the incident at the store this morning."

"What happened at the store?" Addison demanded.

Maggie's heart sank. She should have known Heather wasn't going to take the public smackdown lying down. "Nothing. Addison, we can talk about it later. I'll walk Caleb out to his car."

"What happened?" Addison repeated.

Maggie brushed her away when the footsteps at the bottom of the stairs drew her attention. She turned to see McKenna and Kady standing together, gripping hands, horror filling their white faces.

"It's okay," she quickly reassured them. "No one's hurt. Where's Clare?" she asked Caleb.

"I, uh, locked her in the back of the car," Caleb said sheepishly. "Told her I'd give her ten bucks if she could get out."

Maggie smiled wanly. "You just lost yourself a bet." She was glad Clare wasn't here to see the police question her mother. It was bad enough the others were watching, but Maggie knew there was nothing she could say or do to make them disappear back to their rooms.

"Why is he here?" Kady asked in a quiet voice, so unlike her usual strident tones. "The cops came when Daddy..."

"It's not that," Addison assured them, quicker than Maggie could. "Something happened at the store. With Mom."

Even without glancing at them, Maggie could feel the heat of the three gazes.

"Sorry girls." Caleb took another step into the living room. "I don't mean to scare you. Everyone is fine, that I know of, anyway. I just need to talk to your mom here, for a sec."

"Are you arresting her?" McKenna asked, her voice tremulous like she was on the verge of tears.

Kady stepped forward. "You are *not* arresting her."

"Don't even think about it," Addison added. In a moment, they had grouped around Maggie, shielding, protecting, daring Caleb to come closer.

A hint of a smile darted at the corners of Caleb's mouth. "No one is arresting anyone. And you're not giving Heather Vreeland one penny, Maggie. Dylan is right where he belongs, and it's the only way he's going to get off the drugs. But Maggie, you can't be fighting. Especially at work."

"I know that."

"You were fighting? At work?" Addison asked with confusion.

"When were you going to tell us about that?" Kady demanded.

"I wasn't," Maggie retorted with her back to her girls. "It's none of your business."

"It is if the police are in our house," McKenna said in a staunch voice, making Maggie's heart ache because she sounded exactly like Mike.

She stared at Caleb, refusing to glance at the girls surrounding her until she could figure out what to tell them. They shouldn't be involved; it was her duty as a mother to protect, to shield, not the other way around.

"I talked Heather down," Caleb admitted. "But Maggie, if I hadn't been there...if it had been one of the new guys, who didn't know you..." He didn't have to finish.

"Thank you," she said stiffly.

"She wants an apology."

"Of course."

"Preferably in public. Be prepared to grovel. And Heather insisted I talk to Paul at the store. He's given you an official warning, in writing. However that works; whatever it means."

"It means no more fighting."

"I don't understand *why* you would be fighting," Kady cried. "You don't fight with people. Maybe if it was Aunt Cat—"

Caleb choked back a burst of laughter at the mention of his brother's girlfriend before he quickly sobered. "I'll get out of your way. But Maggie, are we clear? I don't want to be back here about something like this."

"You won't be," she promised.

Caleb backed toward the door. "I'll hold off Clare as long as I can."

Maggie smiled with gratitude, but Kady piped up before she could thank him. "She'll hear about it tonight at the game anyway."

"Game." Caleb nodded at Maggie. "Good luck." With a last smile, he left. The squeal of the screen door the only sound.

"I need to oil those hinges," Maggie mused aloud, looking for anything to break the icy quiet.

"Mom," Addison said sternly. "What happened?"

Maggie bit her lip and raised her eyes to the ceiling, at the crack of peeling paint and faint water stains. She *did not* want to tell them what had happened with Heather. The girls already had a hatred for Dylan Vreeland—understandable, but emotions had bled onto other family members, as they often did in Forest Hills. There had been an incident soon after Mike's death between the hot-tempered Kady and Dylan's sister, another between little Clare and his cousin. Maggie had talked the girls through them, had long discussions about how violence never solved anything.

Even so, it felt so good giving Heather that first shove.

"Heather Vreeland came in the store to ask if I could help bail out Dylan. He's been arrested again." The words tumbled out of her mouth quickly and concisely. She wanted to get this over with. There was no sense trying to hide anything from them since Caleb's visit would have been already reported on by the neighbours.

It had been a while since the police had had to come by one of the Skatt family houses. Maggie's heart sank with dread at the thought that the townsfolk would most likely assume it was one of the girls in trouble.

"Why would you bail him out?" McKenna asked.

"Exactly." Maggie smiled at her confused tone. "Why would I do that?"

"*How* could you do that?" Addison frowned. She might have been self-absorbed, but she knew the financial situation, as much as Maggie had tried to hide it from them. Losing Mike's salary meant things had changed around the house.

They hadn't heard about the insurance settlement. And Maggie needed to be the one to tell them.

"The mushroom farm gave us some money."

"They *paid* you because Daddy died?" Anger and confusion rang in McKenna's voice. Kady had a matching expression on her pretty face.

"No, they paid her so she wouldn't sue them. Right?" Addison asked.

"That's the short end of it. Look, girls, Clare will be back in a minute, and I don't want her to hear about this now."

"It's impossible to keep it from her in this town," Kady said flatly.

"Just about the money. I'll tell her something about the fighting, and why Caleb was here, but let's keep the rest of it quiet and between us as long as we can." She met their blue-eyed gazes, holding until each of them nodded. "Thank you."

"I don't want you to get arrested," McKenna whispered.

Guilt swamped her, and for a moment she felt unsteady on her feet. How could she do that to her girls? She, of all people, knew what it was like to be parentless.

Maggie touched her cheek, McKenna's skin so soft and young, her eyes heartbreaking.

"I'm not going anywhere," Maggie said quietly. "I'm so sorry I scared you."

"I'd look after you." Addison squeezed McKenna's shoulder. "If anything happened to Mom, I'll look after you, just like she did with Aunt Cat and Aunt Brenna."

"And Aunt Dory," Kady chimed in. "I'd help like Aunt Kayleigh did."

"It'd be okay," Addison promised.

Tears threatened in the corners of Maggie's eyes. "You look after yourselves and I'll be here to look after you all. I'm not going anywhere."

A car horn sounded outside and the stomp of footsteps signalled Clare's approach. Maggie blinked furiously as she turned away from the girls, not wanting to sweep them all in her arms in a fierce hug. If Clare walked in on that scene, she'd know something was wrong.

There would be time for more reassurances out of reach of Clare's prying eyes.

"I was in a *cop car*!" the nine-year-old shouted as she slammed open the screen door. "And I almost got out before Caleb came. What are you doing?" Clare's rush halted as she took in the four of them huddled together. "What was Caleb doing here?"

Maggie's mind was blank. "To tell you and Mom good luck with the game," Kady said smoothly.

"We're going to be late!"

Maggie swiped a quick finger under her eye to remove the wetness. "Let's go," she said, using every ounce of what was left of her composure to infuse her voice with fake brightness.

"I want to come," McKenna announced. "Can I?"

"Of course," Maggie said with surprise.

"Me too," Kady interrupted.

"We'll clean up the kitchen and I'll drive us over," Addison said firmly. "We'll be there for the first inning. Now, go."

Maggie swallowed the lump in her throat as she followed Clare out the door.

Chapter Ten

B Y ALLOWING CLARE TO babble about the intricacies of Caleb's OPP cruiser on the way to the game, Maggie got off without a single question about why he had been at the house. There would have to be a conversation with the nine-year-old, but it was one Maggie wasn't looking forward to. It was nice to have distractions.

An hour later, the game was in full swing, with Clare's team up by two runs. Kayleigh, who had agreed to help Maggie coach, stood beside third base.

"Only one out, Emelia; do not step foot off that base if she pops up." Her bellow to the runner on first base could be heard throughout the park. Maggie shook her head with a smile. For someone so wary of the spotlight, Kayleigh had the loudest voice in the ballpark.

Maggie hadn't even had to ask Kayleigh to help her with the team. As soon as Clare had told her aunt what Maggie was doing, Kayleigh had insisted on helping. "You don't think I'm going to let your mom have all the fun without me? I'm going to be your co-coach."

Clare had been delighted. So was Maggie. Once again, Kayleigh had been there for her, solid as a rock for Maggie to stand beside or lean on.

"You should tell her to tag up." The father of one of the girls hovered behind the bench where Maggie stood with her clipboard. Most of the girls on the team had grown up playing baseball, taught by fathers and older siblings, so coaching the group of high-strung nine-year-olds was more of a babysitting job than anything else.

Maggie kept her attention on the field. "Kayleigh will tell her to run," she tossed over her shoulder to the father. Ted? Or was it Tom?

Ted Richardson. Father of...Carson. The blond wanted to play shortstop, even though she had yet to catch a ball and couldn't hit a target if it was painted on the side of a barn.

Mike had always known the names of the fathers because they would line up to talk to him at the end of every game, proud and smug to have the legendary Mike Monroe teach their daughters the skills of the game.

Maggie knew most of the mothers, but the fathers huddled in a group, muttering mutinously at every play. Most of the long-time residents wouldn't dare approach her with complaints, but one or two of the new people, including Ted, didn't hesitate to criticize.

"But you should be teaching her that," he persisted. "You're here to coach them. They should know to tag on a pop fly."

Maggie bit her tongue. Emelia was one of the newer players who hadn't yet grasped some of the more "basic" concepts of the game that Ted was referring to. Whenever she was on base, she would take off in a dead sprint when the ball was hit, resulting in her getting called out several times a game. Maggie's latest idea to help with this was to make Emelia promise not to step foot off the base until Kayleigh told her to.

"What exactly are you teaching them if you're not going over the basic fundamentals," Ted continued.

"Great hit, Chloe!" Maggie shouted. "Run, Emelia, run! Go to third—no home! Run home, all the way!" As the girls danced and cheered around her, Maggie stepped out from the caged dugout to face Ted.

"Do you want to do this?" she demanded, thrusting her clipboard in Ted's face. "Do you want to take the time to make the lineup, and the positions and the snack lists, as well as trying to keep the girls on the bases when they're just aching to run all the way around to get home? Do you want to listen to all of the other fathers second-guess your every decision, even though you know very well that you know more about the game than anyone else?" She ripped off her ball cap and waved it in his face. "Do you want to try this on for size so you can have everyone yell at you when you lose, or when their daughters don't get to play their favourite position?"

Ted stared at her, dumbfounded.

"Because if you don't want to do this, then keep quiet and let me do my job. One that I don't get paid for, I'll remind you."

"Hey, Maggie! Good game, isn't it?"

She whirled around to find Ben standing behind her, holding the hand of a little girl.

What was he doing here?

Her face warmed, but Ben grinned like he hadn't stopped her from pummeling Heather Vreeland among the baked goods in FoodMart only that morning.

"Miranda says she can't wait to play on your team," Ben continued, turning to Ted with a friendly expression. "Is your daughter on the team? She's so lucky. Do you know who Maggie's husband was?" Ted gave a shocked shake of his head and Ben continued. "Mike Monroe: best damn ballplayer to ever come out of this town. I knew him in his heyday. He was this close to playing in the majors. And do you know Maggie here taught him everything he knew about the game? He used to tell anyone who'd listen that Maggie was the best ballplayer in the house. Your girl is really lucky to play on her team."

Maggie's mouth dropped open.

"Well," Ted said awkwardly. "I didn't know that. Thank you for coaching, Maggie." He backed away like a dog with his tail tucked between his legs.

Maggie waited for Ted to return to the throng of fathers before turning back to Ben. "You must think I'm a complete bitch. Oh, sorry," she gasped, realizing Ben still held the hand of the little girl.

She was a pretty child, with a sprinkling of freckles across her tiny, turned-up nose and her father's wavy dark hair. "You must be Miranda."

The girl gave her a ghost of a smile.

"I think he had it coming," Ben said with another grin. "And it seems like you haven't had the best day."

She sighed. "You've no idea. About this morning—"

"Mommy!" Clare called from the dugout.

"Coach Maggie, I'm up to bat next, aren't I? Callia says it's her turn."

"Callia, Mia, Jordan," Maggie called, reading from the lineup on her clipboard. "Get your helmets on." She gave Ben an apologetic glance. "I've got to deal with them. Thanks, for…that." She jerked her chin toward the group of fathers huddled together.

"I'm not sure what I did, but at least he's not chirping in your ear anymore."

"It's nice to have help."

"I think you were handling things just fine."

"Thanks." Maggie took a step back toward the dugout, unable to drag her gaze away from Ben. "I should thank you for this morning too. Without you there—"

"Always happy to help." Ben's grin widened. "Besides, I wouldn't have wanted to miss that. Good luck with the game. We're going to stay and watch the rest of it, aren't we, Miranda?"

"Cheer loud for us. We might need it." She gestured at the bleachers where Addison and McKenna were laughing together, ignoring Kady who was reading her phone intently. They might not be paying attention but at least they were all there. "My other girls are up there."

Ben didn't glance up at the bleachers. "The redheads—I can tell they were yours from a mile away. Especially the youngest one. She looks just like you at that age."

"McKenna." A furrow tightened between her eyes. "I always thought she takes after Mike."

"She's all you." Ben smiled again, and Maggie felt her gaze caught by him. He was the same Ben, but different. Maggie had always laughed and joked with him, confided more than a few things, but back when they studied at the corner of the kitchen table, she never had a problem looking away from his dark eyes.

"She's better in math," Maggie said finally, taking a step backward, needing some distance between them. "I'd better get back to the team."

"Good luck," Ben called after her.

"Who's that man?" Clare demanded as soon as Maggie had resumed her place along the bench.

"Carson's dad?" Maggie avoided her daughter's eyes, even though she knew very well who Clare was talking about.

"No, the other one. The one with the girl."

Maggie didn't even have to glance at Clare to know she now wore the mulish expression she favoured when she wasn't getting her own way, the same expression Cat used to have when she was younger.

"That was Ben," Maggie said carefully, trying to keep any emotion out of her voice. "Mr. Higgins. I went to high school with him. He just moved back and wanted to say hi."

"Did he know Daddy?"

"I think so. Mr. Higgins used to help me with my math. We were friends."

Friends. She had been friends with Ben Higgins, spending countless hours at his dining room table as he patiently coached her in calculus and algebra, going step by step through never-ending word problems until Maggie could solve them in her sleep. They had been good friends, the relationship only cracking when Mike came into the picture because Maggie had wanted to spend all her time with him. And when she'd started back to school, ready to resume her studies with Ben, she'd discovered she was pregnant and didn't see the need for advanced math.

Maggie had been friends with Ben, but why did her stomach have to give such a constant flutter when he stepped before her? It could be the embarrassment of her earlier actions or it could be...?

What else could it be?

Maggie pushed the thought away, pushed it down deep as one of the girls struck out for the final out of the inning. "Okay, girls, your turn to hold them. Jordan, on first..." She raised her voice as she recited the positions twice more until the team had it straight.

Kayleigh joined her in the dugout. "I think we're going to have to use glue to keep Emilia on that base! Every time Chloe swung the bat, she took three steps off the base."

"She's quick, though," Maggie said. "Made it from first to home."

"I saw you talking to Ben," Kayleigh said out of the corner of her mouth as the girls streamed onto the field. "I thought you were just *friends*."

"We are." Maggie rolled her eyes. "That's the last thing I need—the whole town thinking something's going on. Friends." She spelled out the word to make her point. Maybe if she said it enough times she might be able to forget the lurch in her stomach when he had smiled at her. She had no need for silly feelings. No time for them either.

"Yeah, right." Kayleigh smirked.

"Coach Maggie, I can't get my kneepads on."

Maggie knelt beside Mia and helped her on with the shin pads, then the chest protector. She handed the girl the face mask and helmet and finished with a pat on her head. "Catch well, keep your mitt up, and give Callia a good target. Have fun." She turned back to Kayleigh. "What's that supposed to mean? You sound like you're insinuating something."

"Oh, that's a big word." Kayleigh chuckled. "I guess that I am. You didn't see the way he watched you walk away."

"I walked two feet!"

"From the looks of his face, Ben wanted to watch a little longer."

Maggie shook her head and folded her fingers into the netting separating the dugout from the field.

"It's okay, you know."

"What's okay?"

Kayleigh leaned closer. "To look at someone like that. Mike would understand."

Maggie pushed off the fence and stalked to the other end of the bench for the rest of the inning.

Chapter Eleven

WHAT DID KAYLEIGH MEAN? How was Ben looking at her?

Despite her distraction, Maggie's team won the game and celebrated with homemade Rice Krispie squares and juice boxes. Kayleigh helped Maggie pack the bats and bases into the bag without another word, and even carried it to Maggie's car.

It had been a long time since a man had looked at Maggie in any way but as Mike's wife. Or as the mother to one of the girls. Not looking at her like...a woman.

Was that what Kayleigh had meant?

Maggie wasn't sure she was ready to be looked at like a woman. She was still Mike's wife.

But Ben was...Ben was Ben. She knew him. He was nice, and she felt comfortable with him if she could only ignore the flutter in her stomach.

What would Mike think about that?

As the last of the parents stopped by to congratulate Maggie on the win, she spied Ben by the corner of the dugout, now talking easily to Kayleigh, the little girl tugging on his hand. Reluctantly, she walked over to him.

"Good game." Ben turned to her with a smile.

"Thanks. The girls had fun. Do you play, Miranda?" As soon as Maggie spoke, the little girl turned her face into her father's leg.

"What's that, hon?" Ben leaned down to listen as Miranda whispered to him. "Oh. Well...I think Miranda and I are going to head out." He grinned apologetically at Maggie. "It was good to see you...again. And you, Kayleigh. You haven't changed at all."

"I think you need your eyes examined," Kayleigh said with a chortle. "I'm out of here, Mags. See you tomorrow." With a wave at Ben and Miranda, Kayleigh trotted over to her compact car, wasting no time leaving Maggie alone with Ben.

And a little girl who was shifting feet uncomfortably. "I'd better get Clare home too." Guessing the reason for Miranda's fidgeting, Maggie pointed across the road where the house gleamed ghostly in the growing dusk. "If you need somewhere now, stop at the B & B. Either Brenna or Cat are home, and you're welcome to the facilities."

"I spent a lot of time in that house. But it's been a while."

Maggie turned to find Ben looking at her, his dark eyes direct and clear, and suddenly, she didn't know what to say.

Ben broke the moment and glanced down at Miranda. "But thanks; I think we'll be okay. I'll see you around, Maggie."

He wasn't looking at her any differently than he had in the store, but she felt it differently. That crooked smile, the dark eyes locked on her face. Her face flushed in response.

"I'm sure you will." Then she clamped her mouth shut, wondering if that had sounded like she was flirting. Wondering if she wanted to flirt, if she even remembered how to.

As Maggie pulled out of the parking area with Clare still bouncing excitedly in the back seat, her thoughts remained on Ben.

He had stayed to watch the entire game, waited until the end so he could talk to her.

What did that mean?

Then she shook her head. Even nine-year-old Clare would know what it meant. The problem was, what did she want to do about it?

"What's going on at Aunt Cat's?" Clare demanded as the headlights of the car lit up the porch at the house. A group of people stood outside the house.

"Are they fighting again?" Maggie muttered, instinctively pulling into the drive. She had the window open before the car stopped. "What's going on?" she called from the car. "Everything okay?"

"Don't fight without me!" Clare demanded. Maggie turned to see her fumbling with her seatbelt.

"Stay in the car," she said as she opened the door, not recognizing the couple that stood with her sisters.

"This place is haunted!" the man cried. His voice was high-pitched with fear.

"That's why people come," Cat said. Maggie could tell from her expression that exasperation had already turned to anger. All the Skatt sisters had a temper, but Cat had less control over hers than the rest of them.

"Were you not aware...?" Brenna glanced at the man's companion, dressed in only a brief nightdress. Even from a distance, Maggie could tell she looked guilty as sin. "Why don't we change you into another room? Yes, we do advertise as a B &B for the paranormal seekers, but it's only that one room. There's a lovely room on the third floor. Let's get you settled. Come inside. It's chilly out here." With a stern expression toward the girl, Brenna ushered the couple back inside.

With a shake of her head and a rueful smile on her face, Cat headed to the car. "Can you believe that? The girl was all about seeing ghosts, but she forgot to tell the boyfriend what this place was about!" She glanced in the car. "How was the game?"

Cat then listened patiently as Clare took her through every play of the game.

"Sounds great! Wish I could have been there."

"And then Mommy got pissed at—"

"Clare! Language." Maggie shook her head as Cat tried to hide her smile. Clare's potty mouth had been an issue for years and Maggie had found no way to stop her youngest's love of profanity.

"Sorry, you were *angry* at Carson's dad because he was being an asshat."

"Clare!"

"I said asshat, not asshole!"

"We're going home."

Cat stepped away from the car as Maggie buckled her seat belt. "I'll talk to you tomorrow," Cat called. "Clare, be good for your mom. She's had a bad day."

"A real pisser," Clare agreed.

Maggie shook her head as she made an awkward three-point turn in the drive because her focus was on the upper windows in the house. A few were lit—Brenna no doubt showing the disgruntled guests to another room.

Carly's room was on the other side of the house, with a view of the woods and the ancient lilac tree outside the window.

Maggie had been there last night but still wanted nothing more than to hop up the stairs and unload her thoughts to Mike. She wanted to tell him about Addison and Heather and the asshat parent—that was a good word, despite coming from a nine-year-old—and Evie coming home...

Would she tell him about Ben?

Not that there was anything to tell. An old friend...a slight flutter in the stomach...

Nothing to tell.

The high beams of an oncoming car shone straight into her eyes as she waited to pull out. She turned her head away and tried not to glance back at the house behind her.

Maggie had said goodbye to Mike, and there'd been no reaction. No furniture was suddenly thrown across the room, no flashing lights, no doors slamming.

How did ghosts react to unwanted news, anyway?

Maybe it wasn't unwanted news. Maybe he got it.

Maybe he thought it was time for her to move on as well.

Chapter Twelve

T HE QUICK RIDE UP the hill did wonders for lowering Clare's energy level. She took her glove from the car without needing a reminder and even helped Maggie carry the equipment bag to the shed behind the house.

"Jump in the bath and then off to bed," Maggie said as they climbed the stairs to the front door.

"Is that Kady yelling?" Clare demanded, pushing past Maggie to open the door. As soon as the door was open, Maggie was assaulted by the sight of Addison and Kady's angry faces.

Apparently, the earlier reconciliation hadn't lasted. The three of them had *looked* reasonably happy sitting in the stands...

"No, I didn't think of my sister when I was making love!" Addison cried.

"I'm never going to have sex *ever,* and it's *all your fault!*" Kady retorted.

"I don't think that's a bad thing," Maggie said, giving Clare a little push to keep her heading to the waiting bathtub upstairs.

"That's enough, you two. Clare, bath and bed. Where's McKenna?"

"You don't understand!" Kady wailed.

"No, I really don't understand what it's like to be seventeen." Maggie sagged by the doorjamb. What she would give for Brenna and Cat to suddenly appear with a cold bottle of wine to whisk her away from this?

No, on second thought, she wouldn't want them here, since Maggie recalled Cat and Brenna having a similar argument years ago, and they'd probably start rehashing it.

But before she could decide, Kady gave her sister a death glare and stomped down the hall to her room. Addison gave a martyred sigh and turned back into the kitchen.

"Wait, that's it?" Clare asked. "Is it over?"

Maggie heaved her own sigh. "I'm sure there will be another fight soon." Kady and Addison were certainly becoming replicas of Brenna and Cat in the fighting department. "Now, bath and bed, Clare-bear, and that was a really good game." She dropped a kiss on the red head, now smelling faintly of dust from the baseball field. "And make sure you wash your hair."

Giving Clare a push toward the stairs, she stowed her bag in the closet before heading to the kitchen and Addison.

"Don't you have any organic fruit?" Addison demanded as soon as Maggie had stepped into the room.

"If you wanted organic fruit, then you should have stayed in your marriage."

"Don't you care about the chemicals going into your grandchild's body?"

Grandchild. The word sent a shiver through Maggie.

"I'm not old enough to have a grandchild," she muttered as she pushed through the bottles in the cupboard until she found Mike's secret stash of bourbon. "Women my age are still having their own babies."

"You're welcome to this one," Addison said with a grimace on her face. She pressed a hand against her belly. "Won't stop kicking, and I have to pee *all the time.*"

"Welcome to the joys of pregnancy."

The kettle was beginning to whistle. "Aren't you having tea?" Addison asked as Maggie poured herself a hefty shot of Kentucky's finest in the plastic cup Clare had left on the counter.

It was part of Maggie's nighttime ritual to have tea before bed. When they were younger, each of the girls would take turns making her a cup, carefully carrying it to the bedroom for Maggie to drink as she read them a bedtime story. "I put the kettle on for you."

"Thanks, but I think I need something a little stronger than tea first. But yes, I'd like a cup when I'm finished."

Addison fixed two cups of tea as Maggie added a few cubes of ice to the bourbon. "I remember Nana making Daddy tea," she said, handing Maggie a cup.

Maggie reared back, almost spilling the hot liquid. "When was that?"

"When we were living at the house." Addison turned and headed back to the couch, pushing aside the pile of folded laundry before easing herself back against the cushions.

"Sweetie, you were only three years old. There's no way you could remember that. Even if it happened." Maggie tucked herself into the faded and lumpy armchair, the corner still battle-scarred with bite and claw marks from years of pets. Charles, the older of the two black labs, lay at her feet, watching her with sad eyes. As she reached down to scratch his ears, his tail thumped in response.

The dogs still missed Mike. Maggie wondered if the loss would ever fade for them.

"When you went to work early, Nana made tea for Daddy. They would talk," Addison insisted. "I remember."

"Okay," Maggie said, eyebrows raised. "But Carly—Nana—didn't really talk to anyone. And I don't remember her ever making tea for anyone, not even herself."

That wasn't precisely true. Maggie remembered Carly making tea for her once and her heart tightened at the memory. It had been soon after Maggie had told her she was pregnant, one night when she woke up from a nightmare where she'd given birth to a baby with two heads.

There had been quite a few vivid dreams during all of her pregnancies, but none as awful as she'd had with Addison.

Unable to get back to sleep, Maggie had wandered into the kitchen, surprised by the figure of Carly standing by the window, looking ghostly in a long white nightgown. She didn't remember the conversation but recalled that it had been one of the few times Carly had offered any comfort to the teenage girl dealing with the consequences of her actions.

"You know that Carly—Nana—wasn't my real mother, don't you?" Maggie said in a quiet voice.

"But she was still my grandmother. And she's the only one I had. I know Granny Fiona was around a lot, but it's not the same as having a real nana."

"I guess I'm going to be a real nana." Maggie blinked away the sudden wetness in her eyes. She'd known Addison was pregnant from the first blue line on the test, but until that moment, hadn't realized what that meant for her.

She was going to be a grandmother. She was going to have a new little baby to love and cherish and spoil and adore...

For the first time, Maggie's heart lifted as she gazed at her daughter.

Addison rubbed her belly. "You'll spoil her."

"*Her*?"

"With all the girls in this family, there's no way I'd be having a boy. Adam used to say—" She pinched her lips closed after the name escaped.

Maggie took a sip of the bourbon, feeling the warmth of the spirit chasing it down to her belly. "What did Adam say?"

"He really wanted a boy." Addison kept her eyes fixed on the cup in her hands. "We used to joke; I'd say how he had to be extra nice to me so I'd try to make a boy for him."

"You weren't extra special nice to him," Maggie pointed out, trying not to sound judgemental.

Addison didn't reply. Which, Maggie thought, was better than the defensive anger Addison always used whenever she found herself in trouble.

Maggie sipped her drink and waited. The two of them sat there, the only sounds the ticking clock and faint voices from Kady's room.

"So what happened?"

Addison rolled her eyes. "I don't think you want the details."

Maggie shifted in her chair. "I guess I just want to know why. What was so terrible with you and Adam that you had to go looking for someone else? A few someones, if you believe the rumours."

"Billy didn't mean anything," Addison said grimly.

"And Brady did. But what about Adam? Tell me what happened."

Addison sighed and set her cup on the table beside her. She took out her ponytail, letting her bright red waves cascade around her shoulders. Maggie's heart gave a thump of pride as she looked at her girl—so beautiful with her delicate features and turned-down mouth. Addison looked more like her Aunt Dory than either one of her parents, the same calculating blue eyes and smile that could transform her face.

"There was nothing *wrong* with Adam," Addison said finally. "But I don't know what was right about him either. He was fun when we got married; it was fun setting up the house and being together. But then he always had to work, and wasn't happy when I forgot to do things around the house."

Maggie sighed. "Marriage takes a lot of work. It's not always fun."

"I expected that and I put in the work," Addison burst out. "But I missed the fun. Adam was... He got boring."

"Boring."

"I don't know what else to say. I know it makes me look bad."

"I don't really care about you looking bad, I just want to understand."

"One night I went out with the girls in Blind River and Billy was there. That just happened. You know when you're excited about a guy and can't really think straight?"

"It's been a while," Maggie admitted.

"Weren't you ever tempted when you were married?" Addison demanded. "You were with Daddy for years and you're telling me that never once—"

"I loved your father," Maggie interrupted. She remembered once...

She'd been twenty-one, exhausted from Addison, from refereeing Cat and Brenna's endless fighting, from Dory's teenage rebellion. Mike was solid and content, but Maggie had been frustrated, bordering on resentful. There had been once, when she was with Leila at a party, the two of them having a rare night out together.

There had been drinking and dancing and Brett Lyons outside in the moonlight.

There had been one kiss, just one kiss before Maggie had pushed him away and ran inside to the safety of Leila.

But Addison didn't need to know that.

"I get it," she said instead. "It's exciting and new."

"The thing with Brady was different," Addison confessed, her voice low. "He came into the vet with his sister's dog. And we got talking. He was so sweet and different than what he's usually like. He was so worried about the dog. He had to leave him there, and when he came back the next day, we talked again. Then he asked if I wanted to get a coffee on my break."

"Knowing full well you were married," Maggie said grimly.

"We've been friends for years. It meant nothing...until it wasn't nothing. Until we were texting all the time, and he kept making excuses to see me. Nothing happened for so long. I wouldn't let it. I felt bad about letting things with Billy get out of hand and I didn't want... I did, but I *wouldn't*."

"But you did."

"Adam went out of town. We had been fighting—not really fighting, but I could tell he wasn't happy either."

"Did he know about Brady? Or Billy?"

Maggie couldn't believe she was sitting here discussing her daughter's affairs. Affairs. Plural.

Addison shook her head. "I don't think he knew about anything. He never paid any attention to me, so what was I supposed to do?"

"Get in his face. Make him pay attention to you. Do you love him?"

"Adam? More like... a friend. We lived together, but there's no connection anymore."

"And Brady?"

Addison's eyes lit up, and Maggie's heart sank.

Chapter Thirteen

MANAGER PAUL STOOD BY the front doors of FoodMart with a customary scowl on his face as Maggie breezed by him. She often wondered if Paul was especially bad-tempered toward her because he knew once upon a time, Maggie had been offered his job.

She'd declined, even though the pay raise would have helped. But Mike told her she didn't need the extra responsibility, more stress, regardless of what the pay raise would be. They would make do, he'd promised. He'd provide for his family.

And even his death had provided a windfall for them. The insurance cheque sat in the bank, prepared to gain only pennies of interest, a constant reminder that Mike had to die for her to get that money.

She wouldn't think of that this morning. She didn't want to think of anything. Maggie headed for the bakery without her usual cheerful swagger, vowing to find a mindless task that would keep her busy.

She found cakes to decorate.

FoodMart had lost a lot of cake-decorating business thanks to Cat's sideline, the oh-so-originally named Cat's Cakes. Not that Maggie begrudged her sister her success, especially since she had been the one to teach Cat to bake. It had been a while since Maggie had decorated a cake, and as she smoothed the buttercream icing along the sides of the sheet cake, she realized she had forgotten how relaxing it could be. The smell of the sugar surrounded her as she added piping along the top, colourful roses.

Happy retirement!

This was for the loan manager, Mrs. Lewis, who always gave Maggie a cheerful wave when she was in the bank.

She had to figure out something to do with the insurance money. It was just sitting there, only gaining pennies of interest.

But she didn't have to figure that out now. Maggie added an extra rose, knowing Mrs. Lewis' sweet tooth.

"Maggie? You've got someone here, wants to talk to you," April called later as Maggie had finished with a Captain America birthday cake for five-year-old Ashley.

Maggie grimaced, wiping her hands on her white jacket, smearing blue icing along the hem and headed for the counter. She wasn't in the mood to talk to anyone. Her steps faltered when she saw him standing there.

"This is getting to be a habit," she said, embarrassment mixing with uncertainty, giving her a nice fluttery feeling in her stomach. "Yesterday...last night..."

"Yeah, well, just making up for lost time." Ben's smile didn't reach his eyes, which were shadowed with worry. His gaze shifted to April, who wasn't pretending not to listen. "Any chance you have a break coming up?"

Cake forgotten, Maggie checked the clock on the wall. "I've got a couple minutes." She peeked around the counter to see if Paul was nearby and found the coast clear. "Come through and we can go outside. You can leave your basket here."

She led Ben through the back room. The knowing smiles of the other bakery employees gave her a guilty rush, like playing hooky in high school.

There was a lightness in her step as Maggie pushed open the door leading to the little area behind the store. She stopped beside a picnic table and tried to ignore the cigarette butts strewn on the ground. "What's up?"

"I forgot granola bars for Miranda yesterday, so I thought I'd come say hi." He glanced down at the basket he still carried with a rueful smile. "I guess I should have left this inside."

"Don't worry about it. I can vouch that you're not about to run off with a FoodMart basket, as handy as they might be." She smiled at Ben's expression of confusion. "I used to take a few for Mike. They were good for carrying wood into the house, keeping his tools together..." She trailed off, confused by the expression of resignation that flashed across his face.

"Actually, I came to see how you were," he said, his words rushing together. "I was worried after yesterday."

"Yesterday," she repeated. "Not my best day."

"I could see that. Your little altercation here—"

"That sounds so polite."

"And dealing with the arsehole parent at the game."

"I signed up to deal with the arsehole parents," Maggie said. "But I don't think Mike had to deal with as many as I do when he was coaching."

"Yeah, well, it might be different for you. Seeing as how you're a woman."

"So nice that you noticed," Maggie teased. She pulled her ponytail over her shoulder, seeing the grey streaking the red, and flipped it back again.

"Not to offend you," Ben said hastily.

"You must have forgotten that it's nearly impossible to offend me."

Ben smiled, his dimple cutting into his cheek. "I always liked that about you. It was almost like hanging out with one of the guys. Only you weren't a guy," he added quickly.

"No, I wasn't."

"So, look, I got you these," Ben said in a rush, pulling a package of red Twizzlers out of the basket. "I haven't paid for them yet, but I will. I wanted to do something to help, and I remember you used to eat them before a test. Said the sugar relaxed you."

"It did—does." She couldn't stop the smile creeping across her face. "You bought me candy?"

"I'm going to pay for it," Ben said defensively, prompting a laugh from Maggie. A real laugh, with humour, that lightened the weight pressing down on her shoulders.

"Thank you." She ripped open the package with her teeth, inhaling the cherry syrup smell of the licorice. "Want one?"

"I hate the stuff," he admitted. "I didn't get a chance to really talk to you last night, but that was a good game. You're a good coach."

"Thank you," she repeated.

"But the real reason I came by is to see if you were okay. Heather was a piece of work in high school, but she's worse now."

"I'm sorry you had to see it," Maggie began.

"Why? What do you have to be sorry about? Heather was the one out of place."

"I shoved her into a table! And you—you were only trying to help. I broke the mayonnaise..."

"I think it was my elbow that did that." Ben shrugged, a hint of a smile on his face. "I wasn't the one who had to clean it up." The morning sun pushed through the clouds and fell on his face, haloing the dark hair and making him squint. He stepped closer to Maggie.

"Thank you. It's like the only thing I can say to you," Maggie said softly.

"Well, you can stop. And you're welcome. I've only been back a little while, and even I can tell there's a town full of folks who would have loved to give Heather that shove. It was too bad she gave you the cause to do it."

Maggie squinted into the sun as she glanced at Ben. "Thanks." He was so cute when he smiled.

When did she start thinking men were cute?

"It was pretty funny to watch," Ben continued. "Her face...and then when you kicked her shoe."

Maggie covered her face with her hands. "I can't believe I did that."

"It was pretty impressive." Ben paused, and Maggie peeked through her fingers to find him studying her. "But...like I said, I was worried about you."

"You don't have to be. I'm fine."

"The thing is…" Ben narrowed his eyes. "I don't think you are."

"Thanks," she said sarcastically.

"You keep telling yourself that everything is great, and you're handling things, and you start to believe it until everything blows up, and you realize you're not," he said slowly. "Or maybe you are, and I don't know anything."

Maggie was too tired to lie to Ben, so she said nothing, sensing that he knew exactly the turmoil she was feeling under the surface.

"I also came by," he began, shifting his weight awkwardly. "Miranda is trying out Brownies tonight, to see if she wants to join in the fall, and the boys are with my parents, and well, this is the first free night I've had in a while and I wondered if you wanted to get a drink with me?" Ben finished in a rush, and it took Maggie a moment to decipher what he had said.

"I've drunk a lot in the last twenty-four hours." Maggie laughed nervously.

"Or dinner."

Had Ben just asked her for dinner?

"Oh." Maggie looked at the expectant expression on Ben's face, hopeful and nervous, and felt a flutter deep in her belly.

"That was probably the worst invite you've ever gotten," he said ruefully.

"I have to admit, there hasn't been a lot to compare to."

"If you're busy or got things to do with the girls…"

"No… I mean, *no,* I don't have anything on tonight."

"I understand if you don't want to, or if it's too soon."

"Are you trying to convince me *not* to go out with you?" Maggie trailed off, face flaming at the thought that maybe this was purely a friendly invite. Two friends who hadn't seen each other in years, catching up on things, purely friendly things...

Ben appeared just as awkward. "This isn't going like I'd hoped. Maybe I should start over." He took a deep breath and looked her in the face. "Maggie, would you like to have dinner with me tonight?"

She couldn't stop the smile, so wide and big, no matter how she tried to tamp it down. "I'd like that."

"I'd like that too. Great."

"Great."

Maggie grinned at him.

Chapter Fourteen

T HE FIRST THING MAGGIE did when she got home from work was to call her sisters.

"I need something to wear," she bleated, thankful when Brenna answered the phone. It was better to talk to Brenna since Cat still dressed like a teenager, often borrowing clothes from Addison and Evie. Plus, being newly divorced, Brenna probably had more dating experience. Maybe she'd have some advice.

"What's going on?"

Maggie heard Cat's voice in the background. "If that's Maggie, tell her I'm pissed about that cake! I could have done a better job."

"Maggie can do a cake just as well as you can," Brenna shouted back to Cat, thankfully moving the phone away from her mouth. "Why do you need something to wear?" she asked, her attention back to Maggie.

The question wasn't a surprise. Maggie cared little for her appearance, even less since Mike died. But after Ben had asked her out, she'd taken a mental inventory of her closet and realized she had a problem. "Ben's taking me to dinner tonight."

"Whaaaat?"

"Ben's taking me to dinner tonight," Maggie repeated, the enormity of the words sinking deeper with every syllable.

Only eight months after her husband died, and she's already going out with another man? Maggie cringed and gripped the phone tighter.

"Maybe I shouldn't be doing this." From Maggie's reflection in the mirrored closet door, the furrow between her eyes looked like it was threatening to take over her forehead. "Maybe this is a bad idea."

"It's not a bad idea! This is a *date*! You have a *date*! Cat, Maggie has a *date*!"

"It's not a real date. It shouldn't be a date."

"Are you kidding? A man asked you out for dinner. To me, that's a date! Especially if you're going through your closet looking for something to wear."

"I don't know. Maybe I shouldn't be doing this."

"Why not?"

"Because...because," Maggie bleated, sounding like one of the baby goats from the farm on top of the hill.

"Because there's no reason. Seriously, Maggie." Brenna's voice deepened as she lost some of her giddiness. "The girls will be fine."

"I'm not worried about the girls."

She *hadn't* worried about the girls, not until Brenna mentioned them.

"I shouldn't go. I'll call and tell him I'm busy...things got busy. I'll think of something."

"Don't you dare!" Maggie sucked in her breath. Bossy Brenna was back. "You've known Ben Higgins your whole life—"

"Actually, I haven't really, if you consider how long he's been away."

Brenna ignored her argument. "You're a widow, he's a widower. You've known each other forever—"

"Is that the only reason he asked me out?" Maggie felt like she should be outraged but it came out as disappointed.

"Well, I doubt he would have asked you out if he'd been married."

Maggie chewed on the side of her mouth.

"Calm down, Mags," Brenna said as if she could read her thoughts.

"Are you sure?" The question came out so quietly that Maggie didn't recognize her own voice.

"Of course I'm sure," Brenna said, her voice laced with sympathy and equally quiet. Maggie blinked back the sudden dampness in her eyes. "Now, tell me, what's the matter?"

Maggie glanced into her closet, at the hanging shirts and skirts, the fabrics and colours. "I don't even know where to start. Hardly anything fits, and everything's at least ten years old."

"I tried to take you shopping!"

"Well, I can't go now. Help me, please, Bee."

Maggie could hear the swell of pride in Brenna's voice at being asked for help. "Do you have a black dress?"

"Yes, the one I wore to the funeral. Maybe not the most appropriate for this date-not-a-date."

"No...plus, it's Forest Hills, so dresses are out. You have a pair of black pants?"

"Yes, the ones I wear to work every day and they smell like bread. If I wear them, Ben's going to think I have a yeast infection." Maggie giggled.

"Yeast—oh, god, Maggie!"

"Well, it's true. They smell like the bakery."

Brenna was still laughing. "You shouldn't say that."

"Maybe I shouldn't be doing this."

"No, you should. Definitely should. Where's he taking you?"

"I have no idea. Probably Woody's."

"Really?"

"It's not a date, Bee! It's two friends getting together to catch up." There was no answer from Brenna. "Really," Maggie added firmly.

"I'll be over in a minute."

"Why are you dressed like that?" Clare asked later, surprising Maggie in the kitchen. Among the piles of clothes Brenna had brought over was a blue flowing tunic top that flattered the good and hid the bad. Worn over a pair of jeans unearthed from the back of the closet, the outfit wasn't too bad.

Grief had done good things to her body because the muffin top was practically gone, as were the saddlebags once attached to her thighs.

Maggie rubbed her legs, trying to erase the fold marks marring the denim. "Because I'm going out. Addison and Kady will be home."

"Are you going out with Aunt Bee and Cat? Because Cat said I could go over and play with the dogs—"

"I'm not going out with your aunts," Maggie interrupted, adding pasta to the boiling water. If she made them spaghetti now, Addison could heat it up when they were ready to eat.

"Then who are you going with?" Maggie looked up to see Clare with an expression of confusion on her face. "You don't have friends."

McKenna stood behind her with a matching expression. "You're wearing makeup."

Maggie was surprised at how alike the two girls appeared at that moment. All five of them had her red hair, but their features were a mixture of her and Mike.

Now, both Clare and McKenna wore one of Mike's expressions, that of wary uncertainty.

"I have friends," Maggie protested, stirring the pasta. "And yes, I'm wearing a bit of makeup. Do you like it? Aunt Brenna helped me, because you know I'm not used to wearing it."

"Why are you wearing it now?" McKenna asked.

"Pardon?"

Maggie groaned inside. Stalling would only make things worse. No point hiding the truth. She set down the spoon and faced her girls, trying not to wince as they stared back at her. Why did the similarity to Mike have to be so strong *now*? "Look, I'm going out with a friend of mine that I haven't seen in a long time."

"Do I know her?" Clare asked, reaching for the bag of chips on the counter.

"It's not a her. His name is Ben." She wanted casual, she was hoping for casual and failed miserably.

Clare's hand, full of potato chips, stopped midway to her mouth. "Who's *Ben?*"

"Ben Higgins. He's a friend of mine from school."

"Is that the guy from the baseball game last night?"

"Same guy. Remember I said he used to tutor me in high school?"

"He should have worked harder at helping you so you could still help McKenna with her homework," Clare scoffed, losing interest in the conversation. She stuffed the chips in her mouth and made a beeline to the television.

Maggie breathed a sigh of relief when she heard the song from *Paw Patrol* float into the kitchen. One crisis averted, one to go.

"Don't you love Daddy anymore?" McKenna still stood in the doorway, staring at Maggie with accusing eyes.

"Of course I do, McKenna. This has nothing to do with how I feel about Daddy."

"Then why are you going on a date with another man?"

Maggie picked up the spoon and hoped she could still her shaking hand. "It's just supper."

"You're wearing makeup and perfume. It's a date."

"Are you gonna have sex?" Clare asked, suddenly rejoining the conversation.

"No one is having sex with anyone," Maggie said, holding tight to calm. This was a bad idea. She should have known the girls would be upset, even though McKenna would have been the last one she would expect to have issues.

But McKenna was fourteen, and with the age came confusing hormones and issues no parent could understand or relate to.

"I'm going to dinner with a friend," Maggie said, hoping the truth would set her free. "I don't know if that makes it a date because it's been a long time since I've been on one. But I still love your father, and always will. That will never change, no matter who I go to dinner with."

"But Daddy's dead," Clare said cheerfully to her sister. "So it's okay for Momma to hook up with this guy."

"What—no! How do you know about that, when I don't even know what that is?"

"You're hooking up?" McKenna asked, her face aghast with horror.

"No! It's just dinner!" It would have been better to sneak out to Brenna's and get dressed there. Have Ben pick her up there too. What would the girls say when he showed up? Please, don't let them embarrass her?

"But what about Daddy?"

Maggie felt her heart crack at the question asked in McKenna's quiet little voice. She had always been the calm one, standing back in the shadows to let her sisters, and their more exuberant person-alities, take centre stage. Mike had always tried to draw McKenna out, making an effort to spend time with her, just the two of them, but since his death, Maggie had had no time for one-on-one time with their sensitive daughter.

She vowed to do so that weekend. She and McKenna would do something; just the two of them.

But until then, this had to be dealt with.

"I will always love your father," Maggie said, putting her hands on McKenna's shoulders. The girl was already only a few inches shorter than Maggie, growing up so fast. Gone was the fullness of face and stick figure from her pre-teen years. Now McKenna had the beginnings of cheekbones as well as impressive chest measurements, hidden for the most part with baggy sweatshirts. "And I'm not looking for anyone to replace him, because that's just not possible. He was the love of my life." She took a deep breath and willed away the tears. "But I've known Ben a long time, and he's just moved back into town. He lost his wife too, so we have that in common."

"Is he looking for someone to replace his wife?" McKenna asked in a bitter tone.

"I don't think so. I'm sure he still loves her too. But do you remember when Natalie moved away." Natalie and McKenna had been best friends since kindergarten and McKenna had been devastated when Natalie's family moved away two years ago. "You missed her, but you still did things with your other friends. And that was good because you would have been lonely without your other friends."

"Are you lonely?" McKenna's eyes were large and searching. With a sigh, Maggie pulled her close for a hug.

"How can I be lonely when I have my girls? And my sisters." McKenna sniffed a laugh at Maggie's rueful tone. "But that's a lot of women. Sometimes it's nice to talk to a man."

"You can talk to Seamus."

"Seamus is like my little brother. Do you think I want to talk to him all the time?" Maggie moved back to the stove, to the pot that was about to overflow. "Mommas need friends too, and that's what Ben is."

"Is he going to be more than a friend?"

Maggie's first instinct was to soothe, to lie. To tell McKenna that no, of course, Ben was and only would be a friend.

But the giddiness in her stomach as she got dressed told her differently, and she couldn't lie to the girls, especially not McKenna.

"I don't know." She looked McKenna straight in the eye. "I like Ben as a friend but..." She shrugged helplessly. "I think he's really cute too. And he brought me licorice today at the store."

McKenna rolled her eyes. "Oh boy."

"That's a nice thing to do, isn't it? He's a nice guy. You can meet him when he comes to pick me up."

"Are you going to marry him?"

"I'm going to go out to dinner with him. And I'll figure out everything else as I go along. Just like I always do."

Chapter Fifteen

S HE HAD FINISHED WITH the spaghetti, leaving the pot on the stove when the knock on the door sounded.

"He's here!" Clare bellowed, standing two feet away from the front door so there was no chance of Ben not hearing her.

Maggie wiped her sweaty palm down the front of her jeans. What she wouldn't give for five more minutes to wipe the perspiration from her forehead and have another swipe of deodorant.

Ben was here.

And Clare was opening the door, flanked by Kady and McKenna.

Where did they come from?

Ben smiled as he stepped into the house, even though Maggie would have been quaking with fear had the situation been reversed. "Hey," Ben said cheerfully, directing his smile to a suspicious-looking Clare. "That was a great game last night. Your hit was amazing. My daughter Miranda and I were so impressed."

"Thanks." The compliment slightly mollified Clare, but she still stared at Ben with a wary gaze as he turned his attention to Kady.

"You must be Kady. My son Lucas mentioned you, although I'm sure I'm not supposed to tell you that; dark hair, in serious need of a cut?"

"He's the new guy? I saw him on the bus." Kady paused. "I like his hair."

"Of course you do. You're the exact audience he's trying to impress. I think he's a year or so younger than you are."

"I'm in grade eleven."

"He'll be in eleven next year, as long as he gets the history credit. I feel bad pulling him out almost at the end of the school year, but it couldn't be helped."

"He seems to be doing okay, with what I see of him on the bus. I did pretty good in history last year, so if he needs help, just ask."

Maggie's mouth dropped. Ben must have cast some sort of spell over Kady because Maggie had never heard of her offering to help someone with their homework.

Or Lucas Higgins was very cute.

"I'll tell him." Ben's smile faltered when he glanced at McKenna. "Oh, wow. You look so much like your mother back in high school."

"Really?"

Maggie felt a tug on her heartstrings at the surprise in McKenna's voice. No one ever mentioned the similarities between Maggie and McKenna—it was always Kady or Evie that got the attention.

"Really," Ben assured her. "It's actually kind of disconcerting." He gave a rueful chuckle and turned to Maggie.

"Hi," Maggie said as she exhaled. So far, so good. Maybe she'd be able to get out of the house while they were still transfixed.

"You look great. Ready to go?" Maggie could only nod. "It was really nice to meet you, girls."

"It was nice to meet you too."

Maggie raised her eyebrows, kissed the girls and reminded them of the spaghetti before following Ben out the door.

"What did you do to my girls?" she hissed as soon as they were down the steps.

"Nothing, I hope," Ben said with bewilderment.

"That went much better than I expected. They were a little...hostile...earlier."

Ben opened the door for her, and Maggie had to give herself a little push to act like the gentlemanly gesture happened all the time. The last time someone had opened the car door for her, she had been in labour with Kady, carrying a squirming Addison. Mike had—

Stop thinking of Mike.

Maggie settled into the car and lectured herself during the few moments it took Ben to walk around. No Mike. No guilt. Not for leaving the girls, not for enjoying a rare night out with a friend.

She had every right to spend time with a friend.

"Do you get the third degree from your kids when you go out on dates?" Maggie asked before she realized what she'd said. What that implied. "But this isn't a date. Or it doesn't have to be. I don't know what this is."

"I'm okay with it being a date," Ben said in a quiet voice. Maggie glanced sideways and saw his smile. "And I don't go out much myself."

Well, that cleared that question up fairly quickly. Maggie *was* on a date.

"It surprises me how much I drive here," Ben said, dropping the subject of date—or-no date—like it was a hot potato. "When I lived outside Ottawa, I had to drive everywhere. When I came back, I assumed I'd be walking because things are so close, but nope. Driving more than ever."

"It's the hills." Maggie gazed out the side mirror as the top of the hill was visible. "You take your life in your hands if you try and cross the road."

"I got the lecture from my mother. I was only here a day and thought I'd take the kids to the park. Mom went up one side and down the other, practically called me a bad parent to even think about it."

A transport truck passed them, going the other way, too fast for the speed limit. The car swayed from the rush of wind.

"As much as I like a nice walk, it's not something one does around here," Maggie said.

"So what does one do around here?" Ben asked as he turned into Woody's. "Hope this is okay. There's not a lot of choices, and I wasn't sure if you wanted to head out of town."

"Woody's is great," Maggie assured him, even though she inwardly cringed. If she hadn't already given the town enough fodder to send the tongues wagging, showing up with Ben would really take the cake.

She steeled her backbone and lifted her chin as she headed for the door.

Mrs. Patton, from the church, sat at the table near the entrance and glanced up without bothering to hide her curiousity. Amanda, from the Sandwich Shoppe, waved from a corner booth, leaning over to whisper to her husband as Maggie headed for the bar.

Trevor Mackey swiveled on his stool to watch her approach. "Maggie," he said curtly.

Trevor had been one of Mike's closest friends.

"Hey, Mags." Seamus was behind the bar with his usual cheerful expression, but his smile dimmed as he caught sight of Ben. "Two days in a row. What's up?"

"We thought we'd get something to eat. Do you remember Ben Higgins? He was a couple of years ahead of you."

"Sure." Ben stuck out his hand and after a wipe of his own on the towel, Seamus grudgingly shook it. "Table in the back is free. It's a little quieter back there, or it will be until the team comes in."

"We won't be here that late," Maggie said quickly.

Seamus nodded, his eyes wary as he noticed Ben's hand on Maggie's back. "I'll bring you over a couple of drinks. Wine?"

"Please." Maggie glanced at Ben.

"I'll have a pint of Stella." With a nod at Seamus, Ben led them to the table in the back of the restaurant. Maggie breathed a sigh of relief as she sat with her back to the restaurant, hidden from those sitting at the bar. Normally she couldn't care less about what the townsfolk thought, but she was tired of being the centre of attention.

"I remember Seamus as a kid running after your sister," Ben said as he sat across from her.

Maggie rolled her eyes. "Which one? The three of them have a messy history. He's with Cat now." She refused to glance around the restaurant even though she felt the eyes on her.

She was with a friend. She had every right to spend time with whomever she wanted to.

"You okay?" Ben asked in a quiet voice.

"Of course," she said brightly. "Why wouldn't I be?"

"They're not all staring at you. Well, maybe most—oops, that little old lady by the door is actually standing up to get a better look, so maybe all of them."

Maggie groaned.

Ben grinned at her. "Quiet town. Not much excitement."

"And right now I seem to be the cause of most of it."

"You should be flattered."

"Freaked out, more like it."

Seamus brought their drinks and menus, trailed by Fiona.

"I heard you were here and just had to come say hello," she said cheerfully, looking girlish with her close-cropped hair and black Woody's T-shirt. "It's nice to see you back in town, Ben." Fiona gave him a motherly glance. "Your parents must be happy to have you home."

"I think they're more excited about the kids."

"Well, grandchildren are special. I've six now, and a great-grand-baby on the way." She glanced at Maggie in time to see the grimace on her face. "Too soon to brag?" she asked apologetically.

"I'm not talking about this here." Maggie opened her menu, pointedly giving Fiona her shoulder.

"Maggie! Maggie *Maggie*!" Maggie looked up at the chant, trying not to wince as Missy Frew-Farrell barrelled over to the table. Missy had been Brenna's best friend since kindergarten; she was nice as they came, but prided herself on being on top of the news of Forest Hills.

Maggie wondered what Missy would start with—the fight at the store yesterday, or her appearance with Ben?

"I heard about Addison and Adam," she began, her voice heavy with sympathy. "And Brady," she added with a gleeful glance at Fiona.

"I did say I wasn't going to talk about it here," Maggie said ruefully.

"Good luck with that," Seamus threw over his shoulder as he walked away.

"Wait! Can we order?" Maggie called after him. Even though neither of them had opened the menus, maybe Missy and Fiona would take the hint.

No such luck.

"I'll send Cat over," Seamus promised. "Gotta get back to the bar."

"Running away with his tail between his legs," Missy said with a grin. "So how are things with Addison home?"

Maggie was as brief as she could be without being rude and after a few moments, Missy returned to her table. Fiona, after dropping a conciliatory hand on Maggie's shoulder, smiled at Ben and followed Missy.

Maggie exhaled loudly.

"I remember how close you were with Fiona," Ben said.

"Which makes it a little difficult to be angry with Brady. Fiona was Carly's best friend before she took to her room."

"I don't think I ever met your mother. That's kind of strange isn't it, seeing as how we started out in kindergarten together." Ben took a sip of his beer

"Looking back, we think she had bipolar disorder. She never got the help she needed. Besides, she wasn't my real mother." The words slipped out of Maggie's mouth like they were greased.

"She—really? Who was?"

"I have no idea. I really never cared to find out. I had my sisters, and Mike and they were all the family I needed." She sounded bitter, even to her own ears.

"You really don't know? In this town, people must have talked about it."

"It was the best-kept secret in town. Probably the only one." She picked up her menu and flipped it open. "I'm not sure what I want."

That was a lie. She already knew she would order the Meaty Mac 'n'Cheezy because that's what she always ordered when she came to Woody's. It had been Fiona's recipe and she would bring a huge pan of the pasta over for Maggie and her sisters. Her mouth watered just thinking of the cheese, not to mention the bacon and hunks of sausage.

"I was thinking of the chicken burger," Ben offered.

Maggie gave a quick shake of her head. "Mm...no. I wouldn't. I never can put my finger on why. I'd go for the cheeseburger instead."

"If you say so." He shut the menu and smiled at Maggie. "Do you come here a lot?"

"Well, it's really the only place in town."

"Is Forest Hills really a town? I always considered it a village. Allison was from Ottawa, so everything seems small after that."

"Allison. That was your wife?" The easy way his wife's name rolled off his tongue threw Maggie, but she quickly rallied. "Where did you meet?"

"University."

"I heard you were hiding back here."

Maggie looked up with something akin to gratitude as Cat sauntered toward them. She wasn't sure if she was ready for the dead-wife talk, in case it led to the dead-husband one. "See, no secrets," she said to Ben before turning to Cat. "I didn't think you were working tonight."

Cat cocked a hip by the corner of the table. Her dark red hair was swept up in a ponytail and her well-worn jeans fit her like a glove.

Looking like she did, Cat never had to worry about what to wear.

"I'm not. I'm off to the game, but I thought I'd come in first to say hi."

Maggie suspected Seamus had been on the phone to her sister before they had even sat down.

"Hi!" Cat waved at Ben. "Long time no see."

"You look a little...different," Ben offered with a grin. "More mature."

Cat's laugh was loud. "I should hope so. I would have been six or seven when you two were holed up in the kitchen with your math books. Ugh. I bet that's why I hate the subject. So what'll it be tonight?"

"Burger." Ben glanced at Maggie. "Bacon, cheese, and fries. No onion."

"Sweet potato fries. They're awesome. Actually, don't, or Maggie'll eat them all."

"Thank you, sister. Now, go away."

With another laugh and a flick of her red hair, Cat left them, swinging her hips.

"She didn't ask what you wanted."

"She knows."

After Cat left them, Missy rushed back to find out more about Addison, dragging her husband, Colin. And after they left, Leila stopped by.

"Excuse me for a minute," Ben said after he'd greeted Leila.

Maggie watched him walk away before he was swallowed up by the group around the bar.

"How's it going?" Leila demanded in a low voice.

"I don't know because I haven't had a chance to talk to him!" Maggie erupted.

"He looks good. I always thought he was cute in high school," Leila confessed.

"I think he looks better now," Maggie admitted with a sheepish smile.

"Definitely." Leila raised her eyebrows. "So? What's going to happen tonight?"

"We're going to eat." Maggie glanced pointedly at her friend. "Hopefully not be interrupted every five seconds."

Leila held up her hands. "I'll go I'll go." She glanced behind her and leaned forward again. "Are you going to go home with him?"

"What? No," Maggie said firmly. "Kids, Leila. Besides, I hadn't even given it a thought."

"It's been eight months, Maggie. Yes, you have."

"Maybe the tiniest bit of a thought," Maggie admitted. Of course, she'd had thoughts of that nature. Who didn't? It was normal, wasn't it? "But honestly, I haven't had the bandwidth for it since Mike. That's serious stuff."

"It doesn't have to be. It could be a fun romp for you."

"I'm not the fun type. And the last time I had a romp, I got pregnant."

"You're older now, smarter."

"Let's go back to the older part." As Leila laughed, Maggie glanced around her to see Ben returning. "He's coming back. Go away."

"I want details," she hissed as she backed away.

"There won't be any," Maggie mouthed as Ben took his seat. "Sorry about that."

"Don't be. You were always the most popular girl in school, and I see nothing's changed. But I did talk to Seamus about the interruptions." One of the waitresses appeared with a paper bag. "How about we take things to go?"

Chapter Sixteen

T HEY TOOK THEIR MEAL in a take-out bag and left. Ben by-passed the baseball diamond and headed to the river where there was an ancient picnic table under a tree.

"It's not the most romantic," Ben said, gesturing to the cigarette butts strewn on the ground.

"It's fine. It's been a while since I've had romantic."

"Maybe it's time you get some back." He pulled out two Sty-rofoam clamshells. "It's one of the things I regret about Allison. Even before she got sick, we'd let the romance go. Work, running after the kids—we forgot to make time for just us. And then she got sick."

"I think I've always thought of myself as a mother first and a wife second. Or a woman." It was an admission Maggie had never made to anyone, but here, sitting with Ben in the gloaming, it slid out unexpectedly. "Mike and I—I loved him, but romance was never in the forefront. We were so young, and then there were so many kids."

Ben nodded. "I told myself that if I ever had another chance with someone, I'd make it a priority."

"It's because you're mature now. You know what's needed for a relationship. Not that your relationship wasn't good, but you need something different when you're in your forties then when you first start out in your twenties. Or teens."

"You were so young," Ben marvelled. "I remember looking at Mike and wondering how was he going to do it. Never you. You were born to be a mother."

"I didn't really have a choice."

"You raised your sisters. That wasn't just babysitting, was it?"

"No. My—Carly checked out on us even before my father left, so they were my responsibility."

"That was pretty amazing of you."

Maggie shrugged. "They were my sisters. They needed someone to take care of them."

They talked about Cat and Brenna, about Kayleigh's store and her relationship with Erica. They talked about Ben's parents and the difficult decision to move home.

"We don't close on the house for a few more weeks, so I'm a great one to be dating. Not only do I have kids, but I still live with my parents," he said self-deprecatingly.

"I'm going to have a newborn in the house any day now," Maggie countered.

They talked about people they went to school with; who had left and who had stayed. They talked so much that Maggie's pasta was cold long before she was finished.

The night sky darkened to purple as the ball game finished and another started. The lights of the diamond turned on. Ben's face was in shadow which made it easy for Maggie to unload her thoughts.

Mike had listened, but he'd always had his own thoughts and worries competing with hers. With Ben, Maggie could tell he was giving her all his attention.

For once, she was with a person she didn't have to take care of. There was no maternal instinct or wifely duty—there was only attraction and interest and relief.

"Did you know I had the biggest crush on you all through high school?" Ben asked as he offered her the last cold sweet potato fry.

"You didn't. You went out with—what was her name?"

Maggie laughed as Ben clutched his chest. "You never even noticed me."

"You tutored me in math for two years! How could I not notice you? Do you know that because of you, I made sure I got my diploma and took bookkeeping courses? I would have been just another girl bride without any education if you hadn't pushed me so hard."

"I think you would have pushed yourself, but I'll take the credit. I'd rather have taken you out, though."

Maggie caught her breath. "I don't know what to say."

"Don't say anything. Unrequited love—isn't that what high school is all about? Before you got together with Mike, I thought I might have had a chance. After you laid eyes on Mike, every guy in school was out of luck. And he was such a great guy that I couldn't even hate him for stealing you."

"I had no idea," Maggie said softly. But maybe she did; maybe deep down she knew there had been something more than friendship in Ben's eyes when he sat at her table, separated by books and papers and the demands of her sisters.

"I think that's okay because things worked out the way they were supposed to. Maybe not as nice, but..."

Maggie could see his smile in the dusky twilight. "Even if I knew how it would end, I couldn't have changed anything about my life."

"Same. It made me who I am."

Maggie opened her mouth to say something about the man Ben was, but a roar from the baseball field interrupted.

"I hate to say it, but these mosquitoes are eating me alive," Ben said ruefully.

"It is getting late," Maggie agreed just as reluctantly, slapping at a buzz by her ear.

She helped him clean up the Styrofoam containers, flipping on the flashlight on her phone to make sure they had gotten everything. The light illuminated Ben's face, and she saw him smiling at her.

"I had a really good time," he said.

"So did I." The moment stretched between them, but neither of them moved.

Another cheer from the ballpark. "I'd better get you home."

During the drive back home, Maggie ordered herself to relax. It had been a good night. It didn't matter that he hadn't kissed her. It was probably better that way, with her tasting of cheese and sausage and pasta.

Ben pulled into the drive and turned off the car. "I'll walk you to the door."

Even though Maggie was perfectly capable of walking the twenty feet from the driveway to the front door, she allowed it. She didn't want to sit in his car saying goodnight. Every head within spying distance would be craning to see. Out in the open was better. They could shake hands, or hug good night.

"I had a lot of fun tonight," Ben said as they climbed the steps.

"I did too." She gave a bark of laughter. "I was so nervous."

"Thank god. So was I."

"But you must have done this before..." Even before she trailed off, Ben was shaking his head.

"First time. There's never been anyone I've wanted to meet—or reconnect with, in your case. Before I came back, I was happy to be alone with the kids. I gave them all the attention when they needed it and hung out with friends when I needed adult companionship."

"I have my sisters for that."

"My brother's not the best at hanging out," Ben admitted. "It's been getting better since I came home, but we've never been close. Not like you and your sisters."

"I don't know what I would do without them," Maggie confessed. "They got me through this."

Ben paused, the silence broken by the faint sound of cheering from the ball park. "It's a nice night for baseball."

"It's always a good night for ball. That's what Mike used to say."

"You must miss him. And I think that breaks every dating rule."

"Mentioning my dead husband?"

"I brought up Allison earlier."

"It's impossible not to. They were a big part of our lives. Of everyone's life."

"They were."

It was the *were* that did it. The faint emphasis on the word suggested Ben was ready to move on from the pain of the past.

Maggie took a deep breath, a step forward and kissed him—just as Ben was about to say something, so his mouth was wide open under Maggie's lips.

She drew back with a mortified gasp. "Oh god!"

Ben's hand flew to his lips. "You kissed me."

"I think I was trying to. I'm sorry."

"Don't be sorry. You caught me off guard. I didn't expect it."

"I shouldn't have—"

"I'm glad you did." He placed a hand on her waist. "Can you try it again?"

"Maybe you should go first."

"No, I like that you did. It's been a long time since a woman's wanted to kiss me. Or since I've wanted to kiss her back."

"So it's okay..." Maggie took a tentative step closer.

"It's very okay."

She placed a hand on his chest, felt his hand curve around her waist as she leaned forward. Ben met her half way; this time, their lips meeting in the barest touch. Maggie pulled back, considered.

That wouldn't do. She was about to try again, when Ben took matters into hand, suddenly kissing her so thoroughly that Maggie felt like she was being lifted off the floor.

"It is nice when someone wants to kiss you," she murmured when they took a break.

Ben laughed and kissed her again. Maggie felt it all the way down to her toes. How could she have lasted that long without being kissed?

And then the door was pulled open behind her, leaving Maggie pressed up against the screen door.

"What the hell is going on out here?"

Maggie wrenched her mouth away from Ben's, her body out of his embrace, to see Kady on the other side of the screen door with her arms crossed and a fierce expression on her face. "I—why are you—Kady—"

And then her daughter burst out laughing. "Your face! I had to do it–you did it to me once, when Matthew and I–" At the mention of his name, Kady's laughter stopped and her face drooped. She turned away, leaving the door wide open.

Maggie glanced in to see Addison on the couch. "I told her not to do it. We didn't think that you and him were..." Addison trailed off with a smirk on her face.

Maggie's face flamed as she turned back to Ben. "Sorry about that."

"I'm not," he said softly enough so Addison couldn't hear. "Well, maybe about the door."

Any response she might have come up with caught in her throat at Ben's expression. Was that how he had been looking at her at the ball park? Like he was a hungry kid and she was an ice cream sundae?

"I'd better go," he said, backing up.

"I'd better get in," she agreed.

"I'll see you...sometime?"

"Sometime."

"Sometime."

Maggie quickly opened the screen door as Ben made his way back to his car, looking over his shoulder twice before he made it.

Maggie stood framed in the doorway, watching his car pull out of the drive.

"You need to work on your goodbyes," Addison drawled from the couch.

Maggie turned and stared at her daughter, then without a word, headed for the stairs.

"Does that mean you had a good time?" Addison called after her.

Chapter Seventeen

After peeking into Clare's room to find her youngest flat on her back and snoring, Maggie closed herself in her bedroom.

Her cheeks still flamed, torn by glee that *she kissed him and he kissed her back* and humiliation that this had happened under the judgemental eyes of her daughters.

How dare Kady open the door on her!

In another life, Maggie might have thought it was funny but not tonight.

She had *kissed* him—Ben. Maggie pushed her hands through her hair. Awash in guilt, she ignored the little voice that reminded her *Mike was dead*. Not only had she agreed to a date, but she had also taken it one step further.

She had betrayed Mike.

Maggie sank onto the bed as memories loomed, memories of the first time Mike had kissed her. Many of the details had faded, but Maggie remembered how Mike had fumbled with his moves, like he always fumbled gestures of affection. He had never been smooth and suave and confident.

But that was all right because he was Mike.

Six weeks after they first met, Maggie had found herself in the front seat of Mike's truck, freed from her virginity. It had been awkward and slightly painful, but Mike—Mike had been in heaven.

The only thing Maggie could think about was what would it be like if she got pregnant?

What would it be like to have a child of her own?

And so the next time, Maggie had used Mike's enthusiasm to her benefit.

"It's okay," she had whispered when Mike confessed he no longer had a condom in his wallet.

"I'm fine," she assured him the next time.

And the next.

Maggie loved her sisters, but she wasn't their mother, as much as Brenna and Cat would have liked her to be. If she got pregnant, things would change. They would have to. Carly would stop locking herself in her room and come out, taking her place as the mother of the house, because Maggie would have her own child to look after.

Four times was all it took, with the sex getting better each time, and Maggie falling deeper in love with Mike every time she saw him. She loved him, wanted a life with him, but maybe it would be okay if it happened sooner rather than later.

And life with Mike began when Maggie got pregnant.

Maggie shook herself back to the present with a self-deprecating laugh at how naïve she had been. Carly never stepped up, and the only thing sacrificed was Mike's baseball career and what was left of Maggie's childhood.

With a deep sigh, Maggie got ready for bed. Why was she thinking of that now? It didn't matter now how her life with Mike had begun. It had been a good life and had nothing to do with Ben.

Except that she had *liked* kissing Ben.

The feel of his hand pressed against her back, another tangled in her hair, his lips pressed against hers. And yes, even the feel of his tongue in her mouth.

She couldn't remember the last time she'd been kissed like that—with feeling and passion and authority.

Maggie pulled on the well-worn jogging pants she wore to bed, along with an old baseball shirt of Mike's and stood at the side of the bed and stared at the pillow on Mike's side of the bed.

It was still his side of the bed. It would always be his side, even though the pillow no longer had the dent from his head, and the mattress no longer held the warmth from his body.

Mike had always been warm, like a heater tucked in beside her on cold nights. And he never really minded when she pulled her icy feet against his legs.

"Coming for a cuddle?" he'd murmur.

A sob rose, choked in her throat before it could escape. She kissed another man when Mike was alone and cold in the ground. "I'm so sorry," she gasped backing away from the bed like it was on fire.

How could she sleep there tonight when Mike was sleeping in the ground?

Maggie rushed down the stairs, her mind caught in a spiral of Mike. Addison was still up, lounging on the couch like a small hippo lying in the sun.

"I thought you went to bed." Addison struggled to sit up.

"Not yet. I have to talk to your aunts," Maggie muttered, sticking her feet into the nearest pair of shoes that fit, in her race to get out of the house.

"Now? It's the middle of the night!"

Maggie and Addison both looked at the lighted numbers on the cable box. "It's not even ten o'clock," Maggie said. She wanted nothing more than to crawl into bed and find the welcome respite from sleep but that wouldn't happen until she confessed to Mike. To apologize.

To make sure he forgave her.

"What's going on?" Addison wore a confused expression as she finally managed to pull herself into a sitting position. "Are you okay?"

"I won't be long," Maggie said, grabbing the sweater Kady had left by the door.

"I'll leave the light on for you," Addison called after her.

This was crazy. It was late, and there might be guests at the B & B. Maggie had no idea if Carly's room was even empty.

She needed Mike.

There was still a light on at the house as Maggie pulled in. She gave herself a moment to rethink what she was doing.

She'd told Mike she wouldn't be coming back. Their visits were over. It was time for Maggie to move on without him in her life. The only problem was how was she supposed to do that?

One of Cat's dogs gave a bark of warning as Maggie let herself in the front door. Cat appeared from the kitchen with a frown. "What are you doing here?"

"Is there anyone in Carly's room?" Maggie panted like she'd run a race.

"No, it's clear. Are you—? Okay, talk later," she finished as Maggie pushed past her and headed up the stairs.

Maggie slowed her steps as she reached the top, conscious that there might be paying guests tucked into bedrooms. Or possibly Brenna, although her room was on the third floor. She paused before pushing open the door to Carly's room.

Maybe this wasn't a good idea.

It wasn't, but that wouldn't stop her.

She wanted Mike. She wanted him so much that it hurt.

As she sat on the bed, the room began to chill, mixed with the smell of lilacs. "I'm back," she said, her voice almost a whisper.

Goose bumps rose on Maggie's arm's and she hugged Kady's sweater around her. "I need to talk to Mike." The lilac smell grew stronger as well as the chill. "Does that mean he's here, or it's just you?"

No response.

"Are you here, Mike?" She paused before continuing. "I went on a date tonight."

In a quiet voice, Maggie told Mike about Ben coming back to town and their night together and how everyone stared at her at Woody's.

"I felt like I was doing something wrong," she confessed. "Ben's wife died, so he must have understood. We talked about you, a little bit anyway. It felt wrong bringing you up, but I wanted you to be a part of it. That's why I came. I needed to tell you about it. You're still such a big part of my life."

Maggie hadn't realized she was crying until a tear dripped off her chin.

"I love you so much," she whispered. "But I like Ben, and I don't know what to do. I don't want to betray you, but I think I am. I don't know what to do."

"I don't know what to do," she said, the weight lifting with each repetition.

She told him about the fight with Heather at work, and Ben breaking it up. "I've been so mad since you died, but couldn't do anything about it. And then she got in my face and I was so *angry*. I've never felt so angry. It felt so good to let her have it. I pushed her into a table and kicked her shoe and it felt so *good*. I'm supposed to apologize to her, but maybe I need to thank her, instead."

The giggle squeezed out past the tears, the same way it had all the months ago at the funeral. Even that felt good too.

"It's been a really bad week. I know I said Sunday that I wouldn't be back, but I didn't know Heather was going to pull that stunt about Dylan and then Addison. I haven't told you about her, because there's nothing you can do about it and I don't want you to get upset."

Maggie thought about her words. "Do ghosts get upset? How do I know this is even reaching you? It could be like when you're talking on the cell and you go into a dead zone, only you don't realize it and you keep talking. This could be my dead zone."

She glanced around the room. "I guess that's what it is."

The chill in the air seemed to swirl around where she was sitting on the bed. "Does that mean you're getting this? Someone getting this? I can't understand ghost speak?"

Another giggle threatened to escape, this one louder. Maggie was aware of how she looked sitting there on the bed in a cold room, talking to herself. She had to struggle to believe Mike was there with her.

But she knew something was.

"This is so crazy. But...it helps. Somehow it helps. Is it crazy that talking to a ghost makes me feel better? I don't even know if it's you."

The cold air seemed to pulse. "I think it's you."

She took a deep breath. "So, Addison." Maggie told Mike quickly about the pregnancy, about Brady, about Addison moving home. "I know you'll be disappointed in her. I know I am. I can't believe she's capable of acting so callously. She's always been selfish, but this was her *marriage*, and she's ruined it. I look at her and she's so beautiful and loving, but so *stupid*. Such a waste for a little bit of excitement. Such a *Cat* thing to do."

Maggie stilled as her words rang into the room. When had she ever admitted she was disappointed in one of her daughters, or her sisters? Cat's marriage troubles had always upset Maggie, and she'd told Cat on more than one occasion. But never had she admitted that she was disappointed in her behaviour. Divorce was one thing and not always avoidable, but cheating and lying were never acceptable.

"But she's still my baby and I want her to be happy. The problem is that I don't know if Brady's going to be the one to make her happy. He's...Brady. He's practically her cousin, but thank god he's not. I don't know what's going to happen with the two of them, but Addison's back home for now. I doubt Adam will ever forgive her. I know I wouldn't."

For a moment, Maggie was tempted to confess how she herself had intentionally planned to get pregnant but held her tongue. It would serve no purpose to say that out loud.

Taking a deep breath, she felt a sense of calmness flow into her, settling into her core. Talking to Mike had done what she'd hoped. How could he always make her feel life wasn't as overwhelming as she'd thought? Was it his presence, or just talking to someone? As much as Maggie spent time with her sisters, she never really told them how she was feeling. She'd skirt the issue, giving few details about her emotional state, enough for them to feel satisfied that they'd done their sisterly duties by checking in with her.

Another violent shiver had her reaching for the quilt on the bed to pull around her shoulders, but instead, Maggie crawled under the covers.

The sheets were clean and cool, the bed comfortable.

It would be so easy to stay like this, to hide under the covers and let the world go on without her.

That was what Carly had done. What she had allowed herself to do—to stay there, hiding in a room blocked off from her home and family.

"I'm not like you," Maggie said in a wavering voice. "I love my girls. I love my life. Even though... Mike?" She caught herself at the sound of her voice. It sounded eerily like McKenna's.

"What do I do about Ben?"

Chapter Eighteen

The next morning, Maggie woke with a horrified gasp to find she was still in Carly's room, tangled under the covers. The room was warmer and the early morning sun eased through the curtains, but Maggie didn't linger. And even a painfully full bladder didn't stop her from racing out of the room, leaving the rumpled bed behind her.

Cat met her at the bottom with a confused expression. "You sound like a freight train coming down those stairs. Did you sleep here?"

"I fell asleep!" Maggie's voice was loud and accusatory like it was Cat's fault. It had been the fault of a cold room and a warm blanket and Maggie somehow giving in to the exhaustion rather than going another round with an uncommunicative ghost.

How could she have left the girls alone? Clare, so little, and Addison, so pregnant. They didn't know where she was. What if something—what if the police came again, or Heather Vreeland or—

"That's okay. The girls are fine. Addison is there." Cat touched her shoulder, somehow pulling her out of the turmoil of terror. "Maggie, it's fine."

Maggie leaned against the wall, heart racing. She hadn't spent a night away from her own house since she and Mike had taken the girls to Disneyland when Clare had been a baby. "But I never went home!"

"There's a first for everything. Want some coffee?"

Despite Maggie's pull toward the door, she couldn't help but be tempted by the smells coming from the kitchen. "What time is it?"

"Just after six. No one will be up for another hour."

Maggie's alarm wouldn't be going off for another half hour. "Can I have one to go? And I need the bathroom."

She took her time, trying to calm her racing heart. The girls would still be asleep; no one would know she was gone. Last night didn't have to mean anything.

Maggie had spent the night with Mike. The thought calmed her more than anything.

Cat was waiting for her with a worried expression on her face.

"Stop freaking out in there."

"How did–I'm not," Maggie protested. "I'm waking up. It takes a while."

"Not for you." Cat smirked. "I made you a coffee to go. Come and get muffins for the girls."

Maggie hadn't slept in the house for over twenty years but it still felt natural to follow Cat into the big kitchen, counter already busy with the ingredients for the apple oatmeal muffins she made fresh for guests.

Back when Maggie had lived there, it had always been *her* waking early in the morning to make muffins for her sisters, or whip up a batch of pancakes to ensure Brenna ate enough during the day. Her heart gave a painful throb as she recalled the years she acted as their mother, the love they gave her in return.

"You okay?" Cat asked, covering a plate of muffins with plastic wrap.

"I'm fine." It was her usual response, but was she really? She'd had a partial breakdown after being kissed, spent the night in a room with a ghost. But at least the overwhelming thoughts and worries that plagued her seemed to be at bay. Maggie was still confused but she'd lost the sickening heaviness that had threatened to weight her down. "I'm good."

"What happened?"

Maggie had no desire to talk about why she had come over. Admitting she talked to ghosts was embarrassing enough but having to come over to confess that she'd kissed another man was even worse.

But it had helped. She couldn't deny that she felt better.

Maggie shook her head as she accepted the plate. "Long, silly story. Don't worry about it."

Cat kept hold of the plate, forcing Maggie to meet her gaze. "Is this something we need to worry about? I know you like your visits to Mom's room, but last night felt different. You looked different. Scared."

Maggie tugged the plate away from Cat. "When have I ever given you something to worry about?"

Cat's eyebrows rose to peaked teepees on her forehead. "Should I make a list?"

Maggie gave her sister a reassuring smile. "I'm good," she repeated. "Thanks for the coffee."

She took the to-go cup full of coffee and muffins and headed to the minivan, still parked at a haphazard angle in front of the house, blocking Cat's little compact. The early morning sun was already bright, promising a warm day ahead. Maggie paused, listening to the birds singing and the chatter of forest creatures in the woods surrounding the house.

It was a nice day. When was the last time she'd noticed it was a nice day?

When was the last time she took to the woods to clear her mind, tramping through the paths that led up the hills? When was the last time she'd had time for herself? To relax and enjoy a nice day?

Monday she had sat on the porch with her sisters, but it had been the wine and the weed that had forced Maggie to relax.

She needed some Maggie time.

But that wasn't in the cards today. As Maggie made the quick drive to her own house, she ran through her list.

Work. That was constant. An eight-to-four job, five days a week had been her life for as long as she could remember. It had stopped being a challenge years ago, but Maggie enjoyed the interactions with the customers, the other employees.

Except for the Heather Vreelands who came in.

Maggie pulled into the drive with a sigh, dreading another day with Paul on her case. He'd pulled her aside Tuesday morning, giving her a lecture that had been more about listening to himself talk more than anything.

But still, Maggie had felt her manager's anxious gaze hovering over everything she had done yesterday, wondering if someone would push her over the edge again.

That wasn't going to happen.

The dogs met her at the door, stiff-legged and sleepy, but wide awake once they shuffled off the porch. Maggie stood on the porch watching them sniff every flower and blade of grass.

Mike had loved those dogs.

He'd gotten the two of them as puppies when Maggie had been pregnant with Clare. They had had dogs before, but always older dogs that didn't need to be trained. Maggie hadn't wanted the puppies, thought they'd be too much work with a new baby on the way, but Mike had done everything, treating the fat little bodies with as much care and concern as he did his own daughters.

The dogs were almost ten years old and slowing down. Maggie didn't want to think about what would happen when they stopped.

As the dogs bounded toward the woods and the hidden bounty of squirrels to chase, Maggie quietly opened the door, mindful of the squeak.

To find McKenna standing there.

Maggie jumped and hoped her smile hid the expression of guilt as she carefully closed the door, mindful of the noise. Hopefully, McKenna would think she was only letting the dogs out.

"Morning. You're up early." She reached out to kiss the top of McKenna's head and was met with a scowl and folded arms.

"Are you just coming home from your *date* now?" A mixture of scorn and horror and sadness coated McKenna's voice, and Maggie's heart sank.

"Oh, no, I—" At least she wore her pajamas, proof that she had been home. Been home and left…

"You spent the night with him! You spent the night with another man!"

"I didn't, McKenna. No! I came home last night, but I went back out."

"To see *him*?"

Maggie had no idea McKenna's voice could be so cold. She reached for her, but McKenna swerved away. "No, I didn't go to Ben's," she said, speaking clearly and firmly so there was no chance of misunderstanding. The kiss was one thing, but for McKenna to think she'd *slept* with Ben—

Would a fourteen-year-old think that about her mother?

Apparently, yes.

"I went to Cat and Brenna's." Maggie held up her coffee cup and the plate of muffins as proof. "Aunt Cat's takeout."

"Why?"

"Why was I there?"

At McKenna's emphatic nod, Maggie took a deep breath. This had always been the dilemma—what to hide from the girls and what to be honest about. Since Mike's death, Maggie felt taking a more truthful approach was best, especially as the girls were getting older, rather than hiding the worst things, like Mike always preferred. "Because I needed to talk to your father."

McKenna didn't respond, just stared at her with accusing eyes. Maggie was used to expressions like that from seventeen-year-old Kady but not McKenna and she didn't know how to deal with it. "Look, I promise you that I wasn't at Ben's last night. You know how I've been sort of talking with Daddy—"

"With his ghost," McKenna interrupted. Some of the hostility was leaving McKenna's expression, which gave Maggie a frisson of hope.

"Yes, his ghost. As silly as that sounds."

"It doesn't sound silly." McKenna dropped her head. "I talk to him in the woods."

"You do?" At Maggie's incredulous tone, McKenna glanced up with a sheepish half smile.

"When I go for a walk, I pretend he's there with me. And I...talk."

Maggie set the plate of muffins and her coffee down on the side table and reached out a hand to smooth McKenna's sleep-mussed hair. "Because you used to go for walks together. I'm glad. I think he'd like that. I know you miss him."

McKenna's blue eyes were already full of tears. "A lot." She swiped her hand under her nose. Maggie pulled her close for a hug, relieved when McKenna wrapped her thin arms around her waist.

One crisis averted, on to the next.

"I know. It's hard, sweetie. You know, they say it gets easier with time, but I think they're just full of shit, don't you?" McKenna gave a surprised bark of laughter against Maggie's shoulder.

"It doesn't feel like it's getting easier."

"But it will." She ran her hand down McKenna's hair, wanting to smooth out the tangles in McKenna's heart as easy as she could brush her hair. "I promise."

"Was it this hard for you when Nana died?" McKenna asked.

Maggie sighed. "That was different. I wasn't as close to her as you were to your father. And I'd already kind of lost her when she got sick."

McKenna pulled back and wiped a fist across her cheek. "You didn't have anyone."

"I had my sisters, same as you. We looked after each other."

"Kady wouldn't look after me."

Maggie gave a shaky laugh. This was unexpected. She knew she needed to reconnect with McKenna but now?

"You'd be surprised what Kady would do. But you'll never have to worry about that because I'm not going anywhere. Except to work." She squeezed McKenna's shoulder. "I have to get ready. Unfortunately."

"Evie's coming home today."

Evie! In all the excitement and nerves of the date, Maggie had forgotten about Evie's arrival. Her second oldest would be home from her last year of university, arriving by supper today, and Maggie had completely pushed it out of her mind, like some boy-crazy teenager.

"You forgot, didn't you?"

Maggie couldn't hide the expression of guilt that raced across her face. "There's been a lot going on this week. But I'm glad she's coming. I'll make lasagna for supper, okay? She'll like that."

McKenna nodded, looking marginally happier. Having Evie home would be good for McKenna. Despite the eight-year age difference, they had always gotten along, both quiet and studious in a house of loud personalities.

Maggie shooed McKenna away with a playful slap on her bum. "Go get ready for school. I'll have my shower and see what I can do about breakfast for you. And McKenna–"

McKenna turned and Maggie's heart nearly broke with love. "I love you."

There were love and affection in the house, but they didn't say it nearly enough. That would change now.

"Love you too."

Chapter Nineteen

MAGGIE TIPTOED UP THE stairs, hoping no one else would wake up. She felt strange, off-balance, like walking on the deck of a boat. The day had started wrong. Her routine had shifted, and as much as Maggie tried to pull it upright, it wasn't working. She needed a shower, breakfast.

Instead, she took two steps into her room and lay down on the bed.

There was no denying she needed a moment—and it was only Wednesday.

She counted to ten, relishing the quiet of the house. Maggie wished she could go down and sit at the kitchen table with her coffee, but McKenna might want to talk more, and the others would be awake soon. If she wanted a moment to herself, she had to take it now, because tonight, there'd be another person in the house, someone who would want her time and energy as well.

Another moment and Maggie sat up.

Before heading for the shower, she checked her phone sitting on the nightstand. She'd run over to Cat's without taking it. Maggie didn't use her cell often but knew it was the lifeline for her daughters, and she'd left the house without even thinking about it.

For a moment, Maggie allowed the emotions swirling to inch closer, feeling her shoulders tighten at the thoughts of sad daughters and first dates and dead husbands mix with the daily pressures, and then with a firm shake of her head, she pushed them away.

She would not let herself be overwhelmed.

But when she read the text waiting for her, the tightness of her shoulders intensified, as did the smile on her face.

Wanted to let you know I had a GREAT time last night.

Before she had time to dwell and worry and relish, the door to her bedroom burst open.

"Evie's coming home today!" Clare bellowed at the top of her lungs.

"You're better than any alarm clock." Maggie winced at the muffled curse from Kady's room across the hall. "Get out of here and I'll be down soon to make breakfast."

"Evie, Evie, Evie," Clare chanted, darting toward the stairs as Kady's door banged open.

"I'm going to *kill* you," Kady muttered, heading after her little sister.

"Not before breakfast," Maggie called after her.

She took a deep breath, the little exchange helping to steady her. She may be off-balance, but the girls still needed her.

She took the quickest shower she could, hoping her refereeing skills wouldn't be necessary before she finished, and was pleasantly surprised to find Clare and Kady calmly eating breakfast in the kitchen when she came down.

"Evie's coming home today!" Clare chirped as Maggie got a bowl out of the cupboard.

"So I heard."

"Did you forget?" Clare demanded.

"Of course I didn't forget."

"How was your *date*?"

Maggie sighed inwardly. She suspected that would be the topic of conversation with everyone today, regardless of the distraction Evie's homecoming would provide. "It was nice. We talked, and it was nice to catch up with him."

"You kissed him. Kady said you kissed him."

Clare's expression was gleeful, and for a moment Maggie wished her reaction was more like McKenna's. She didn't know if she had the energy to deal with Clare's excitement any more that morning.

"I did kiss him," Maggie admitted, keeping her voice even as her cheeks heated.

"Kady says you were making out," Clare accused.

"I'm not sure what 'making out' entails these days." She felt her cheeks flush even more as she remembered the details, his hands on her back, the feel of his chest pressed against her, his lips.

His mouth.

"Are you going on another date?" Clare asked, her spoon still poised above the cereal soaking in milk.

Maggie shook her head to clear her mind of the thoughts of Ben's mouth. "Eat your breakfast," she said automatically. "And I don't know."

"He hasn't asked her," Kady said, her mouth full of one of Cat's muffins.

"You could ask him." Her heart burst at Clare's suggestion. There was support, even encouragement and from the daughter she'd never imagined giving it.

McKenna appeared in the doorway. "*Are* you going out with him again?"

Maggie stared at her, seeing Mike's determination in her eyes, the way the girl tilted her chin. "I don't know. What would you think of that?"

The table fell silent as the girls digested her question.

"He said I was good at baseball," Clare announced. "I like him. You can go out with him but I don't want to see any kissing."

Maggie directed a glare at Kady. "I would rather no one had seen any kissing last night," she said archly. "Let's not do that again."

"You did it to me!"

Maggie bit her tongue. The one time she had opened the door to Kady and Matthew, a quick peek out the window had shown the boy practically dry humping Kady against the door. "It's a little different."

"Well, I'm okay with you hooking up with Ben, so don't get mad at me about the door," Kady said imperiously.

Clare scrunched her face. "Hooking up is gross."

"I went on a date. Let's leave it like that," Maggie said.

"What if we don't want you to date him?" McKenna asked quietly.

Maggie glanced up at her. She thought they had settled things earlier but had that only been the beginning? "I'm not sure what you do want me to do, McKenna?"

"I want you to say that you won't see him again."

"Would you do that?" Clare asked in a hushed voice.

"Of course," Maggie said immediately, even though the pang in her heart forced her to clutch the table. "Your father dying has been hard on all of us. I don't want to make it worse. And this was only a date."

"You were making out with him, so that's more than a date!"

The guilt of enjoying being in Ben's arms, the feel of his lips on hers rushed back. "Is that what's bothering you?"

McKenna stared at Maggie with accusing eyes. "Yes," she spat.

Maggie blew out her breath. "Do you feel like I'm cheating on your dad?"

"Yes."

She sat down heavily at the table. "Truth?" She glanced at each of them in turn. "That's why I went to Aunt Cat's last night. To talk to your dad and tell him what happened. I know it's not cheating, but I'm not going to lie to you—it felt weird."

"Maybe he's not doing it right?" Clare asked with utter seriousness. "Maybe he's a bad kisser."

Maggie's mouth fell open as she stared at Clare. There was silence, and then in perfect unison, she burst into laughter at the same time as Kady and McKenna.

"What?" Clara demanded. "Is he a good kisser?"

"I'm not telling you that!" Maggie wiped her eyes. It felt good to laugh with her girls. Humour had been missing from her house lately. "But I think I need your help." She held up her hand as Clare opened her mouth. "Not help about kissing. I'm not going to lie to you about this. I like Ben. We were good friends when we were younger, and it's been good to reconnect with him. I had no idea there would be kissing last night, so I'm as surprised as you. But I'm new at this too."

Footsteps sounded on the stairs, and Addison appeared with tired eyes and an arm wrapped around her belly. Maggie stood with a concerned frown. "Are you okay?"

"She didn't let me sleep much last night," Addison admitted, rubbing slow circles on the belly that peeked out from beneath her T-shirt. "I called work, told them I wasn't coming in."

"Work!" Maggie glanced at the clock on the stove. Despite her early start, she only had a few minutes before she needed to leave. "I'd better get going, so should you. Finish your breakfast."

"But you need our help with the kissing!" Clare cried.

"We'll talk about it later," Maggie promised, dropping a kiss on the top of the little girl's red head. "But I think I'm okay with that."

"Mom?" Maggie paused at the door and glanced back at McKenna. "If we didn't like it—if we didn't like Ben, would you still go out with him?"

Maggie needed no time to answer. "Of course not. My girls come first."

"But you like him."

"I do."

"You'd be sad if it was just a one-time thing?"

"I'd get over it."

"I don't want you to be sad anymore."

Maggie pulled McKenna into a hug. "Oh, sweetie, I don't want you to be sad either. If you're not okay with it, then how can I be? You come first."

"I'll be okay with it," McKenna said into Maggie's shoulder.

"I'm fine," Kady said in a bored voice.

"I don't want you to be sad either!"

Maggie glanced at Clare's eager voice and keeping one arm around McKenna, she ruffled Clare's hair. "I can't be sad if I have my girls," she promised.

"And Evie. Evie's coming home today," Clare cried, pulling away to dance around the kitchen.

Chapter Twenty

MAGGIE RACED THROUGH THE store to the bakery, already a few minutes late. She avoided eye contact with Paul but knew he was checking his watch as she disappeared between the aisles. She had a list of things to do that day and hoped they would be able to keep her mind off the countless emotional whirlwinds.

She prayed for a quiet day; one without any drama or conflict or fighting.

"Maggie!" April called soon as Maggie had disappeared into the bowels of the bakery, to check on orders. "You've got a visitor!"

Ben!

Maggie changed direction and hurried back to the counter, only to find Kayleigh chatting easily with Leila. The smile slid off her face.

"How'd it go?" Kayleigh said as she spotted Maggie, speaking as casually as if she was asking about the weather, not asking Maggie about the first date she'd gone on since Mike.

She shouldn't be surprised to see Kayleigh. There had been little contact with her sisters since Brenna left yesterday which always meant a face-to-face attack had been planned. Maggie wondered if Cat had tattled yet about her sleep-over last night.

She shrugged, choosing to keep her myriad of emotions to herself. "Everyone stared."

"You're a Skatt," Leila pointed out. "Everyone always stares."

"Kayleigh Skatt, is that you?"

Kayleigh turned at the older woman approaching, pushing a shopping cart. "Hi, Mrs. Jibb."

Mrs. Jibb smiled brightly at Kayleigh. "I was just on your website this morning and fell in love with those little mice ornaments you've got. Do you have any in the store?"

"I've got the whole set."

Mrs. Jibb clapped her hands. "Oh, goody. I'll be right over as soon as I've finished my grocery shopping. Maggie, dear, it was lovely to hear you were out with Ben Higgins last night," she said as she pushed her cart past.

"I—I'm glad it made you happy," Maggie stammered, unsure of how to respond. "Have a nice day."

"Does the woman know it's six months until Christmas?" Leila muttered.

"One hundred and ninety-three days," Kayleigh corrected with a grin. "And it's people like that who keep me and my shop in business. Let's finish up so I can open up and get the mice ready for her. So are you going out with him again? Is this going to be a thing?"

Maggie couldn't be sure if Kayleigh thought that was a good idea or not. "He's busy; I'm busy. Between Evie coming home and the girls' activities, I'm not sure it's a good idea."

"He didn't ask her," Leila cut in.

But he'd had a *GREAT* time, Maggie recalled. Maybe Ben was just being nice. Maybe he really thought her boring and old and—

Maybe she was overthinking things.

"Why didn't you ask him?" Kayleigh demanded.

"You sound like Clare." For once, Maggie wished another customer would appear so she could stop talking to her sister.

"She's a smart girl. Why didn't you?" At Maggie's shrug, Kayleigh narrowed her eyes. "Who had the issue with him? Kady? She's still pouting about her own breakup, so Mom can't have any fun?"

Kayleigh knew the girls too well. "It wasn't Kady. McKenna," Maggie admitted. "I thought she was fine when he picked me up, but this morning she was a little hostile."

"She's a teenager. They're always hostile," Leila cut in.

"Not McKenna."

"No, not McKenna," Kayleigh agreed.

"You can't let them dictate your life," Leila argued.

"They're my daughters," Maggie said coolly. "They are my life."

"Yes, but you need something more."

Maggie was about to protest when she caught sight of Paul lurking at the end of the cereal aisle, pretending to tidy the endcap. "Get back to work," she hissed to Leila.

Leila glanced furtively over her shoulder. "Stalker Paul on the prowl?"

"He's still mad at me from the thing with Heather on Monday," Maggie said, hands moving aimlessly pretending to look for something on the counter. "He wrote me up, and I really don't want another talking to."

Kayleigh examined the fresh loaves of bread on display and chose one. "This is exactly the loaf of bread I was looking for," she said loudly, backing away from the counter. "Thank you for the amazing service this morning, Ms. Bakery Manager."

Maggie was laughing as she waved Kayleigh away.

A few hours later, Brenna showed up. Like Kayleigh, Leila escorted her over to the bakery department.

Leila didn't know Brenna as well as Cat and Kayleigh but had an odd fascination with her. Maggie had noticed Brenna produced the same reaction from quite a few of the women in town. They stood up straighter, spoke a little clearer, and used bigger words like they were leafing through a thesaurus whenever Brenna was around.

"So," Brenna said, almost rubbing her hands together with excitement. "How was it? But first, when is Evie coming home?"

"She didn't give me a time," Maggie admitted. "But she said she'll be here for supper."

"Do you want to come to the house? We have guests, but they're out for dinner."

"Thanks, but I think I'd like to keep my girl to myself for the night," Maggie said with a sheepish smile. Evie hadn't been home since Christmas and while FaceTime and text worked for short-term absences, they weren't good at giving hugs.

"We get her Thursday night, then," Brenna said.

"Sounds good. She'll want to see you too."

Maggie finished setting up the display of muffins, checking to see if yesterday's baked goods were on the top of the pile. Maybe that was all Brenna wanted to know.

"How was last night?" Brenna demanded, dashing Maggie's hopes.

"It was a date."

"Yes, but seeing as how that was the first date you've been on—in, like, forever—I need more." She motioned with her hands. "How was it?"

"It was okay."

"Brenna, I hate to interrupt, but I have a legal question."

The three of them turned with surprise to find Mr. Quilliams standing behind the muffin table, ball cap folded in his hand. "I saw your car out front. I've been meaning to call you. It's about my son."

"Sure, Mr. Quilliams, just give me a minute here." Not a blink signalled Brenna was anything but delighted to be interrupted by a potential client. "Why don't you meet me outside by my car? I just need to talk to Maggie about some family issues."

Mr. Mason gave a solemn nod. "I'll be outside."

"That's not creepy," Leila said under her breath.

"It's the same as Paul skulking around, which he has been doing all morning. Make this quick, Bee."

"It was just *okay*?"

Maggie frowned. "What do you want me to tell you?"

"Tell me what you did, what he said, how you felt. Tell me *everything*!"

"There isn't anything to tell and no time. I'm not sure what *to* tell you. He picked me up and Clare gave him the fish-eye. We went to Woody's and everyone in the place stared. We had a steady stream of visitors come to say hi. He drove me home and—"

"And?" Brenna screeched, before glancing around with embarrassment. Maggie looked around and saw Paul disappear down the canned vegetable aisle. She definitely needed to make this a quick visit.

"And he kissed me."

"You didn't tell me that!" Leila cried.

"You didn't ask!"

"I most certainly did! I asked if you got any action and you said no."

"You meant did I sleep with him and I didn't."

"I meant, did you have that perfect movie kiss, where you stare at each other with longing in your eyes before your lips lock together in a frenzy of passion."

Both Maggie and Brenna stared at Leila, who stood with hands clasped before her chest, making decidedly kissy fish faces.

"It definitely wasn't a movie kiss if that's what it looks like," Maggie drawled. "At least I hope it didn't look like that!"

Cat was the last to arrive at the store. She made the rounds through the aisles with her cart before appearing at the bakery.

"You look like crap," she announced.

"Thanks." Maggie rubbed at the beginnings of a headache that had been threatening all day.

She glanced around, searching for Paul. She'd lost count of how many times she'd seen Paul that day; normally, he barricaded himself in the tiny office upstairs, but today she felt like she had a babysitter.

Cat followed Maggie's scrutiny. "What's going on here? You seem stressed."

"Paul," Maggie sighed. "He's been on my case since Monday."

"You can't really blame him," Cat said.

"I thought you, out of everyone, would be more sympathetic."

Cat grinned. "I'm still pissed I missed out. You can't let him get to you." She glanced around. FoodMart was the only grocery store in Forest Hills and Cat knew it almost as intimately as Maggie did. "I can't believe you still work here. You've been here, what, twenty years?"

Maggie sighed again. "Closer to thirty."

"Jesus." Cat shivered. "That's almost my whole life. I think I'd kill myself if I had the same job for that long."

"Why can I see Addison saying the same thing?" Maggie asked with a frown.

Cat waved away Maggie's displeasure. "Whatever. So, how was the date?" she asked, a perfect balance between Brenna's needy excitement and Kayleigh's careless questioning. "You weren't much for details this morning."

"Sorry about that."

"Is that it? Because you know I can stop by the hardware and ask Ben how it went."

"Just like you somehow appeared at Woody's last night even though you didn't have a shift?"

Cat grinned. "Seamus needed me for something."

"Cat!" Grandmotherly Mrs. Bignell waved as she approached. "Just the person I wanted to see. I need a cake."

"We do cakes here too, Mrs. Bignell," Maggie reminded her.

"Yes, but Cat has more time to put into the details," Mrs. Bignell said. "You're good too, Maggie, but I know how busy you are."

At least Cat had the courtesy to lead the woman away before taking any details about the cake order. Maggie was proud of her sister's talents, but Paul would definitely not appreciate her poaching the customers.

She glanced around with a worried frown. Hopefully, her manager had missed Cat's visit and now that her sisters had been there to speak their piece, Maggie could go back to work.

Chapter Twenty-One

LATER DURING HER BREAK, Maggie again raced through the store, this time to pick up a few things for supper that night. After all the talk about Ben, she wanted to focus on Evie.

It had been six months since Evie's last visit; six long months without those lanky arms wrapped around her in a tight hug. No mother could ever have a favourite child but at times Evie's goodness shone just a little bit brighter than her sisters.

Lasagna would be perfect, Maggie decided and picked up one of the apple crisps that Evie liked. And she'd make some cookies when she got home. And there were the makings for a salad in the fridge.

Maggie was lost in thought as she took her things to the cashier. As she rounded the corner by the produce, she looked out the automatic doors in time to see Heather Vreeland heading across the parking lot.

The woman had been in the store. Anger rose; had she been there to make another plea for her son's behalf? Or had she been there solely to pick up groceries, scurrying through the aisle to keep out of Maggie's sight?

Giving a muttered curse, Maggie dumped her groceries in the apple bin and hurried out the door after her.

"Heather!"

The woman turned at the sound of her name. "Leave me alone," Heather said automatically.

Maggie wanted to curse again at the frightened expression that crossed Heather's face. "I'm not going to hurt you." There was more than a little satisfaction in that realization, but Maggie focused on her annoyance at the fact. How could *anyone* be afraid of *her*? "I want to apologize."

"You assaulted me in public!"

Maggie glanced around, making note of the few customers lingering in the parking lot, waiting for more to gossip about.

"And I'm apologizing to you in public, just like you wanted. I'm sorry about the other day," Maggie said, trying to remember the words she'd coached Clare the last time the nine-year-old had to apologize for hitting Kady. "I was upset and I lost control of my temper."

"I was upset too, and I didn't hit you!"

"Thank you for being the bigger person."

"I was only asking for your help, and you assaulted me."

Maggie took a deep breath. "You were asking me to help with the son that kill—" She caught herself before she said the words because if she went down that road, it would only lead to another shoving match. And this time, Ben wasn't around to pull her off Heather.

"I can't help with Dylan's bail," Maggie said shortly, wanting to end with that. End the whole miserable experience and go back in the store to buy her ground beef and finish her shift.

"But I don't see why not? You have the money. I'd pay you back."

The money. The insurance money sitting in the bank waiting for her to make a decision on what to do with it.

"Do you really need me to explain why I won't be using that money to help Dylan?" Maggie's voice was quiet and still, and if any of her girls had heard it, they would have run for the hills.

This was never going to end.

Fiona's words suddenly echoed in Maggie's mind. Heather was a mother too, Fiona had reminded her, implying Maggie would have fought with everything she had for her girls.

"We're family," Heather said.

Maggie used all her willpower to take a step back when all she wanted to do was tackle Heather into the nearest car and bang some sense into her head. "No, we're not. And if you don't understand what you're asking me to do, then I can't help you. But I'm telling you right now, Heather, I will not now, nor ever, be contributing one penny to your family's problems. Because your family problems created my family problems, and I will never forgive you for that."

Heather stared with fearful eyes.

"I apologize for the incident in the store on Monday," Maggie said stiffly. "I shouldn't have reacted like that. But that's the end of it."

She turned and walked away, with her eyes filling with tears and a hitch in her breath. Giving her head a shake to pull herself together before she entered the store, the air conditioning was a welcome change from the heat of the afternoon.

She automatically smiled in response to Mrs. Lawson's greeting and collected her meat and cheese from where she'd left them among the apples, and headed to the express line.

"What did you do?" Paul was suddenly at her side. "I saw you talking to Heather Vreeland outside. I don't want any more trouble. I've had enough, Maggie. Do you know she could sue the store?"

"No one is going to sue the store."

"You don't know that. We'd take a huge hit, and our reputation—"

"This is the only grocery store in town," Maggie reminded him, setting her things on the conveyor belt. "Nothing will happen to the store. And I apologized to her. Nothing more."

"Apologized. Good," Paul said nervously. "That's good. That's what you should have done."

"That's why I did it." The exhaustion hit Maggie then. She was so tired of Paul, of this place, of doing the right thing for everyone. Why couldn't she have tackled Heather into the car? "I need to pay for this now, Paul, and get back to work. My break is about over."

"Good. You should get back to work," he repeated and hurried off.

Maggie met the gaze of Mavis, the older cashier who had worked at the store longer than anyone could remember. "I think you should have decked her."

"I'll remember that for next time." She gave Mavis a tired grin. "Although I don't think Paul could handle it if I did."

"Oh, Paul can't handle what's in his pants, so what makes him think he can handle us in this store?" Mavis' dark eyes almost disappeared among the wrinkles as she guffawed.

"Guess not," Maggie said hurriedly as she swiped her debit card, wondering if there were stories about what was in Paul's pants that she hadn't heard.

Maybe it was better that way.

With her bags in hand, Maggie headed back to the bakery and the last of her shift. There was a refrigerator in the bakery that she could store the bags in, a good idea as long as she remembered to take them home.

So deep in thought, Maggie didn't notice the woman standing at the bakery counter.

"Hello, Maggie."

Maggie stilled, the voice sparking recognition, like something from a long-ago dream. As if slow-motion, she turned.

It was Addison, but Addison without the pregnant belly and aged about ten years. Who–?

"Dory?" Maggie demanded incredulously. "What are you doing here?"

Dory smiled, a welcome, friendly smile, not the smug grin Maggie remembered. "How's it going, big sis?"

Maggie set down her bags behind the counter, gobsmacked at the sight of her sister. Cat would have been cool with her welcome, and Kayleigh would have kept on walking, but Brenna would have hugged Dory, despite the years of bad blood. Maggie had no idea how to react. "Dory?" she repeated.

Dory—it was really Dory, arriving like a bad period the day after the tampon sale had ended; tall and slim and dressed to the nines in a simple shirtdress and booties.

"Mom?"

And then Maggie forgot about everything because there, rushing up behind Dory toward the counter with an expression of joy on her face was Evie. With a choked cry, Maggie rushed towards her with arms wide open, grabbed on and held on tight.

"I thought you wouldn't be here until later!" Maggie hugged her girl hard, feeling the missed meals and stress of exams in her thin frame. Oh, she would feed her up, bring back the curves, the apples of her cheeks.

"We got an earlier start! It's so good to see you. And Dory–Aunt Dory–insisted on coming to find you at the store."

There was wetness under Maggie's eyes by the time she released Evie. "I *missed* you." She breathed deep, kissing the top of Evie's head. Her daughter's hair was shorter than it had been at Christmas, stopping at her shoulders instead of red waves cascading down her back. She had Brenna's hair; Brenna, whose locks were the envy of the rest of them.

"I missed you too," Evie said happily. "It's so good to be home."

"I don't understand." Maggie hugged her again, glancing over her shoulder to where Dory was watching, along with the rest of the bakery staff. She couldn't be bothered to tell them to go back to work. "Why is Dory here? Did you come here together?"

"I've been checking in with my niece since she moved to the big city," Dory said with a casual shrug of her slim shoulders. Slimmer than what they had been the last time Maggie had seen her, almost three years ago. Her hair was back to her natural red, no longer dyed black or blond or bubblegum pink as it had been in her youth. Shorter now, and curly. "They told me they were coming, and I asked to hitch a ride."

"They?" She looked past Evie at the man standing beside the hamburger buns; handsome, well dressed. Evie pulled him forward by the hand.

"Mom, I want you to meet Malcolm."

"Malcolm," Maggie repeated, dumbly searching Evie's face for some sign of the joke. He was handsome but with wrinkles. Laugh lines, really, but lines etched in his face that wasn't apparent in the usual twentysomething's face unless they had an aging problem. And the grey hair suggested that it had been more than a few years since Malcolm had seen his twenties. "Evie, you didn't tell me you were bringing someone. Two someones, actually." Maggie gave her sister a sideways glance of distrust.

"I wanted it to be a surprise." Evie's words tripped out of her mouth in their haste. "Malcolm and I have been together since school ended, but we've known each other for years. He wanted to see where I lived, meet all of you, and when I told Dory about our trip, she asked for a ride back."

"Maggie!"

Heads turned to see Manager Paul with an expression as thunderous as his voice. "You said you were going back to work and here I find you once again, socializing with your family. This is a place of business, not a place for a reunion. In *my* FoodMart, we pride ourselves on our exemplary customer service, not skills at gossiping."

"Paul, it's just Evie back from school. She'll be—"

"And yet another sister," Paul said archly, with a sideways glance at Dory. "Really, Maggie, you need to keep your family business private. This is neither the time nor place."

"But–"

"Back to work, Maggie. I pay you to manage the bakery, not stand around and talk all day."

Maggie stared at Paul, her cheeks flaming as hot as the anger rising within her.

"I'll go," Evie said hurriedly. "We'll meet you at home, Mom."

Maggie ignored her. "I haven't been standing around talking all day, Paul."

"Really? Every time I was at the back of the store, I saw you holding court with one of your sisters. Customers who were in the store to shop were milling about, listening to you gossip about your love life. I can only imagine the salacious reports you were giving them."

"I wasn't gossiping about anything," she retorted heatedly. "And there was definitely nothing salacious about what I was saying. If you were so interested in what was going on, you could have joined in."

Maggie regretted the words as soon as they flew out of her mouth. No one knew that the recently divorced Paul had made a half-hearted attempt to coerce her into dinner with him soon after Mike died.

Paul's face creased into an ugly grimace. "This is your second warning, Maggie, in as many days. I let the incident with Heather Vreeland slide because it was clearly an emotional altercation, but I can't today. You're slacking off, letting your responsibilities suf-fer—"

Heather Vreeland. It was like the name was a can of gasoline being thrown on a fire. Maggie's face burned with anger. How dare Paul—?

How dare Heather—?

"You know nothing about my responsibilities," she said, rage making her voice quiet and still.

Maggie heard an intake of breath from behind her. "Uh oh," Dory whispered.

"You know nothing about what happened with Heather," Maggie continued, taking a step forward. "That shouldn't have been brought into the store, but I didn't start it."

"And yet you had to finish it by using violence." Paul raised his voice, causing nearby shoppers to glance over with interest. Maggie had no doubt that after today FoodMart was going to be *the* place to go for gossip. "I was absolutely disgusted with your behaviour. Childish, immature—"

"I don't care."

Fury bubbled inside Maggie, giving her the ability to block out everything but Paul's face; red blotched and weak-chinned, with hair thinner more every year.

She didn't care what he thought of her.

She only cared about Mike, and Mike was gone. Heather Vreeland was the cause of that, and if Paul was defending Heather...

Maggie didn't want to be here. She couldn't, not anymore.

It came from nowhere, from deep inside. Maggie had no idea she was capable of speaking the words until they were there, bursting out of her mouth.

There was only one thing to do.

"I quit."

Chapter Twenty-Two

"WHAT?" PAUL'S EYES BULGED.

"Shut up, Maggie," Dory hissed. "She takes it back; she doesn't quit."

Maggie swung to her face her sister. "Don't tell me what to do!"

"Let him fire you," Dory mouthed.

"I am not letting him fire me," Maggie protested. "I'm quitting. I've leaving. Right now. Because I'm sick of this." With suddenly shaking hands, she took off her jacket and slipped behind the counter to grab her purse and her groceries.

"Maggie?" Behind the bakery counter, April had been watching with an expression of concern. And...was that a tiny hint of elation? The rest of the bakery staff were grouped around, all with similar expressions.

Maggie smiled tremulously. "You're in charge now, April. Call me if you need anything."

And then flanked by Dory, with a nervous Evie following, holding the hand of mysterious Malcolm, Maggie walked silently out of FoodMart,. With each step, she listened in horror to her words echoing in her head.

I quit.

I quit.

I *quit.*

The elation of seeing the sour grapes expression on Paul's face died as she walked out of the store. The afternoon was hot and made her wish she wasn't wearing black polyester pants.

She wouldn't be wearing them much longer.

"Mom...your job." Evie glanced from Maggie to Dory, who stood with her arms crossed and the corner of her mouth turned up in a smile.

Did she find the situation funny?

Evie looked to Malcolm like he was the adult who would make everything all right. "Your mother knows what she's doing," Malcolm assured Evie.

Maggie didn't, but it was nice for Malcolm to give her credit.

"We don't need to do this in the parking lot. I'm going to drive home and I'll meet you there," Maggie said, walking stiffly to her car with a sinking feeling in her stomach. Part of her wanted to run back in and beg Paul for her job back. The other part wanted to drive her car straight into the big window through which the cashiers had clustered, watching her exit.

Maggie climbed in the van in a daze and started when Dory opened the door to the passenger side.

"What are you doing?" Maggie asked. Across the asphalt surface, Malcolm started his sleek sports car with a roar and pulled out of the parking lot.

"Catching a ride back with you. Malcolm's got a sweet ride but it's not the most comfortable in the backseat." Dory spoke in a nonchalant voice like she hadn't witnessed Maggie self-destruct only moments earlier.

Maggie managed to turn on the car but couldn't bring herself to pull out of the FoodMart's parking lot. If she left, then it was all over. There was no getting her job back.

She had really fixed things for herself.

Leaning forward, she rested her head against the steering wheel. What had she done? How was she going to look after the girls without a paycheque?

"You're an idiot."

Still with her head on the steering wheel, she glanced at Dory staring affectionately at her.

Affectionately? Dory never did affection, but now there was no doubt about the certain fondness in her expression.

Which was why Maggie didn't automatically tell her where to go. "You're not helping," she muttered instead.

"What did you quit for?"

Maggie heaved a sigh and sat up. "I have no idea. I was so mad at Paul and tried to think of what would piss him off the most."

"There might have been a better option. You should get out of here. People are starting to stare."

"People always stare." But Maggie put the minivan in gear and drove through the parking lot, giving the gas pedal an extra kick as she pulled out onto the road, smiling when the tires squealed.

"You worked there forever," Dory commented.

"Feels like it." Already the fear of being unemployed was creeping toward her like a low-lying mist on the ground. Maggie had known her share of townsfolk who'd dealt with layoffs and forced retirements, the odd person who'd been fired. No one ever quit, at least not without another job waiting in the wings.

Maggie didn't have another job. She didn't even have the potential for another job. She'd worked at the FoodMart since she was sixteen, staying through her pregnancies. Store management had always been generous with her hours and maternity leave and promoted her along the way.

"I've never worked anywhere else," Maggie said in a hollow voice.

"Well, then you've definitely worn out your welcome. I'm sure there's something else you can do in this town. Didn't you go to school for something? I remember you and Brenna studying together."

"I got my bookkeeping certificate," Maggie said shortly. She had done the online course between Addison and Evie, but when the babies had kept coming, it was easier to keep her job at the store. "I used to help Fiona with the books for Woody's."

"Maybe you can do that again. Or take some time off."

Maggie pulled into the driveway. Never had the house looked more tired and in need of care than it did today. Shingles in need of repair, peeling paint on the porch, flower beds full of weeds. No one would ever know she'd planted tulips under the kitchen window.

"Time off isn't usually a *thing* here," she said sarcastically.

Malcolm had parked by the corner of the house, and Maggie pulled up beside him, momentarily pushing away the slithering fear of being unemployed until later.

There'd be time enough later to figure out what she was going to do. There was money in her bank account, not much, but enough for a rainy day. There was her RRSP that she could dip into to pay for Kady's school—

The settlement from the insurance company. The money the mushroom farm paid. Nearly a million dollars sat in her bank account.

The realization sent a flush of relief through her body, like a cool shower on a hot day.

"Are you okay?" Evie called as soon as Maggie stepped out of the van. Evie's pretty face wore an expression of concern.

She would not let Evie see her own concern.

"Your mom'll be fine, Evie. Don't worry about it," Dory said blithely before Maggie had time to respond. "It's something she should have done a long time ago."

Malcolm stepped forward as Maggie headed for the stairs. "Mrs. Monroe, I realize these aren't the best circumstances to be meeting—"

She interrupted him with a snort. "Call me Maggie." Appraising him through narrowed eyes, she saw a tall, well-dressed man with an easy smile. There was no doubt Malcolm was good-looking, but how could he attract a twentysomething like Evie, used to hipster beards and beat-up sneakers?

Malcolm wore boots and slim-cut khakis with a preppy button-down.

Maggie guessed there was something athletic in Malcolm's routine to keep him so fit. Swimming, or maybe some racquet sport, like squash. With that car, he looked like he could afford it.

"How old are you?" Maggie demanded.

"Mom," Evie hissed.

"Forty-two," Malcolm replied evenly.

She respected how Malcolm stood tall and proud before her—proud but not cocky. Self-assured. She may not appreciate his age, but she'd had enough of cocky kids to last a lifetime. "Then definitely call me Maggie. Come in."

"Actually, I think I'll be off," Malcolm said. "I'll leave Evie here to catch up, but I'm sure it'll be better without me hovering. I've booked a room at the B &B down the hill. I'll go get settled."

"Thank you," Maggie said with surprise. "I would like some time with my daughter. Why don't you come back for supper? About five thirty. We eat early here, and Clare has a game tonight."

"You have to come to Clare's game," Evie begged, her fingers tangling with his.

"I'd love to," Malcolm said, looking down at Evie with a smile. "See you in a couple of hours, then."

Maggie nodded and headed into the house, giving Evie privacy to say goodbye. From the footsteps, she knew Dory was following her.

The dogs met her at the door with wagging tails. The bus delivering Kady and McKenna wouldn't be there for another hour, Clare a little later.

"Addison?" Maggie called. The living room was empty, but Addison's car was parked haphazardly at the side of the house, so she knew she was home.

Now that Maggie thought of it, wasn't that Brady's truck parked at the neighbours? There was no telltale sound of his lawn mower.

"Mom?" Addison appeared in the doorway to the kitchen, with a banana popsicle in her hand. "What are you doing home? And—Aunt Dory?"

"Hey, Addison," Dory said with a wave. "You look very pregnant." She stepped forward and embraced Addison, who met Maggie's gaze with an expression of shock.

"Is Brady hiding in the kitchen?" Maggie asked drily, moving past her with her bags of groceries.

"He brought me a popsicle," Addison said defensively as a shuffle in the kitchen brought Brady forward.

"Hi, Maggie," he said, sheepishly. His eyebrows jerked as he saw Dory with Addison. "Dory! Aren't you a sight for sore eyes?"

Dory released Addison and made no move to disguise her obvious appraisal of Brady, tanned and smilingly handsome, even in his grass-stained jeans and dirty shirt. "Well, haven't you grown up nicely?"

"Don't," Maggie snapped, feeling her stomach turn. "Just don't."

"What are you doing here?" Addison asked in bewilderment. "I thought Evie—" Her question was cut off with the squeal of the screen door and Evie's cry of joy.

"You're so pregnant!" Evie bounded across the room to sweep a laughing Addison into a hug. "You look so great."

"I don't feel it," Addison complained. "At least not today."

"I think it's great that—" Evie halted as she noticed Brady standing behind her sister. "Brady? What are you—?" She turned to her sister with questioning eyes.

"Hey, Evie," Brady said, missing all the cues and easily sweeping her into a hug. "You look amazing. Home for good?"

"I—thinks—I don't know," she stammered.

"I'm going to put these things away," Maggie announced. "Evie, where are your things? You couldn't have fit much in that car of Malcolm's?"

"Who's Malcolm?" Addison asked.

"My bag is still in his trunk." Maggie didn't miss the defensive note in Evie's voice.

"I got mine," Dory half lifted her suitcase. "Where can I stash it?"

"I guess you're staying here," Maggie muttered.

"I thought I'd start out here," Dory said cheerfully. "Then when you throw me out, I'll try over at Cat's."

"That's thinking positive." Maggie gave the sleeping arrangements some thought. "Evie, I thought you and Addison could share, and Dory, then you could stay in Kady's room," I guess."

"I'm staying with Malcolm at the B & B," Evie said. Silence greeted her words—Dory, who no doubt knew of the plan, and Addison and Brady, who still hadn't a clue who Malcolm was.

"Are you, now?" Maggie was satisfied to see Evie's flinch, but not nearly satisfied enough. "Brady, don't you have work to do over at Mrs. Patton's?"

"Oops, lost track of time," he said quickly. "Thanks for reminding me. Addie." He pressed a hand against Addison's stomach and Maggie felt her own stomach roll over at the adoring smile Addison gave him. "Hang in there. I'll talk to you later. Bye, baby."

She wasn't sure if Brady meant that as a term of affection to Addison, or if he was speaking to the child in her belly.

Evie stared at him with wide eyes. "What's going on?" she demanded as the side door slammed behind Brady. "Where's *Adam*?"

Addison waddled into the living room, frantically licking her dripping popsicle. "It's a long story. I'm going to need to sit down for it."

"I have to go to the bathroom first." Evie laughed. "That was a long drive."

"You can put your bag upstairs," Maggie said to Dory, ducking into the kitchen. She needed to put the groceries away, and she needed to start the sauce for the lasagna and she needed—

Maggie needed a minute.

She placed the bags on the counter and stood there, head bowed, hands still entwined in the plastic handles.

What the hell had she done?

And what was she supposed to do now?

Chapter Twenty-Three

"**M**om?"

Maggie had managed to put the groceries away and fill the kettle by the time Evie came to find her.

"Don't worry about it," Maggie said immediately, hating the expression of concern on Evie's face. "I'm so glad you're home, and I wish you hadn't witnessed that, but it's under control."

"How can you say that? You just quit your job!"

"And we're not going to talk about it right now," Maggie said, pulling cups and tea bags out of the cupboards. "We're going to talk about you. And this Malcolm person, because I can do the math, Evie, and he's *twenty* years older than you. I'd like to know how you came to be involved with him and why I haven't heard about it. I definitely want to talk about that." Maggie raised her eyebrow and Evie looked suitably guilty. "And I'm sure Addison's going to fill you in on the dirty details about what's going on with her and Brady. And then Clare and McKenna and Kady will be home soon, so they'll be no discussions about my job."

"Are you sure?"

Maggie twisted her mouth into a smile. "I'm your mother. Of course I'm sure."

Evie helped her carry the teacups to the living room.

"So tell me about Malcolm," Maggie invited after they were settled in the living room. Dory set down the magazine she'd been leafing through. She sat across from Maggie in the extra chair, the one only the dogs found comfortable. "Since this is the first time I've even heard of his existence."

"He's so great," Evie bubbled. "Isn't he, Dory? Dory's met him a bunch of times."

Maggie would get into Evie's connection with Dory later. She couldn't deal with everything at once. Dory's appearance would cause conflict—much conflict—so Maggie pushed it away until later.

Still, there was a tiny part of her that was glad to see her sister.

"He's a professor at the school, but not from one of *my* classes!" Evie laughed nervously. "And nothing happened until I finished my exams. There's nothing wrong with this. He may be a bit older—"

"How old are we talking about?" Addison asked, waddling into the room and straight into the sudden tension. "Older than me?"

"Older than me," Dory laughed. "But your mom's still got him beat."

"You're dating a man in his..." Addison glanced at Dory, mentally calculating. "In his forties?"

"You shouldn't talk," Evie shot back. "What were you doing with Brady here? You're married to *Adam*?"

"Not for long." Addison's mouth twisted into a frown. "He called earlier," she said to Maggie. "He's talked to a lawyer."

Maggie sighed and said nothing. Another expense.

"You're getting a divorce? Are you trying to tell me you're with Brady now?" Evie exclaimed in horror. "What about the baby?"

"It's Brady's baby." Addison held up a hand to ward off Evie's explosion. "Don't bother getting mad, it'll only upset the baby. You liked him like a hundred years ago."

"This isn't about me liking him. You're having Brady Todd's baby and you didn't bother to tell me! I'm your sister!"

"You didn't tell me you were dating an old guy," Addison countered, both hands holding her belly like she was trying to cover the baby's ears. "I'm your sister too!"

"That has nothing to do with it!"

Dory turned to Maggie, not bothering to hide her smile. "This remind you of anyone?"

Maggie rolled her eyes. "Almost every day with Brenna and Cat." She was torn between stopping the argument between Addison and Evie which was quickly escalating and letting them fight it out.

Dory decided for her. "Didn't you say something about making lasagna? I could help you with that."

Maggie stood, cup in hand. "When the two of you finish your bickering, join us in the kitchen," she said loudly. "Until then, keep it to a dull roar."

"Why don't you get changed?" Dory offered as she followed Maggie out of the room. "I'll poke around and start things."

"Thanks," Maggie said, grateful to be given an escape.

Once alone in her room, Maggie pulled off the polyester pants and T-shirt and tossed them into the hamper. If she could burn them, she would.

Instead of rushing back downstairs, Maggie took a few moments to text Kayleigh, Cat and Brenna to tell them Dory was home.

The responses were instantaneous, and not very welcoming.

She couldn't blame them. The last time Dory had been home, she'd tried to finagle her way to sole ownership of the family home. The time before that, she'd left in the middle of the night with the contents of Kayleigh's wallet, Brenna's piggy bank and Kirby Conlin, Cat's crush at the time. The time before that—

Why now? Maggie lay on the bed, exhaustion creeping along her limbs. Couldn't she get through a day without any problems to deal with?

Her phone buzzed. Please, no more from Cat or Kayleigh about Dory. But when Maggie reluctantly glanced at the screen she saw a text from Ben.

How's your day?

There was no denying the flutter in her stomach the few words produced. It had been a long time since anyone had asked how her day was.

Without thinking about it, Maggie typed an abridged version of her day, complete with how she had quit.

She watched the ellipsis on the screen as Ben typed his response. It came quicker than she expected.

Are you okay?

Yes. No. A little shaky, but all right. Plus, Evie is home. Brought a much older man, and my sister Dory with her. The job situation has to wait.

Wow. Wow. Do you ever have calm, quiet days?

Not lately.

Let me know if I can do anything to help.

This helps.

Was that too much to admit?

Then I'll keep texting you.

Don't because I have to make supper. Clare has a game tonight.

I'll be there. Or will it be awkward?

Why awkward?

Because I'll want to kiss you again. I don't think you

want an audience this time. I know I don't.

She laughed out loud. Ben wanted to kiss her again. Her life was falling apart and she had a man who wanted to kiss her.

Maybe no audience

But another kiss?

Maggie imagined the hopeful expression on Ben's face and couldn't help but laugh again.

Not at the ball diamond.

What if you win? I'll need to congratulate you.

Maybe find a different way.

She was so bad at this. But it made her smile so hard. How could a person make her feel so good with such few words?

I can think of many different ways. G-rated ways!

Well, that's no fun

Maggie flopped on the bed, holding her phone in the air as she reread the words. The sounds of Evie and Addison's bickering faded from her mind as she laughed to herself and wondered how to respond.

Customer came in □ Gotta go. See you tonight

Is it bad to say that I can't wait?

You can say anything. I won't think anything is bad.

Enjoy your family and see you soon

Chapter Twenty-Four

MAGGIE CLUNG TO HER Ben-induced lighter mood for the rest of the night. She kept the conversation focused on Evie or Addison until Kady, Clare, and McKenna got home from school, and then it was easy to avoid what had happened with the house full of infectious laughter and nonstop chatter. Maggie faded into the background as she watched her girls, her heart bursting with happiness to have them together.

She served the lasagna and salad as she tried to make conversation with Malcolm during dinner, asking polite questions even when she wanted to give her attention to her girls. Maggie couldn't help but notice the way Malcolm kept touching Evie's arm resting on the table beside him, and the way Clare glared at him every time he did.

Dory, she ignored altogether.

She had no idea what had brought her sister home, and right now, she didn't care. There would be time enough to get to the bottom of why Dory was here with her sisters, if only so Maggie didn't have to listen to it twice.

With supper over, Maggie shooed Clare out of the kitchen to get ready for her baseball game. Without a word, Malcolm began clearing dishes, working in tandem with Evie, leaving no doubt in Maggie's mind the two had been on kitchen duty before. She pictured them in Malcolm's apartment, or house, making dinner together, or entertaining friends.

Evie had been living on her own in Toronto for four years. Maggie knew none of her friends or her daily activities, other than the morsels Evie handed out about her life like min chocolate bars at Halloween. Single bites and not very satisfying. Maggie had to trust her.

But why did Malcolm have to be so old? And what did Evie see in him?

Maggie was going to have to dance around carefully with this one.

When the day was over, Maggie tucked a freshly bathed Clare into bed, cutting off her story of the game with the reminder that she had school the next day. It had been another good game.

"Your dad would have been proud of you tonight," Maggie said, dropping a kiss on Clare's head.

"Do you think he watches me?" Clare called as Maggie was closing the door. Out of the girls, she was the most curious about Mike's ghost.

"I don't know," Maggie said truthfully. "But your dad loved baseball and he loved you, so if he could figure out a way to watch you play, I bet he would."

Clare snuggled into her covers. "I like thinking that."

"So do I."

Maggie's next stop was to check in with McKenna, who put down her book when Maggie poked her head in.

She couldn't help but notice McKenna's happiness had increased tenfold since Evie had arrived. Maybe that's what she needed; someone to talk to. Maggie vowed to be more of that person.

In the room across the hall, Kady was caught up on some Instagram drama.

"Night, honey," Maggie said from the doorway.

Kady looked up. "I saw you with that guy again at the game. Are you going to go out with him again?"

"I don't know. I keep thinking about him, though. Is that normal?" Maggie confessed, leaning against the doorframe. Talking about a man with her daughters was strange territory but maybe she could learn something.

"I love it when guys keep popping into your thoughts," Kady said in a dreamy voice.

"And who keeps popping in for you?" Two days ago Kady had been devastated by her breakup with Matthew Todd, but by the looks of things, he had already been forgotten. Or replaced.

Oh, to have a seventeen-year-old's attention span.

"No one." But Kady wouldn't look at Maggie, her fingers plucking at the bedspread.

"Uh huh. Well, let me know when there is something to tell."

"Lucas is really nice," Kady called as Maggie stepped out into the hall. "You know, Ben's son?"

"I haven't met him yet." Maggie closed her eyes with dread.

"Cute too."

"That's nice." The fake joviality sounded strange even to her own ears.

Addison's door was open as Maggie headed for the stairs. The room had been empty since Evie had left for university and it was nice to see it come alive again with Addison's clothes already strewn around.

Messy, but nice.

Maggie's gaze targeted Dory's bag sitting on Evie's old bed. She would much rather have Evie's things here than over at Cat's, but clearly, she hadn't been given that option.

And then she looked at Addison, already dressed for bed. "Are you okay?" she asked with concern.

"She's kicking a lot. And it feels weird here." Addison touched her chest.

"Heartburn. That was probably because of the lasagna."

Addison closed her eyes. "Ugh. It's—" Her eyes flew open. "Want to feel?" Maggie jumped across the room with hand outstretched. "There." Addison grabbed Maggie's hand and pressed it against her side. "Can you—?"

Maggie's eyes filled with tears as she felt the kick of the little foot. "Oh, Addison," she said. "There she is."

A new life to love, a precious new member of her family. Her hand still pressed against her stomach, Maggie used her other hand to smooth the hair off Addison's forehead.

"I can't wait to meet her," Maggie whispered. "Or him."

Addison's eyes were heavy as she gazed down at her. "Really? Even after all the mess I made?"

"Of course. You love your babies no matter what, and I'll love this one, no matter what I think of your decisions."

Addison smirked. "At least I didn't come home with an old guy."

Maggie rolled her eyes and dropped a kiss on her forehead. "Get some sleep."

When Maggie went downstairs, she planned on telling Dory she was going to bed, having decided the questions of why she was there could wait until the next day.

But instead of her early bedtime, she found all four of her sisters in her living room.

It should have been a pleasant sight. Brenna brought wine and had already poured generous glasses. Her favourite potato chips were in a bowl on the coffee table, courtesy of Cat. And Maggie suspected Kayleigh might have a little something in her pocket, ready to light up when the time was right.

Dory sat on the couch, looking as relaxed as if she owned the place.

"I guess we're doing this," Maggie said ruefully, reaching for her glass of wine and handful of chips before sinking into the chair closest to Dory. "I was going to bed."

"Hang in there another couple of minutes." Brenna sat on the couch beside Dory. Cat and Kayleigh sat across the room. As Maggie sipped her wine, Brenna pulled the basket beside her and began folding laundry. Maggie had long ago learned not to feel guilty about Brenna helping her with the laundry. Brenna insisted that the chore relaxed her, so why would Maggie want to take that away from her? "The girls in bed?"

"Except for the one probably kissing her boyfriend good night over at your place." Maggie grimaced. Even though it would have been a tight fit to have Evie and Malcolm stay with her, she wished Evie was under her roof.

Malcolm could stay at the B & B.

"I like Malcolm," Cat announced. "Once you get past the shock of Evie dating a man older than me, he seems like a good guy."

"I've known him for a few years," Dory said. Maggie noticed she held her wineglass by the stem like Brenna. Brenna once told them that it was so her hand didn't heat the wine, but Cat's response to that was to drink the wine quickly before it got warm. "He'll treat her well."

"Well, now if *you* give him the stamp of approval, I'll think he's an asshole," Cat drawled, glaring at Dory with laserlike intensity. Maggie might have been nervous had Cat been looking at her like that, but Dory only rested her arm on the back of the couch, being careful not to disturb the piles of clothes surrounding Brenna.

"So what's new around here?" Dory asked in a bored voice. "Who's with Seamus this week?"

Kayleigh made a noise in her throat. "I don't want to listen to the two of you snipping at each other. Get to the point—what are you doing here, Dory?"

Maggie took a mouthful of wine, readying herself to wade through Dory's blithe answer to find the truth.

"I thought it was time for a visit with my sisters."

"Bullshit. You don't give a damn about us, you never have. What do you want this time? We bought Dad out, and the house is mine and Brenna's now. You can't touch it. There's nothing for you here."

"You'd be surprised." Dory nibbled a potato chip. She was slim, almost dangerously slim. Maggie would guess that she'd lost more than twenty pounds on an already thin frame since she'd last seen her.

"What? I can't believe you have friends anywhere," Cat said rudely.

"Cat," Brenna admonished, stopping in the middle of folding Clare's T-shirt. "She deserves the benefit of the doubt."

"You really think so? Because the way *I* remember it was that Dory tried to con our father into pulling the house—*my* house—out from under us. Did I get that wrong?"

"I can't do this tonight," Maggie said loudly. "Cat, the past is in the past, and whatever reason Dory has for being back isn't important. She's our sister and she's here. Let's just enjoy that."

Dory lifted her wine glass. "Let's talk about what happened with Maggie today instead. You should have seen her in action."

Maggie groaned. She should have let Cat have another go at Dory.

"What's going on?" Kayleigh asked with a concerned frown.

"You haven't heard? You mean there's something going on with my life that isn't public news?"

"I was doing inventory all day." Kayleigh turned to Cat.

"I was doing cake orders. I've barely talked to Seamus today." Cat looked at Brenna.

"I was up the hill at the camp," Brenna frowned. "What did we miss?"

"I quit my job," Maggie said baldly. "Paul was lecturing me and I up and *quit*." Her laughter had a touch of hysteria in it.

"It was pretty impressive," Dory said casually. "I had front-row seat."

"How could you do that?" Brenna whispered. "Why?"

Maggie stared at the glass of wine, hoping it might give her an answer. "I really don't know."

"You must—"

"I'm tired? Tired of working, of being the responsible, dependable one? Of taking shit from Paul? I'm tired of missing my husband and justifying my interest in Ben to my girls? I'm tired of holding things together for everyone. I'm so fucking tired all the time."

"Maggie..."

She waved away Brenna's attempt to reach for her, Kayleigh's shift in the chair, the expression of pity in Cat's eyes. "No, don't say anything. This is the hand I was dealt, and I'll deal with it. I always do."

"We can help."

"What, exactly, can you do? It's great that you're here to pitch in when I need something, but really, Cat, what can you do? I quit my job. It was a stupid thing to do. I have to support my girls, and now I'm on my own." The fear rushed at her like a linebacker; the thought of being penniless, homeless, her girls alone and scared. She swung out her chair to pace across the room with angry strides.

"You have that insurance money," Brenna said, watching her with a worried gaze.

"It won't last forever. You know, that cheque was the last thing that flashed through my mind before I told Paul, so I guess I'll blame that. Because I have a chunk of change sitting patiently in the bank for me. Oops." Maggie covered her mouth with her hand and glanced at Dory. "You're not going to try to steal that money from me, are you, Dory? Because I may forgive more than these two, but I certainly don't forget."

She regretted the words as soon as they were out of her mouth.

Dory's mouth tightened, and her eyes were hard glints of green light. "This was a mistake."

"You think?" Cat laughed, a rough bark that rang through the room like a bell had been rung.

"I thought maybe enough time had passed."

"How much time does need to pass after you try and cheat your family?" Kayleigh asked, a finger on her chin. "Before you can be welcomed back into the fold?"

"Stop it," Brenna said quietly.

"Brenna and I had to fight it out before I forgave her," Cat offered. "You up for it, Dory? Because I'd love to go a round with you."

"This escalated quickly," Brenna said wryly, as she pressed a neatly folded T-shirt to Clare's pile.

"No one is fighting," Maggie announced. "I can't deal with this tonight. I had the cops at my door Monday night and I don't want them back." She raised her eyes to the ceiling. "It was only Caleb, but still. Not fun."

"How is Caleb?" Dory asked.

Maggie glanced at her with amazement. Dory was still here, not as relaxed as she started out, but still sitting with Brenna. Back when they were growing up, arguing with Dory was like arguing with an imaginary friend—Dory would make her digs and sniped remarks and then escape before anyone could turn the tables on her.

Maybe she had changed.

Why, are you planning on going through all the Todd boys?" Cat raised an eyebrow as she reached for the wine bottle. "You asked about Seamus and now Caleb. Liam's good, by the way, but his son's on the shit list with Maggie because he knocked up her daughter. Now, let's get back to what you think you have planned for us."

"Those boys always seemed to be of interest to this family," Dory said, ignoring Cat's last words.

Maggie didn't hear the car pull in but saw the headlights just as the dogs barked a warning. "Who else is here?" she muttered as she headed for the door. Her wish for an early bedtime seemed like a forgotten dream.

She made it to the door in time to see Fiona Todd hop up the steps to the porch.

"You don't look happy to see me," Fiona said with a smile.

"Surprised is more like it." Maggie held the screen door open for her. "Look who's here," she announced to the room.

"I heard the five of you were here," Fiona said. "I thought someone better come and check on you, just in case things got out of hand."

Maggie met Cat's gaze. "That's scary timing," Cat said.

Chapter Twenty-Five

"Wine?" Brenna invited. She quickly swept the piles of clothes back into the basket as Cat got another wineglass from the kitchen. Maggie hovered by the door as Fiona smiled at the gathering.

She still wore her Woody's shirt, her short dark hair greying more every year. Maggie thought Fiona looked too young for having a great-grandchild on the way. "It's good to see you together," she said. "And good to see *you*, Dory."

Dory stood to hug Fiona, giving the woman more affection than she'd given Maggie or the others that day. Fiona settled on the couch beside Dory, accepting the glass of wine Brenna poured. "What'd I miss?"

Maggie took her chair, hating the thought that Fiona was intruding. Fiona had always been in their lives, so why did she suddenly wish she hadn't stopped by?

"Cat and Dory were about to go a round," Kayleigh said, her hand reaching for the bowl of potato chips.

"That's not the best idea, is it?" Fiona admonished. "You'd wake the girls. I assume they're all tucked into bed by now." She turned to Maggie. "Good job. That's pretty early." A wistful smile crossed her face. "This reminds me of when Carly used to put you girls down early so she could come over for a glass of wine. It didn't happen often, only when Roger was home."

"She left the house?" The image of bedridden Carly out of the house, engaged in normal activities struck Maggie as odd.

"That was when Dory was a baby, I think. Maybe Brenna."

"When did she start staying in bed all day?" Cat asked quietly.

Maggie realized their positions had changed since Fiona arrived. The surge of hostility and tempers had dissipated as quickly as they had come. Now, they sat hunched, leaning forward toward Fiona. Dory's arrival faded into the background, Maggie forgot about her job for a moment. There were so many stories and rumours about Carly Skatt but no one ever *talked* about her to them.

It was like the town wanted them to forget about her.

Fiona took a sip of wine and settled into the couch. "I didn't come over here to talk about your mother."

"What if we want you to?" Brenna asked. "There's so little we know about her. Cat and I—" She waved her hand between them. "We hardly remember anything."

"I don't know what there is for you to remember." She glanced apologetically at Maggie, swept her gaze to the others. "It's been so long since I've been in the same room with all of you. I have to admit it's nice. I'd rather catch up with you than talk about old times."

"I'm glad you stopped by," Maggie said politely. She wanted the conversation to go back to Carly. Why was Fiona stalling?

"Seamus tell you we were here?" Cat asked.

"He was a little worried," Fiona admitted.

"He had no reason to be," Dory said.

Cat guffawed rudely. "Oh, you think you have nothing to be worried about? You better stay away from my house."

"It's my house too," Brenna reminded her. "*Our* B & B."

"How's that going?" Fiona asked, sounding eager to change the subject.

Kayleigh shook her head. "Uh uh. You were going on a Carly rant, so let's hear it."

"I wasn't going to rant about her." Fiona leaned back against the couch, shoulders slumping as if in defeat.

"What if *we* need to?" Cat asked. "Go on a rant."

"I don't think you do." Fiona smiled knowingly. "That wouldn't be good for any of you."

"I think that's up to us to decide," Maggie said. Fiona glanced at Maggie at the sound of coolness in her voice and nodded.

"Carly took to her room whenever she found out about one of Roger's affairs," Fiona began with no preamble. "He was not a good husband."

"That's putting it lightly."

Maggie raised her eyebrows at Dory's words. Dory had always been their father's champion, even spending years chasing him down. It might have been more touching had she been trying to get to know him, rather than setting up a plan to con her sisters.

"Every time he cheated, it hit her a little harder," Fiona continued. "I'm not saying that was the reason. You all know the same as I do that she was most likely bipolar. But it was his fault she started hiding in her room."

"How many affairs?" Brenna asked hoarsely.

Fiona shook her head. "That's ancient history and he's not worth talking about. You want to know about your mother." She stared across the room like she was looking into the past. "When we were young, about Clare's age, we got lost in the woods. We had to stay out all night, and I've never been so scared. But Carly kept talking and telling me stories so I wouldn't be afraid. And as soon as the sun came up, she found our way home."

She turned to Kayleigh. "She loved Christmas. I think that's where you got it. She always had decorations up at the end of November and every night for the week before Christmas, she'd read *Twas the Night Before Christmas* to you."

"What else?" Cat whispered as if she was starving for another bite of food.

"She was an amazing cook. She never had a cookbook, said she couldn't be bothered. She'd figure it out herself. But she was a horrible baker. She made me a birthday cake once, and I swear it chipped the floor when she dropped it, it was so hard." Fiona laughed at the memory.

"What else?" Kayleigh asked eagerly.

Maggie wanted to join in but couldn't shake the realization that she was listening to talk about a person she didn't know. Carly wasn't her mother. Maggie was the result of her father's infidelity, a story that had never been told.

It was time to find out why.

Maggie's heart began to race at the idea of knowing more, knowing the who and where and what about her life. She'd always pushed away the thought of finding out the truth of her biological mother, of sweeping aside the questions because there had always been more to focus on.

She opened her mouth, ready to interrupt another of Fiona's stories when heavy footsteps on the stairs distracted her. "Mom?"

Maggie was out of the chair in an instant. "Addison. What's wrong?"

"It hurts." Addison's face was in a grimace of pain. Fiona was there before Addison was halfway down the stairs.

"Are you in labour?" Cat demanded. "I thought you weren't due for another couple of weeks."

"I don't know." Maggie helped Addison down the stairs, one arm around her daughter's waist, the other holding her hand. Addison groaned as she took the last step and squeezed Maggie's hand.

"It hurts—here." Addison pressed her side.

"Did your water break?" Maggie asked.

"No, it just hurts." Addison hissed through her teeth. "Now it's really bad."

"Breathe, just like you learned in your classes," Fiona said.

"Adam knew how to do the breathing."

"Well, Adam's not here," Maggie said briskly. "But we are and we'll get you through it. Do you want to sit?"

"No, it's better standing up. Ow..." Addison panted like a dog, complete with tongue hanging out. The sight made Maggie fight down a giggle. Had Addison learned anything from prenatal classes?

"What do you want us to do?" Brenna asked, wringing her hands, hovering at Addison's side.

"Give her some room to start," Maggie snapped. "Can you stay with the girls if I take her to the hospital?" She rubbed Addison's back, her mind racing to what was needed. Brenna could stay with the girls, Maggie would back a small bag for Addison—

"I can't go to the hospital," Addison shrieked. Maggie reared back. "Brady's out with his friends, and he'll never be able to get there in time."

"I don't think your baby's going to care," Maggie said grimly. "*You're* having the baby, not Brady. He doesn't even have to be there."

"Seamus can find him," Cat promised.

"I don't want to go," Addison wailed, tears beginning to fall. "I'll wait and—oh god it hurt—she can get there and..." She trailed off suddenly. "It stopped."

"Don't you pretend you're not in labour if you are," Maggie cried. "Brady can get there when he can."

"I'm not. It, the pain, it just stopped." Addison took a deep breath, and then another, straightening her back. "That's all. Is there going to be more?"

"If you're in labour there will be." Maggie checked the clock on the wall.

"It might be Braxton Hicks," Fiona said knowingly, taking a step back.

"That hurt like hell," Addison announced. "I don't think I'm going to like this giving birth stuff."

"Nobody does," Dory said.

They waited, still grouped around Addison, each checking the clock. Kayleigh counted down each minute that passed, while

Brenna peppered Addison with questions about how she was feeling.

Fiona returned to the couch with Dory, chatting quietly.

"That's five minutes," Maggie announced. "Any more pains?"

Addison shook her head with wide eyes. "Is that it? Those Braxton Hicks things?"

"Maybe. Give it a couple more minutes." Maggie pushed a stray hair behind Addison's ear and looked at her closely. "You've been out of sorts for the past couple of days. I wouldn't be surprised if you went early."

"She left her husband and moved home," Cat said dryly. "That'd make anyone out of sorts."

"What's Adam think about all of this?" Brenna asked.

"He called a lawyer," Addison said matter-of-factly. "So he doesn't think much of it."

Brenna sighed. "Get me the name of the lawyer, and I'll sort things out for you. If that's what you want?" She looked earnestly at Addison.

"Has anyone asked if we're sure that it is *Brady's*?" Cat looked around, shrugging her shoulders. "It's a good question."

"It's Brady's baby," Addison said firmly. "It's been over with Adam for a while, but neither of us wanted to admit it."

"So you decided to do something to make him admit it."

"Cat," Brenna hissed.

"What? I'm the queen of failed marriages in these parts, so I'm allowed to make the nasty comments."

"No one is making nasty comments to my daughter." Maggie glared at Cat, tucked her arm around Addison. "It's been seven minutes without another pain. I think it's safe to say you're not in labour. Let's get you back to bed."

Chapter Twenty-Six

W HEN MAGGIE RETURNED AFTER seeing Addison back to bed, only Brenna and Dory were still there. Maggie smiled with amazement as the two of them finished folding her basket of laundry. She'd never seen Dory do laundry, even when she lived at home. She used to convince Brenna to do it for her.

"Fiona went to track down Brady." Brenna giggled, carefully moving Kady's pile of clothes back into the basket. "I almost feel sorry for him. Seamus came to get Cat and took Kayleigh. Joss is coming for me."

Maggie took a seat and reached for the bowl of potato chips.

"Is that the big guy you were with when I was back before?" Dory asked, handing Brenna Clare's pile. "The bald guy, with the motorcycle?"

"That's the one," Brenna admitted with a smile.

"He doesn't seem your type."

"Before I came back, he was definitely not my type." Brenna laughed. "But he's sort of grown on me."

"That's good. I'm glad you're happy."

"Thanks." Brenna narrowed her eyes and gave Maggie a sideways glance, which Maggie understood all too clearly. She couldn't remember Dory ever being concerned with their happiness. Growing up, Dory would do what she could to *ruin* happiness.

Dory was different. She was making an effort, and it was making Maggie nervous.

"I'm serious," Dory insisted. "I know I've done a lot that I have to make up for, but I want you to be happy. I want Cat to be happy, and Kayleigh." She turned to Maggie. "And you. I'm sorry I wasn't here for the funeral."

Maggie stilled her hand in the potato chip bowl and stared at Dory. Now? Eight months after Maggie's life exploded, and Dory couldn't be bothered to come or to send word—*now* she was getting an explanation? "No, you weren't here."

"I...couldn't." Dory lifted her chin and glanced imploringly at Maggie. "I had things going on in my life that couldn't wait. I'm sorry." Her gaze took in Brenna, who sank into the couch with an almost imperceptible shake of her head. "I'm so sorry I couldn't take the time to be there for you."

Maggie had managed to push away the disappointment and hurt that Dory's absence caused, but now that it was in front of her again, the tightness around her heart squeezed painfully. "You didn't even call."

"You didn't need me." There was no bitterness in Dory's voice, only sadness.

"You don't know what I need."

"Have you ever needed me?" In the past, such a question from Dory would have been thrown with the added power of resentment and antagonism. Now, it was simply a question.

One that Maggie couldn't answer. "You should have been here," she said instead. "Mike loved you."

Dory nodded, a sad smile at the corners of her mouth. "He was always good to me, no matter what I did. He'd only get mad at me when I talked back to you. The time you tried to stop me going out with Burt Kenny and we had that screaming match..."

"You were only fifteen. Burt Kenny was ten years older than you." Maggie recalled the night as clearly as it was yesterday. Catching Dory crawling out her bedroom window, dressed in tight jeans and a top that barely covered the essentials, their shouting waking up the others.

"It was actually illegal," Brenna said in a quiet voice.

"I'm sure he thought what I did to him when he tried to put his hands on me was illegal too." Dory grinned wolfishly. "I could look after myself."

"That was supposed to be my job," Maggie said ruefully.

"You had enough on your plate." Dory took a sip of wine, and then another. "Asking you to be a mother to all four of us wasn't fair."

Brenna laughed ruefully. "I don't remember anyone ever asking."

"Maybe. I did what I needed to do," Maggie said simply. "I'm not trying to be a martyr, but I had to take care of you because I was afraid of what would happen if I didn't."

"That I would end up wilder than I did?" Dory asked.

"That they would take you away." Maggie swallowed her long-ago fear of losing her sisters. "They could have—Children's Aid could have stepped in. I couldn't let that happen."

"I asked Fiona about it once," Brenna offered. "She said basically, the town decided that you were mature enough and you were doing a good job, and it was best for us all to leave things the way they were. Plus, they all thought Carly would eventually snap out of it."

"I wonder if she would have "snapped out" of it if they'd taken us away?" Dory mused. "I'm glad they didn't try. Staying with you was the best thing for us. I can't imagine what I would've turned out like if it hadn't been for you, Maggie. And Mike. I loved him, despite how I treated him. I should have told him. I should have told you too."

Maggie glanced sideways at Brenna, who had the same expression of disbelief as Maggie did. "Tell me what?"

"That I love you."

The room was silent save for the soft clink of Dory's glass as she set it on the table before her. Maggie's throat grew tight. She knew her sisters loved her; she loved them with all her heart. But they never said the words.

"I'm grateful for you taking care of me," Dory continued. "I wasn't the easiest kid." She smiled ruefully.

"No. No, not really." Maggie didn't know what else to say. "Dory..."

"I need to apologize for that," she interrupted. "And for a lot of other things, but that's a start." Dory yawned. "I've had enough excitement for one day. Is it still okay that I stay in Addison's room?"

Maggie was startled at the abrupt change of topic. Maybe Dory could only handle so much. "You may not get much sleep. She'll be tossing and turning for a while yet."

"And you're sure that wasn't labour?" Brenna asked nervously. "If she starts and you're in the room…"

"I can deal with a little labour pain," Dory said with a laugh. She pulled herself off the couch. As she stretched, Maggie realized how beautiful her sister was. Cat and Brenna were attractive, especially Brenna when she smiled, but Dory's delicate features and big green eyes put the rest of them to shame.

Brenna laughed, pulling Maggie's attention away from Dory. "Addison was a bit of a bridezilla when she got married. I can't imagine what she's going to be like when she goes into labour."

"She was pretty horrible," Maggie agreed. "But I think she'll be okay tonight. Her due date isn't for a few weeks."

"Addison came three weeks early," Dory reminded her.

Maggie looked at Dory with astonishment. "You remember that?"

Dory rolled her eyes. "How could I forget? Mike was somewhere playing ball, and Kayleigh took you to the hospital. She'd only had her license for about a week."

"She was a total trouper," Maggie said fondly. "I was yelling at her to speed up one minute and slow down the next."

"You made me stay at home with Cat and Brenna," Dory said, her face falling into the characteristic sullen pout from their childhood.

Maggie gave Brenna a sideways glance. Maybe Dory hadn't changed so much after all. "Sorry to have wrecked your plans."

"I was leaving that night."

Maggie froze. "What are you talking about?"

"Leaving where?" Brenna asked.

Dory shrugged and began picking up the wine glasses on the coffee table. Maggie rose and touched her arm. "What do you mean?"

Dory took a deep breath. "That had been the night that I first planned to leave. Run away, if you want to call it that."

Maggie swallowed, trying to get moisture into her suddenly dry throat. "You were fourteen. Where were you going?"

Dory shrugged again and took the glasses to the kitchen without answering. Maggie turned to Brenna. "Did you know about this?"

"I was eight. She barely talked to me, so no, I knew nothing." Headlights flashed against the window. "That's Joss. Are you going to be okay with her?"

"What choice do I have? It's not like Cat's going to take her in."

"I meant Addison."

Maggie smiled grimly. "I've had five children. I think I'm okay." She walked Brenna to the door, waved at Joss on the back of his motorcycle.

"Brenna gone?" Dory asked, coming out of the kitchen to the roar of Joss' departing bike.

Maggie locked the door, turned off the outside lights. "What did you mean about that? That you were going to leave?" she demanded.

Dory smiled ruefully. "I'll save that for another day. I'm going to get some sleep. Night, Maggie."

Maggie huffed with impatience. Dory might have changed, but her flair for the dramatic hadn't. "Good night."

Dory climbed the stairs, her slim hips moving under her dress. Maggie waited until she was at the top before she turned out the lights and made her way up in the dark.

She took her time getting ready for bed, knowing that sleep would evade her that night. Her mind whirled with questions about Malcolm, replaying the expression on Paul's face and how it felt when Evie hugged her.

Maggie did what she could to turn her mind off as she lay in bed, focusing on the cool sheets, the soft breeze floating in through the window. The smell of freshly cut grass drifted in, courtesy of Brady's visit to the neighbours, as well as the faint aroma of the lilac trees in bloom. She'd left the curtains open enough for a sliver of moonlight to cut through the darkness, creating shadows in the corners.

As she rolled onto her side, the room was lit enough for her to see the smoothness of Mike's side of the bed, the pillowcase faded from repeated washings.

It took Maggie a moment to realize Mike's pillow held a faint indent like a head had laid down on it.

She stared at it for a long moment. One of the girls must have been in the room. It would be something McKenna would do—lie on her father's side of the bed to feel close to him. Slowly, she reached out a hand, not noticing her fingers were trembling slightly and touched the indent.

It was warm.

Maggie sucked in her breath but didn't move. Instead, she spread out her fingers, covering a few of the flowers on the pillowcase.

"Mike?" She held her breath as she listened, but only the sounds of the night intruded on the silence. A floorboard creaked somewhere in the house, and the pipes groaned.

They were the usual sounds of the house, but each one lifted the hairs on the back of Maggie's neck.

"Are you here?"

The room didn't turn cold, and there was no overpowering scent like in Carly's room. But something told Maggie not to be afraid.

It'll be okay.

Maggie knew the voice was in her head, but it was Mike's voice. *It'll be okay* had been his catchphrase, his answer to everything.

When Kady had come home from school in tears in grade three, after fighting with her best friend, Mike had given Kady a big hug and taken her outside to play catch. *"It'll be okay,"* he'd told her.

When Maggie had been six months pregnant with Clare and began to bleed, Mike had found her in tears in the bathroom, unwilling to move in case she somehow did something to the baby. He had hugged her tightly. *"It'll be okay."*

"How do you know?" she had cried into his shoulder.

"Because I do."

When, two days before her wedding, Addison had erupted in frightened tears, it had been Mike who had comforted her.

"It'll be okay," Mike had said.

"You can't know that!"

"But I do. Because it has to. It'll be okay, Addie; it always is."

And it always was.

"You're here," Maggie said aloud.

The only reply was the night breeze through the crack in the window, fluttering the curtains like they were sheets on a clothesline on a windy day.

I love you.

It'll be okay.

Maggie fell asleep, her face wet with tears, and her hand fisting the corner of the pillow.

Chapter Twenty-Seven

MAGGIE WOKE UP FEELING more cheerful than she had in a long time. Even the early morning chaos didn't faze her. She shushed Kady and Clare's squabbling, asked them to be quiet to let Addison and Dory sleep. No one noticed she wasn't rushing to get to work, or that she wore a faded pair of jeans instead of the basic black work pants that always smelled faintly of bread.

When the bus had driven off, Maggie let the dogs out the back door, then poured herself a second cup of coffee and joined them on the deck.

It was going to be okay.

The sun was shining and a breeze ruffled Maggie's hair, loose and damp against her shoulders. It was nice not to have it pulled back into her ponytail. She could hear the cars laboring to get up the hill, the neighbours to the right talking loudly by their car.

Voices rose from the trails in the woods that wound behind the house. She craned her neck to see who it was but only caught a glimpse of a blue shirt, probably someone taking an early morning walk.

Mike and McKenna used to go for walks nearly every weekend. Maggie never joined them, enjoying the thought that they could have something together. McKenna was the only one of the girls who didn't play baseball, as much as Mike had encouraged her. So he had made sure they still shared something.

Maybe Maggie would take McKenna for a walk in the woods this weekend. It had been so long since she had stretched her legs doing anything other than rushing around FoodMart.

It would do them both good.

Sometime later, Addison found her on the deck, with a page ripped out of Kady's forgotten math notebook and one of Clare's glittery pens, making plans.

"What are you doing out here?" Addison asked, still in an old nightshirt and bare feet. One of the dogs rushed back from where he was sniffing the grass around the deck to say hello.

"How are you feeling?" Maggie asked, gesturing to the chair beside her. Addison sank into it with a groan, dropping her hand to rub Charles' ears.

"Everything hurts," Addison complained. "I'm so tired all the time. I told them I couldn't come into work again."

"You should stop working now, anyway." Maggie capped her pen and set the notebook on the table at her side. She reached out to touch Addison's belly, swollen and straining her nightshirt. "You'll need all the rest you can for when the baby comes. How did you sleep?"

Addison glanced at her with purple-shadowed eyes. "What's sleep?"

"Is Dory still in bed?"

"Yeah. We were up talking for a while, so I don't know how much sleep she got."

Maggie pushed away the momentary swell of jealousy. "We'll let her sleep. Listen, we need to talk about the baby."

"Having the baby?" Addison frowned with confusion.

"I meant when she's born. Are you staying here, or will you and Brady..." Maggie was unwilling to finish the thought. "You said you talked to Adam. You need to figure this out. Hopefully before the baby comes."

Addison was quiet for a moment, and Maggie watched her formulate her thoughts. Brady lived over his parents' garage, and Maggie hated the thought of Addison and the baby being shuffled there. She and Adam had been saving to buy a house, but still lived in a nice apartment in nearby Elliot Lake.

"Can I stay here?" Addison asked in a quiet voice.

"Of course. Is that what you want? Is there any chance with you and Adam?"

"Adam..." Addison swallowed, and Maggie saw the hurt in her eyes. "Adam's been seeing someone else for a while. I knew about it but didn't want to admit it because it's embarrassing. I didn't want to say anything in front of everyone last night."

"You were seeing someone too," Maggie pointed out.

"Yes, but I couldn't make him happy. What's that say about me?"

"It doesn't say anything about you. Marriage doesn't always work, Addison. Look at your aunts."

"Look at you and Daddy," Addison pointed out.

Maggie smiled fondly and leaned back into her chair. "No one is the man your father was. But even he wasn't perfect. You know what used to drive me crazy about him? He'd always pull off his underwear with his pants, so it would end up in this tangled mess I'd have to pull apart when I did the laundry. It drove me crazy!"

"I guess I never did the laundry," Addison said ruefully.

"I remember I exploded at him once," Maggie continued, her thoughts in the past. "I yelled and threw his underwear at him. Do you know what he did?"

Addison shook her head.

"Went out and bought a new washing machine. The old one kept leaking, but I was making do with it. We didn't have the money saved up yet for a new one. But your dad took the money we had, and some of the money he'd saved for a new truck, and went and bought one.

He said, "I know my dirty underwear causes trouble, but maybe this'll help."

Addison smiled. "I remember the new washing machine. Evie and I played with the box for days."

"Until you left it out in the rain and it fell apart," Maggie said fondly. "I was going to make the two of you pick up all the pieces of soggy cardboard, but your dad got out there first. I never said another word about his underwear being attached to his pants."

She didn't talk about Mike enough with the girls. They were so sad for so long that Maggie never wanted to bring him up. But now, things were getting better and it was time to remember happiness, not just the sadness.

"I want the type of marriage you had," Addison said quietly, her eyes on the trees.

"I want that for you too, and I'm so sorry that it didn't work out with Adam. But do you think Brady—"

Addison held up her hand. "I know you don't like him."

Maggie took Addison's hand and folded her fingers over hers. "Addison, I adore Brady. It's impossible not to. I remember the day he was born, of your dad taking me to the hospital to see him. I had a stuffed bunny as a present. I was pregnant with you and had no idea what to get for a baby boy. When we walked in, Liam was trying to change him." She shook her head with a smile. "Brady peed all over him, and Emily was laughing, too sore to get up and help. Mike jumped in and that's when I found out he had no idea how to change a diaper. I waddled over and fixed Brady up. He was a beautiful baby."

Addison laughed. "I have to tell him that you saw him naked!" She clutched her belly. "Oh, it even hurts to laugh."

Maggie laughed with her. "It was pretty funny, but I don't think Brady would appreciate it as much as we do." They were silent for a moment. "Addison, I need you to be happy," Maggie said slowly. "I need to make sure Brady is the one who can make you happy. I know he's fun and cute, but to be honest, his reputation makes me a bit nervous."

"It's pretty ironic since *our* family was always the one with a reputation. You and Aunt Cat, and Aunt Dory."

Maggie rolled her eyes. "We were the talk of the town in our day," she said ruefully. "But not much has changed, has it?"

"Brady's settled down," Addison said reassuringly. "He still likes to go out, but there's no one else. No other women. He told me."

"Okay."

"I trust him."

"That's a good thing."

"I really love him."

Maggie glanced over, realized she was still holding Addison's hand. "I hope he really loves you too."

"I like the thought of being here, with you," Addison admitted, sounding young and afraid. "Brady doesn't know anything about babies."

"He'll learn."

"He will. He wants to. But for now, until I figure things out, I'd like to stay."

"Of course." Maggie gave Addison's hand a squeeze. "It'll be okay."

Addison glanced at her with surprise. "That's what Dad always said."

"He did." Maggie shrugged with a rueful smile. "And he was right."

After her talk with Addison, Maggie made more notes before heading into town. Her first stop was the bank.

"Maggie. I wondered when I'd be seeing you." Ted Brooks, the manager of the only bank in Forest Hills and Maggie's financial advisor, escorted her into his office the next morning. "How are things?"

"Not great," she replied with a cheerful smile. "But I think they're going to get better."

An hour later, Maggie left Ted's office with a clear plan for the insurance money, involving trust funds and GICs, shares giving her dividends, and education accounts for McKenna, Kady, and Clare. Another one would be set up for Addison's baby, whenever she was born. There was money set aside for a new roof and a few other things that needed to be done around the house. There would be a new car, as soon as Maggie found another job.

The best news, according to the financial advisor, was that she didn't have to find work for six months.

Heady with relief, her footsteps felt light as she left the bank. Now that was taken care of, Maggie felt like she could do anything.

She had the whole day ahead of her, free of any commitments, and it was a dizzying experience, one that kept the smile on her face.

Why had she never thought of quitting her job before?

She left the minivan in the bank's tiny parking lot and crossed the street. When had she ever stopped into the Sandwich Shoppe during the day? She was seeing a new side of Forest Hills. She had time to spare, wasn't rushing to get somewhere, to get something finished.

"Have a great day," she called over her shoulder as she left the Shoppe, the enticing coffee aroma mixing with the sugary smell of the pie, making her mouth water.

Her next stop was Higgins' Hardware.

The store was small and packed to the rooftops with everything a person could need to fix anything, including the kitchen sink. As the bell above the door signaled her arrival, Maggie blinked into the dimness, needing a moment for her eyes to adjust.

"Morning!" She heard Ben's voice in the distance but he was nowhere to be seen. "I'll be with you in a minute."

"Take your time," she called, placing the takeout coffee cups on the counter beside the bag holding the pie.

"Maggie?" Ben appeared from an aisle, a box in his hand. "What are you doing here?"

"Are you the only one who can visit at work?"

Ben's smile was wide, reaching his eyes. Something down in the pit of Maggie woke up and stretched. "I love visits at work." His eyes lit on the coffee beside Maggie. "You brought coffee?"

Maggie picked up a cup and let their fingers touch as she handed it to him. "Do you know I hold you responsible for my coffee addiction? Every time you'd come over to tutor me, you'd bring a Thermos of coffee."

"But you never drank it."

"I loved the smell, but I didn't like the taste. Then. It took a while, but I got the hang of it. For years after, I thought of you every time I smelled coffee."

Maggie didn't think it was possible for Ben's smile to grow any bigger. "What's in the bag?"

"Pie. But it's not for sharing."

"But I like pie."

"I'll remember that for next time. This one is for Cat. We're going for dinner tonight."

Ben sipped his coffee. "A real family dinner with all the sisters. Was it a surprise to see Dory?"

"You could say that. Yesterday was full of surprises. Dory, Evie bringing a boyfriend home, one that's almost the same age as me."

Ben winced. "I saw them at the game last night and wondered. It's so easy to tell who belongs to you." He reached out and smoothed a strand of hair off her temple.

"We were blessed with the colour."

"My favourite." He caught Maggie's gaze and held it over the edge of the cup. "How're you doing?"

Maggie thought for a moment. "Surprisingly well. I assume you mean the job or lack of one."

"Did you mean to quit?"

Maggie laughed. "Does anyone ever really mean to quit their job?"

"So—no."

She shook her head. "No." When he prompted, Maggie gave him a few more details of the previous day. "I think it's a good thing," she finished. "Or it will be when I find another job. Right now I'm afraid I'm going to enjoy this free time a little too much to start looking."

"Maybe you don't have to look."

"That would be too good to be true."

"Maybe not. You're a bookkeeper, aren't you? You took all the courses? I need someone to help me with the books."

"I've never actually helped someone with their books," Maggie admitted. "Other than Cat. And Seamus with Woody's."

"Perfect. I've never run a hardware store. Can't be too different than doing the books for a restaurant."

"Are you serious?"

"Sure, why not? We can figure it out together." Ben winked. "Think of how much fun we can have working together."

Maggie hesitated. She liked Ben, would like to spend more time with him. And yet... even if that had been Mike giving his blessing last night, it didn't feel right. Darn it, Maggie silently cursed, what's holding you back?

"What did I say?" Ben asked with a worried expression in his eyes.

Maggie shook her head. "It's nothing. Nothing that you said."

"Am I pushing you too much?"

She blinked with surprise, gave a nervous laugh. How could Ben know exactly what she had been thinking? "You're not. Yet. I've never... This is all new to me."

"It's new to me too. Tell me if I'm doing something wrong."

"Nothing is wrong. I like...spending time with you," she finished, not ready for a full confession of her feelings. "But Mike was the only other relationship I had and that started in a bit of a rush. I went from zero to sixty pretty quick."

Ben held her gaze again. "Are you telling me you don't want this to go anywhere?"

"No!" Her denial was quick and loud, and Ben gave her a relieved smile. "I don't mean that at all. I don't know what I mean."

"I might know." He put his coffee on the counter and took her cup from her hand before putting his hand on her waist and drawing her close.

Very close. Maggie felt the warmth from his body, smelled the coffee on his breath. "That kiss scared you." He kissed her cheekbone under her eye, a soft brush of his lips.

"I think it scared my girls." Her voice was shaky, probably from the proximity of Ben.

"Not you?"

"No." Her answer was little more than a breath of air. Had it scared her?

It brought her to life.

Eight months of being without Mike had dulled her senses. Made her believe that the touch of another wasn't important. She thought she was ready to move on, but until Ben, Maggie didn't have anywhere to move on to.

"So we'll take it slow?" Ben asked huskily. "If this is something you want."

"I want," she said, not caring if she sounded too eager, too excited.

They laughed softly together and Ben nodded. "So we'll take it slow. Because Maggie, I like this."

"I like you," Maggie blurted.

"I like you too." Leaning forward Ben pressed his lips against hers for a brief moment. "But we'll take it slow."

"Not that slow." Maggie claimed his mouth in a lingering kiss. When she pulled back with a smile, she liked the expression on Ben's face. Content and happy, and hungry for more.

It had been a long time since a man had looked at her like that.

"I thought your girls were scared," Ben said in a low voice, his hand tightening around her waist.

"They're not here, are they? Is anyone here?"

"I hope not."

Maggie kissed Ben again, winding her arms around his neck as he pulled her close.

They stood kissing in the hardware store until the bell signaled the next customer.

Chapter Twenty-Eight

MAGGIE'S NEXT STOP WAS the B & B. As she let herself in, she heard singing from the kitchen.

She paused to listen. Possibly the Spice Girls. It was hard to tell.

Trying not to wince from the assault on her ears, she ignored the stairs a longing glance before heading into the kitchen.

Cat was at the counter, ingredients spread around her in neat order. For someone so laid back, Cat was meticulous when it came to her kitchen, more like Brenna.

She had the mixer on high, as well as earbuds in, so Maggie was able to sneak up. Cat looked up to see Maggie standing almost on top of her and jumped back in shock.

"Your face!" Maggie cried, bursting into laughter. She slid past Cat to put the pie into the refrigerator.

"That's mean." Cat pulled out the headphones. "I could have had a knife in my hand and then where would you be?"

"Skewered by my sister?" Reaching past Cat wielding a wooden spoon as a weapon, Maggie scooped a fingerful of chocolaty batter out of the bowl.

"I'm making that for someone, you know," Cat said drily.

"My fingers are clean. I haven't picked my nose all morning," Maggie joked.

Cat gave her a surprised glance. "You're in a good mood."

"I am. Strange, isn't it?" Maggie grinned around the finger in her mouth.

"A little. Other than Evie coming home, you've had kind of a shitty week."

"I have." She contemplated sneaking more batter but thought better of it. There had to be cookies around here somewhere.

"What have you been doing today?"

"I've got to get a baby room set up, so I was figuring out what I need." Maggie ticked off her fingers as she spied the full cookie jar. "I went to the bank, dealt with my money issues. Bought a pie for supper tonight. And I saw Ben."

"Aha!" Cat waved the spatula and a dollop of batter fell onto the counter. "Ben. Is that why you're so cheerful? What have you been doing with him?"

"Nothing!" Maggie pretended to be affronted, but the smile quickly broke through her guise. "I was talking to him, but nothing."

"Nothing?" Cat narrowed her eyes, and Maggie broke.

"Maybe something," she hedged. "A little kissing."

"Break-the-door-down kissing, like the other night?" Cat asked with a grin.

"No, nothing like that. And we didn't break the door. Kady just opened it on us." Even with the memory of the embarrassment of getting caught by her daughters, Maggie couldn't wipe the smile from her face. "He offered me a job."

"A real job?"

"Doing the books for the hardware store. He says they're a bit of a mess."

"I was thinking about that. You do the books for me and Woody and no one pays you. So we should. And other people will too."

"That's wishful thinking."

"I'm serious." Cat turned on the mixer, drowning out her next words.

Maggie swiped at the blob of batter on the counter that Cat hadn't gotten to and sucked on her finger. "I think Dory's changed," she said when Cat switched the mixer off again.

"Well, that's a pleasant change of topic. She's here, you know. Showed up about twenty minutes ago."

"Have you talked to her yet?"

"Why would I do that?

"Cat." Maggie gave her a disapproving stare. "She's our sister."

Cat gave her an incredulous stare. "What did Ben do to you? Are there some black magic in his kisses?"

"No." Why did the memory of Ben's kiss make her smile?

"Dory's the sister who couldn't be bothered to come home for Mike's funeral. Have you forgotten?"

"No, I haven't forgotten. But what if she's here for a reason, as a cry for help?" She shook her head at Cat's expression of disbelief. "Plus, she seems to know this Malcolm."

Cat's face relaxed. "Ulterior motive. I get it now. They went out, by the way. The two little lovebirds, all smiley and holding hands."

Maggie winced at the image. "Do you really think Malcolm's a nice guy? I haven't had a chance to get to know him."

"I do," Cat said, her expression earnest. "I love Evie, and I wouldn't stand for her being with a guy who wasn't."

"It's not like you to make such a quick judgement about a person." Now Cat looked sheepish and Maggie frowned. "What is it about him that makes you like him?"

"He kind of reminds me of Perry."

"Ah." Perry MacLeod had been Cat's second husband. Their marriage had only lasted a short time before Cat had strayed. "Perry was so nice. He was too good for you."

Cat frowned. "Thanks for the vote of confidence."

"You know you treated him like shit." Maggie pushed off against the counter. "So where is she?"

"Dory? In her room? I have no idea. She's just *here.*" Cat ran the spatula around the bowl.

"I'll let you get back to it. Who's that for?"

Cat's eyes shone with triumph. "Mrs. Fields called when she heard you quit the store. She still needs a cake for her doggies and thought she might take a chance with me."

"I'm glad my quitting got you a job." Maggie grinned over her shoulder.

"I think it will probably save those dogs' lives." She gestured to the counter. "I'm using animal-friendly ingredients and a lot less sugar. Mrs. Fields might not like it, but her fur babies will."

"Every cloud has a silver lining," Maggie said with a smile. "But unfortunately Mrs. Fields won't think so when you don't give her the sugar high."

Leaving Cat to her cake, Maggie checked Dory's room, the library, Brenna's office on the third floor but found no sign of her sister. It wasn't until Maggie walked past Carly's room that she heard a murmur. Knowing there were no guests at the inn, she pushed open the door without knocking.

"Jesus!" Dory's eyes were wide and shocked. "Did you forget about knocking around here?" The shadows under her eyes matched Addison's, but her appearance gave no other indication of a sleepless night. She was dressed in navy shorts, showcasing her long, pale legs, and a cream-coloured sweater, her short curls dropping around her face.

Maggie glanced around the room. Other than the quilt wrinkled underneath Dory, the room was clean and bright, ready for the next guest. The temperature was normal and no floral scent.

"She's not here?"

"Hasn't been yet. Why? Feel like a chat?"

Maggie stepped in. "With you, not her."

"To what do I owe the pleasure?" Dory patted the bed but Maggie remained standing.

"Why are you back?"

"You don't beat around the bush much, do you?" Instead of meeting Maggie's gaze, Dory leaned forward and pulled open the drawer on the little nightstand. It was empty, save for a pad of paper and a pen. "No Bible? Seems pretty sacrilegious for Brenna. She was always the good churchgoer. Maybe that's changed since she's been home."

"No, Bee still goes to church most Sundays."

"That's nice. I've never seen the point. Organized religion has never been my thing."

"Organized anything has never been your thing." Maggie crossed her arms. "But I'm not here for your views on religion."

Dory nodded with a knowing smile. "You want to know about Malcolm. He really *is* a nice guy. Evie's mature enough for an older guy."

Maggie frowned. "How do you know how mature my daughter is? How can you know anything about her?"

"We're Facebook friends."

"Are you serious?"

Dory shrugged. "I looked up your girls when I joined Facebook. I thought I might have more luck with them than the rest of you. Evie lived close to me, and I suggested we meet."

"So you've been living in Toronto." Because of their conversation last night, Maggie tried to remain calm with Dory. Patient.

But she couldn't forget the past—the fights, the arguments, the frustration with her younger sister. Dory could always push her buttons, and Maggie prayed that it wouldn't come to that.

"For the last few years. Malcolm lives in my building. Evie met him when the two of us were out for brunch."

Dory's words stabbed through Maggie. "Did the two of you go out for brunch often?" There was no denying the iciness of her tone. Maggie knew it was jealousy, plain and simple, but couldn't help it.

"You're mad." Dory heaved a sigh. "So shoot me, I wanted to spend time with my niece and I knew what you'd say. Evie did too." She shrugged. "Evie is a great kid—an amazing woman, but being alone in a city isn't the easiest thing. You always took care of me. I wanted to return the favour. I thought I could help."

Maggie looked searchingly at Dory. "Do you expect me to thank you? For convincing my daughter to lie to me?"

"I don't expect anything from you, Maggie."

The sadness in Dory's voice cut Maggie to the quick. "What's that supposed to mean?"

Dory shifted on the bed, curled one bare leg under her. "Nothing. Just that growing up, I expected more love and attention than I got. I wanted more—all of it, probably. And when I didn't get it, I turned on you." She made a noise in her throat that might have been rueful laughter. "I can't believe some of the stuff I pulled."

Maggie leaned back to fully look at her sister. "Who are you, and what did you do to my sister?"

"I've changed."

"Forgive me, but you can't expect me to fall for that after a few little heart-to-hearts. After what you pulled last time—"

"I know, I know. I felt like I deserved more. It wasn't fair. It wasn't good. It wasn't...sisterly."

"No, it wasn't."

The room fell silent as Maggie mulled over Dory's words. She could see the changes in Dory, but were they real? Was this the true Dory, or was she pretending? Maggie hated to be so untrusting, but it was difficult to forget the past, as much as she might have wanted to.

"Is Dad still in Toronto?" Maggie asked hesitantly. She hadn't seen or spoken to their father for three years. She'd received a sympathy card from him when Mike died, but no more. His silence had been the last nail in the coffin for their relationship.

"No," Dory said shortly.

Maggie bit her lip. She couldn't care less about Roger Ebans' whereabouts but had to ask the question. "When you were speaking with Dad, did he ever say anything about my mother? My real mother? Not Carly?"

Dory shook her head. "Never. And I asked. I really tried to get it out of him. Why?"

"I've been spending a bit of time here, in this room."

"With Mom? Carly?"

Maggie took a deep breath. "I tried to convince myself it was Mike, that I was talking to Mike, but I knew it wasn't. If he was a ghost, there'd be no way he'd hang around here. He'd come home, to us."

It had been something Maggie had known in the back of her mind but never wanted to admit. After last night, she was ready to accept it. Her visits had been with Carly, not Mike. She'd poured her heart out to Carly, not Mike.

She was surprised how little the thought of it bothered her. Carly had offered little for Maggie while she had been alive—forcing Maggie to grow up early, take responsibilities above and beyond what a young girl should have had to take. It seemed almost ironic that in death, Carly had finally stepped up.

Dory glanced at her with a curious expression. "I guess."

"I liked believing he was here. I would come every week and talk to him. I don't know why I'm telling you this."

"Because you need to tell someone, and I just happen to be here?"

"I don't need anything," Maggie said quietly. "I never did."

"You never let yourself need," Dory corrected, her voice firm. "You needed more than any of us, but you never allowed yourself to admit it."

"How could I?" Maggie asked. She shook her head. "I don't want to talk about this. It's not about what I need or don't need. I want to know if you know who my real mother is."

Each second the pause became longer, more drawn out, the tighter Maggie's nerves stretched. "Who?" she finally demanded.

"I don't know for sure," Dory said reluctantly. "He would never tell me."

"Who do *you* think?"

Dory took a deep breath and met Maggie's anguished gaze. "I've always thought it was Fiona," she admitted.

"Fiona! Fiona...Todd?" Maggie's emotions erupted. Relief, happiness, understanding was the first to hit, like a gentle wave hitting the shore. Fiona had been more of a mother to Maggie than Carly ever had been. It wasn't a shock; she wasn't a stranger. It would be good if Fiona was her mother.

Then the tsunami hit.

Maggie leaped off the bed. "That can't be possible. No. "

"But it makes sense, doesn't it?" Dory pressed. "She was here all the time. She really looked out for us; she helped you."

"But she can't be!"

"I'm not saying she is. But I think—"

"Addison and Brady are having a baby!" Maggie cried her expression one of anguish. "If Fiona—that would make Liam my brother. That would make Addison and Brady cousins."

Dory's expression mirrored her own "They'd only be half-cousins and that's not... It's not great. It would be like when we found out about Dad and Colin Farrell's mom. Colin was going out with Brenna at the time."

"That was bad enough, but they were just kids! Addison and Brady are having a baby." Maggie shook her head, remembering how upset Brenna had been to discover her new boyfriend was actually her half-brother. Thank goodness Colin and Brenna had done nothing more than share a few kisses.

"Do you think there might be more of us out there? That Dad had more kids?"

"I think this is bad enough."

Maggie paced to the door. She desperately wanted Fiona to be her mother, but the thought made her sick to her stomach. It would make Seamus her half-brother; her half-brother marrying her sister. Liam's sons would be her nephews.

Brady would be her nephew. Brady and Addison would be cousins having a baby, like some medieval times plot twist.

How could Fiona let this happen?

"How can you even suggest such a thing?"

"You asked!" Dory cried. "Talk to Fiona. This is only what I think. I'm probably wrong. She wouldn't let Addison and Brady—she wouldn't let it happen if she knew."

Maggie missed the pounding of footsteps on the stairs, but the hammering on the door yanked her back to reality.

Maggie pulled it open, expecting Cat or Brenna, only to find Malcolm. "I'm sorry to interrupt," he began, holding up his phone. "Evie's trying to reach you. Addison has gone into labour. She says it's not like last night. She's had a bunch of contractions and they're coming fast."

Cat rushed up behind Malcolm, holding Maggie's phone. "Maggie, Addison's tried to call. She's having the baby! You've got to go!"

Chapter Twenty-Nine

M AGGIE'S ONLY THOUGHT WAS Addison.

She forgot about Fiona, her father, and any possible unknown siblings out in the world. Flying down the stairs with Dory and Cat in full pursuit, Maggie was ready to run back home to get to her daughter. Brenna stopped her at the door.

"Hang on a second, let me get my keys," Brenna said frantically. "I'll drive, and Cat can—" She rushed away without finishing her thought.

"She's having the baby!" Cat jumped up and down. "Right now! We've got to go!"

"Let me drive you home," Malcolm said, his voice calm in the face of the excitement.

Maggie took a deep breath. She had been through five of her own births without issue but this was *Addison.* This was her daughter.

"We can pick up Addison and Evie and go right to the hospital," Malcolm continued. He touched Maggie's arm. "Let me help."

Maggie handed him her keys as if she was in a dream. Her baby was about to have a baby.

"We'll be right behind you," Cat promised, still jumping up and down. "You're going to be a grandmother!"

"You're going to be a great-aunt," Maggie shot back over her shoulder.

"I'll call Kayleigh," Brenna called as Maggie raced out of the house, tripping over the dogs. "And I'll wait until the girls get home from school. Go!"

Malcolm had the car started, and as soon as she hopped in, took off with a squeal of tires.

"It'll be okay," Malcolm said with a reassuring smile. "We can get her there in time."

Maggie thought her heart was about to pound its way out of her chest. "Do you have kids?"

"Not yet," he said apologetically.

"Then don't tell me it's going to be okay because you have no idea what it's like to have your daughter going through this," she snapped.

Malcolm was silent as he pulled into the drive.

Maggie rushed into the house, expecting to find Addison in pieces. Instead, it was Evie who was wringing her hands with an expression of terror on her face.

"Her contractions are three minutes apart," Evie cried as soon as she saw Maggie. "We need to go now."

"We've got time," Addison said, more calmly than Maggie would have thought possible for her eldest daughter. "I called Brady, and he's meeting us—" She stopped suddenly, gripping her stomach.

"Breathe," Evie shouted. "Breathe through it."

"I'm trying." Addison panted through gritted teeth.

"Malcolm's in the car." Maggie did her best to remain calm, but the sight of Addison in pain tore through her heart like nothing she'd ever thought. "We need her bag."

"I got one ready," Evie cried, holding up Clare's pink-and-purple knapsack.

"Then let's go," Maggie ordered, putting her arm around Addison.

"No, wait."

"Addison, there's no time to wait for Brady!"

"No, what about Kady and McKenna? And Clare?"

"Brenna will be here in a minute to wait for them. They'll meet us at the hospital." Maggie did her best to shuffle Addison toward the door, but the girl wasn't budging.

"I want them with me."

Maggie stared at Addison with astonishment. "Addison, we don't have time."

"I'm not having this baby without my sisters." She took a deep breath and straightened. "That's over. I have to go to the bathroom, so we'll wait for them." She waddled off to the tiny bathroom beside the kitchen without waiting for a response.

"Addison," Maggie called after her.

"The bus is here!" Evie shouted. A moment later, McKenna burst into the house with Kady right behind her.

"Why is Evie's boyfriend in our car?" Kady demanded.

"Is Addison having the baby? McKenna cried.

"Get in the car," Maggie said. "She wants you with her."

By the time everyone had piled into the car, Clare's bus had arrived, and the little girl jumped into the van with a gleeful yell.

Malcolm insisted on driving, and Evie sat beside him to give directions.

Maggie sat in one of the two middle seats and held Addison's hand. "You'll be okay," she kept repeating, her teeth practically chattering with fear. Remembering the pain of her own deliveries, realizing Addison was going to have to go through that, sent terror through her. How could Addison handle it?

"I'm fine." Addison exhaled, clutching her stomach. "It hurts a bit more than I expected, but it's okay."

"It's only the beginning," Maggie said apologetically.

"It's gonna feel like you're pooping out a watermelon," Clare called cheerfully from the back seat.

By the time Brady got to the hospital, Addison was settled in a birthing room, her contractions coming quickly.

"It hurts," she moaned as Brady rushed to her side. The contractions had become intense on the drive, and Addison quickly lost her calm composure as the fear of the unknown set in.

Maggie saw the terror in Brady's eyes as he took in Addison, writhing in pain on the bed. Evie hovered at her side offering her ice chips, and Clare hopped about at the foot of her bed, cheering her on. Kady lounged on the chair, intent on her phone, but McKenna stood by Maggie, gripping her hand every time Addison cried out with pain.

Brady slowly backed away from the bed, his eyes growing wide, making him look younger than his twenty-six years. "You've got your sisters—maybe you don't need me in here."

Maggie caught him by the collar as he turned to bolt.

"You're right where you need to be," she said grimly. "Clare, go find your sister some more ice, and get something for me to drink." Clare's eyes rounded as Maggie handed over her wallet. "A Pepsi or something."

Clare laughed. "I thought you meant wine or something."

"There'll be time enough for that when this is over. Get some for everyone." Clare slipped out of the room as Maggie hauled Brady closer to the bed. "She's already eight centimeters."

"Eight—that's good, right?" He stared in horror at the monitor strapped to Addison's stomach, the IV attached to her arm.

"It means it's going to go fast. You'll have your baby soon."

"My baby." At Brady's hushed tone, Evie moved from Addison's side to allow Brady in. He took Addison's hand. "*Our* baby."

"You don't even want to be here! You'd better be ready to help out," Addison cried.

Maggie almost laughed at the shock on Brady's handsome face. "Of course I want to be here."

"Bullshit. You were ready to run." Addison panted as another contraction began.

Brady winced as she squeezed his hand. "What do I do?"

"No other women," Addison grunted. It took a moment for Maggie to realize what she was saying. "No more screwing around."

"No, of course not."

"Don't lie. I know what you're like. No other women," she repeated. "If I give you this baby, it's only me. Promise?"

"I don't think you have a choice," Kady put in. "You're having the baby whether he agrees or not."

"If he wants any part of this baby, he'll agree. If not, I'm kicking him out of the room." Addison bared her teeth, looking fearsome.

"Addie, you can't kick me out," Brady protested weakly.

"No, but I will," Evie said staunchly.

"And I will," McKenna added, stepping forward.

"I'm so giving your ass the boot if you don't tell her what she wants to hear," Kady promised, without lifting her eyes from her screen. "Then I'll give one to your brother for being a stupid jerk."

Maggie couldn't hold back her laughter.

"Addie, I love you," Brady promised. "Only you. Only ever you. I want this. So much." He dropped to his knees on the floor beside the bed.

Please don't let him propose, Maggie pleaded inwardly.

But the moment was cut short by Addison's shout of pain. "Let me stay," Brady begged. "What can I do?"

"Get this baby out of me!"

Forty-five minutes later, Maggie entered the waiting room. It was a crowded place, full of coffee smells and anticipation. Cat, Brenna, and Kayleigh had arrived, along with Seamus and Fiona, joining Malcolm and Dory. "It's a boy!" Maggie announced, her eyes still full of tears of happiness.

"A boy?" Cat gasped.

"We Todds are known for our boys," Fiona said with a happy smile.

Chapter Thirty

"H E'S GOT YOUR RED hair." Maggie cuddled her grandson with one arm, smoothing the soft down on his head with gentle fingers. She'd experienced instant maternal love before, but this was different. This was love for Addison and the baby. Admiration and gratitude for presenting her with the gift of a grandchild.

She even felt friendly toward Brady.

"But he looks like Brady," Addison said. "So if you were wondering if he really is the father…"

"I'm not wondering. I can tell he loves you," Maggie conceded. "Is the dutiful dad back?"

Malcolm had taken the van home with the girls, and Seamus had taken Brady to pick up his truck as well as clothes for Addison and the baby. Evie, in her excitement, had packed a pair of jeans and a towel for Addison.

"He'll be back soon. He keeps texting me." Addison held up her phone.

"I think you scared him with your talk of kicking him out of the delivery room." Maggie smiled proudly.

"When you said I needed to plan, I knew I had to talk to him," Addison said seriously. "I thought I'd have more time."

"I didn't know there was a need to talk to him about that."

"There wasn't. Not really. He says he loves me, and I believe him, but I've been so fat and ugly lately—"

"You were never fat and ugly," Maggie interrupted in a stern voice. "You were pregnant. With this beautiful miracle." She cuddled the baby closer.

"I trust him," Addison said with a tired smile. "And I love him."

"I know."

"It's going to be okay."

Maggie looked at her daughter, at her grandson, who already had her heart. "Of course it will. So have you decided what to name this little guy? Since all you had were girls' names picked out?"

"I really thought I was having a girl," Addison said ruefully. "But I—we—decided on Keegan. Keegan Michael. After Dad."

Maggie pressed her lips to Keegan's head so Addison wouldn't notice the tears in her eyes.

~

Fiona was still in the waiting room. "You stayed," Maggie said with surprise.

"It's my first great-grandchild." Fiona shivered. "That's going to take some getting used to."

"Grandmother is bad enough."

"That's what happens when you start young." She smiled fondly at Maggie, but Maggie didn't return it. "Maggie, what's wrong?"

"I need to ask you something," Maggie said urgently.

There would be no easy way to ask, no easy way to hear the answer. She had pushed the thought from her mind during the delivery, but now it was back, staring her in the face like a Peeping Tom.

As much as Maggie wanted Fiona to be her mother, she wanted it to be true even less. And if it happened to be true, Maggie would never tell a soul. Addison and Brady—she could never do that to them.

"What is it?" Fiona asked, concern evident on her face.

"Are you my birth mother?"

Fiona blinked with surprise. "What are you asking me?"

"Am I your child? Did you and Roger Ebans—"

"*No!*" Fiona cried. "Oh, Maggie, no. Not that I wouldn't love to be your mother, but no. Just no."

A mix of relief and disappointment nearly brought her to her knees. Fiona reached for her arm.

"I would have told you," Fiona continued, her voice gentle. "I could never keep that from you."

"Okay." Maggie pulled away to sit down on the closest chair. She breathed deep, fighting the urge to put her head between her legs.

Fiona knelt by the chair. "Are you okay?"

Maggie gave a shaky laugh. "I didn't know if I wanted it or was scared about it. With Addison and Brady—"

"It would have never gotten that far," Fiona promised. She touched Maggie's head, smoothing her hair like Maggie was a little girl. For a moment, Maggie wanted nothing more than to sit and have Fiona soothe her as a mother would.

"Then who is?" Maggie demanded. She heard Fiona's sigh.

"Do you really want to know?"

"I do. I think it's time. Don't you?"

Fiona smiled grimly. "Good thing we've got the drive back to talk."

Maggie waited impatiently as Fiona slipped into the room to say goodbye to Addison and Brady. Was she really about to find out the truth?

Did she really want to know?

Maggie was quiet as Fiona led the way to her car. As Fiona drove out of the parking garage, her heart hammered more than a pneumatic drill.

She needed to know.

She waited until they were speeding along the highway, the headlights casting shadows along the rocky shoulder. Her voice was tired, resigned. "Who gave birth to me?"

In the faint light from the dashboard, Maggie saw Fiona's shoulders slump. "As much as I'd love to claim that title, Maggie, I'm not your mother. But she *was* a friend of mine. And Carly's. Her name was Elizabeth Connors. Beth. We were good friends."

Beth Connors. She'd never heard that name before. How could the name of her biological mother not produce an iota of recognition?

She took a deep breath, wanting more. "You said you *were* friends. What happened?"

"It's not a nice story, Maggie."

"I don't care."

"Okay, then." Maggie saw that Fiona was gripping the steering wheel, Maybe talking now wasn't the best idea. Fiona wasn't young, and the road was dark...

"Your father–Roger–had chased after Carly for years," Fiona began, and Maggie instantly forgot about any hesitation. "He was completely head over heels for her, mainly because Carly wouldn't give him the time of day. She knew what he was like; everyone did. Roger wanted something until he got it—toys, women, cars, and then he didn't want it anymore. Carly wouldn't let him get her. She kept him at arm's length for years, teasing and playing and flirting, just enough to hold his interest, but nothing more.

"The three of us—Carly, Beth, and I—were the closest of friends. BFFs, you'd call us now. Beth's home life wasn't the best, and we tried to protect her as much as we could, letting her stay at our places when her father was on a bender. It was just her and her father. Her mother had left years ago."

"That's sad," Maggie offered when Fiona paused. Maggie tried to feel sympathy for the woman she'd never met, but it was like pitying a stranger.

"What's really sad is that the three of us were so close, but neither of us knew Beth was in love with Roger."

"In love with him," Maggie echoed.

"So she said. She'd been in love with Roger almost as long as Roger had been chasing Carly. Beth never said a word."

"Why not, if you were such good friends?" For a moment Maggie felt like she was talking to Kady about some high school drama. She had to shake her head to remind herself that this was her mother they were discussing.

"I never got to ask her," Fiona said sadly. "Apparently they'd been sleeping together for most of high school." She heaved a sigh. "We had no idea. I wish we did. I really wish she'd told us."

Maggie swallowed the dryness of her throat. "She got pregnant?"

"Just before we graduated high school, Carly finally decided to give Roger a chance. Maybe she thought she could settle him down, make a man out of him. They dated for about six months, all the while he was still sleeping with Beth."

Maggie made a sound in her throat. "Did he not know Beth was pregnant?"

"She wasn't—not yet. Beth was wonderful, so sweet and funny, but living with her father..." Fiona glanced over at Maggie. "You know how parents can mess you up."

"I do."

"So I don't want you to blame her. She really loved your father, but he treated her appallingly."

"She can join the club. What happened?"

"Roger and Carly got engaged. And Beth got pregnant."

Maggie's heart broke for the mother she never knew, thinking of the pain of heartbreak she must have gone through.

"She hid it from us, hid the pregnancy from everyone. She'd always worn baggy clothes, mainly because they couldn't afford the latest style, but I think it was to hide her body from her father. He was a drunk, a mean one, and Beth probably didn't want him to look at her in...that way."

"What happened to him? My *grandfather*?" She cringed at the word, at the man she pictured in her mind.

"Drank himself to death. He died just before Carly's wedding. She must have felt so alone. Seven months pregnant, and no one in the world knew about it."

"What happened?" Maggie felt like a broken record. "Did my father take the baby from her?"

"Yes, but not like you think." Fiona pulled the car into the right-hand lane to let an impatient pickup roar past them. "Carly and Roger got married. They were happy at first. I don't know what was happening with Beth and Roger—possibly Roger broke it off with her. Roger moved into the house with Carly. They talked about getting their own place, but it never happened. Beth had the baby—"

"What happened?" Maggie stared at Fiona, seeing her expression lit by the dashboard lights. Tears slowly rolled down her cheeks, and Maggie felt like crying herself.

"Three months after Carly got married, Beth had the baby, all alone in the bathroom."

"All by herself? Maggie asked in horror. She'd watched Addison give birth not four hours ago, given birth five times herself, and she couldn't possibly imagine doing it alone.

"I don't know the details. Beth left me a letter. She left one for both me and Carly, but didn't get into what happened with the birth."

"*Left* you a letter?" The pang in Maggie's heart shifted to grief as she realized what Fiona was going to say.

"She died, Maggie. I'm sorry."

Maggie turned to the window. She'd known, deep down, that her biological mother must be dead. Why else would she let someone else raise her baby, someone who wasn't fit to be a parent?

The truth hurt, like a wound poked while still healing.

"How?" she asked in a hollow voice.

Fiona shook her head. "Hemorrhage. I don't know why she didn't call 9-1-1. She obviously knew what was happening because she wrote us letters. It said you were Roger's, that she'd never been with anyone else. Maybe she thought Roger would deny it."

"I'm sure he would've if he could," Maggie said bitterly.

Fiona shrugged. "Maybe. Beth eventually called for help. She must have been so scared. By the time Roger and Carly got there, it was too late." She sniffed and wiped the tears with the back of her hand. "I wish I'd known. I still miss her."

Maggie thought of her mother, alone and scared, in pain, and her heart cracked a little. "That's it?" Her voice felt like it had been scraped raw.

"Carly never forgave him. She stayed because by then she really loved him, but it was never the same between them. In the letter, Beth asked her to raise you like her own. I know she did the best she could."

"Why didn't you take me?"

"I thought of it, more than once, when Carly began to get sick. But Maggie, I couldn't take you away from your sisters, and Roger would never let me take you all. I couldn't. I had three boys and a bad husband. It wasn't the place to bring you into. I did as much as I could for you."

"I know. I know you did."

But what would her life have been like had Fiona been the one to take her in? Or if her mother had lived?

Maggie was silent for the rest of the trip home.

Chapter Thirty-One

T HREE DAYS LATER, THE family gathered for Sunday supper at Cat and Bee's.

Addison was out of the hospital. She watched baby Keegan be passed around to doting aunts and great-aunts with a new mother's worry. Brady hovered over whoever was holding him.

"I'm going upstairs for a minute," Maggie said quietly to Brenna. She had told her sisters the story of her biological mother two days ago but hadn't had a chance to visit Carly's room.

She wasn't sure why she felt the need to visit, only that things needed to be said.

"Everything okay?" Brenna glanced at her warily.

Maggie nodded and tried to smile. Things would be okay, she knew that, but the thoughts of her mother had kept her awake the last few nights. Thinking of what Beth had gone through, what she must have felt, haunted Maggie almost as much as Mike's death.

But she was glad to know the truth at last.

Maggie slipped away and up the stairs. Cat said the room would be empty for the next few days, implying Maggie could visit any time she liked. They had never discussed Maggie's last visit, but Maggie found Cat watching her whenever Ben's name came up.

It came up with more frequency each day. Maggie wasn't sure what was going to happen with her and Ben, but as long as they took it slow, she could figure it out as they went along.

They had plans for next Tuesday. He was taking her to dinner in Elliott Lake, away from the prying eyes of the town.

Maggie resisted the urge to knock as she slowly pushed open the door to Carly's room. The curtains were drawn and fluttered from the open window. Outside the window, the scent of the lilac tree, thick with blooms, filled the air.

Maggie sat on the bed and wondered how to start.

"I know about Beth."

She paused, waiting. Birds chirped. She could hear the sounds of Clare running around the yard with the dogs. Maybe Carly didn't want to hear about it.

Maybe she was hiding, the way she'd hid all through Maggie's childhood. Maggie knew there might have been mental issues, but what she could never forgive Carly for, was that she never tried to help herself.

Carly let herself waste away, knowing her daughters needed her.

Maggie could never do such a thing. She waited another minute, told herself she'd give her a few more.

But as she sat picking at a loose thread on the quilt, the room began to chill and the scent of the flowers heightened.

"Fiona told me about Beth," Maggie said slowly. "It was time I asked about her. I should have done it a long time ago."

She took a deep breath, for once unsure of what to say. Before, when Maggie had visited, she had unloaded her feelings, her thoughts bubbling out in her haste to unburden herself. But this time, she didn't know what to say. "I don't know how to do this. What to say to you. Should I thank you? Of course I appreciate you taking me in like that. It couldn't have been easy."

But it hadn't been easy for Maggie either, living with a woman who was reminded of her husband's infidelity every time she looked at her.

It explained so much.

"I think that's all I need to say to you." Maggie stood up quickly. For years she'd wished she could tell Carly all the things she needed to get off her chest. About how Carly's neglect had hurt, her refusal to care had damaged them all. She'd had anger and resentment simmering all her life.

But there was nothing boiling today. Now there was an empty spot where her anger had been. Maggie would never truly forgive Carly, but the rage was gone.

Maggie had become the woman she was because of Carly. She was strong and dependable, responsible. Maggie was the mother she was today because Carly hadn't been much of one.

"Thank you for taking me in." She paused, unsure of what to say.

Nothing more needed to be said. Carly had helped Maggie through the last months, but now... now Maggie knew she'd be fine on her own.

"I won't be back," she said stiffly. "This time, I really mean it. Goodbye, Carly, and good luck wherever you are." As she stood, the room grew warmer as the scent of the lilacs faded. Would Carly be back?

Maggie lingered in the hallway, staring at the closed door for a long time before she forced herself to go downstairs and join the others.

Supper at Cat's was always a loud event, but that night was even more boisterous than usual. All five of Maggie's daughters were there, as well as the five sisters.

Seamus pointed out that there was a lot of estrogen in the room.

But they fit happily around the heavy oak table. Under the table, Cat's dogs wove around legs, silently begging for scraps of roast chicken.

Brady was teased mercilessly by Seamus and Joss, with little Clare joining in with the hope of making Joss laugh. Maggie saw how she idolized him, making Maggie wish Ben was there so they could begin to get to know him.

"Everything okay upstairs?" Brenna asked, pouring herself another glass of wine. Seamus had shooed the sisters out of the kitchen and they'd taken the wine to the living room, including Dory. Dory had slid into place with the family. Maggie had stopped being surprised to see her, and Cat had let go of some of her hostility. She seemed to fit in better, more naturally, no pushing buttons and causing conflict. It was as if Dory actually wanted to be around her sisters.

"I said my goodbyes." Maggie settled against the couch, happily full from the meal. "No more visits."

"Until the next crisis?" Cat asked.

"I think I can handle the next one on my own."

"What makes you think there'll be another crisis?" Kayleigh asked.

Brenna laughed. "Isn't there always?"

"Well," Cat began. Maggie noticed she was pleating the hem of her shirt, a telltale sign something was bothering her. "I might have the next crisis."

"Sounds ominous." Dory reached for the wine bottle.

"Not really, but there's the potential for a few scary scenes." Cat paused for a long moment, and just as Maggie was about to demand answers, Cat blurted out. "Seamus and I are getting married."

Maggie glanced first at Brenna but seeing as her sister looked calm and composed, turned to Cat with a smile. "You've been getting married for a while now."

"We actually picked a date."

"That's great!" Maggie was the first to reach her, and there was laughter and excited voices as they congratulated her.

It wasn't until they were seated around the table again that Maggie noticed Dory had tears in her eyes. "Are those happy tears?" she demanded.

"Sure." Dory wiped under her eyes. "I'm really happy for you, Cat."

"But..." Kayleigh drawled.

Cat threw up her hands. "You're going to pull a Dory. You're going to say something mean, or tell us something about Dad that will give you all the attention."

"I don't want to do that. I'll tell you another day." Her chair scraped along the floor as she stood up. "I'm going to head back to your place," she said to Maggie.

Brenna caught her hand. "You can't go after that."

"I've spoiled enough over the years. I'm not spoiling this for Cat."

Cat rolled her eyes, her expression mutinous. "We've been engaged for over a year so there's nothing to spoil, but you are ruining things with your drama queen act. *I'm not telling you.*" Her mocking impression of Dory rang through the kitchen.

Brenna tugged her hand until Dory sat down. Maggie watched her with a heavy feeling of dread.

"I was going to tell you tonight," Dory began, gazing at the table before her. "It's the reason I came back. It's not a good one." She raised her head and glanced at each of them. "Two years ago, I had breast cancer. They caught it early, and I beat it. But it's back."

The room was silent until Cat groaned. "You know, that's such a *Dory* thing to do. Tell us this; make us love you again."

Dory looked up at Cat. "Did it work?"

"*Yes,*" Cat said scornfully. "That sucks. The cancer, I mean, not us having to love you again."

"We never stopped loving her," Maggie corrected. "We're sisters. We may not like each other all the time, but we'll always love each other. We'll get through this as we get through everything else."

It was Kayleigh who first reached for Dory's hand. Kayleigh with all of her pent-up resentment towards Dory fading in the wake of Dory's announcement. "It'll be okay," she said with a grim smile.

"It has to be," Cat said, covering their hands with her own.

Chapter Thirty-Two

LATER THAT NIGHT, AFTER Maggie had taken her daughters home, and when her girls were curled up with books or baby phone or an old stuffed duck, she stepped outside.

She turned off the porch light in the hopes of keeping away the bugs and sat on the step to wait.

Her excuse was that she was taking the dogs for the last walk, but the girls knew the dogs were fine on their own outside. Maggie squinted into the darkness as the dogs lifted stiff legs on every blade of grass. The white petunias she had planted that morning glowed in the moonlight. Kady had helped her weed the gardens, surprising both of them with how much she enjoyed it.

A figure appeared, hurrying along the road. Maggie jumped up to meet him as he turned into the driveway. "You walked?"

"My mother told me in no uncertain terms that I was nuts," Ben said with a grin. "But I didn't think you wanted the headlights waking up the girls."

"Clare's the only one asleep," Maggie admitted, leading him back to the porch. "And maybe Addison. I know it's not a big deal, but after everything that's gone on…" She hadn't wanted the girls to know Ben was there, not because she was afraid of his visit bothering them, but more because she didn't want another discussion about him. She didn't want another discussion about anything, period.

"I'm glad you texted." Ben sat on the porch step beside her, sliding closer when the wood gave a warning groan. "How's Addison?"

"She's good." Maggie's voice rang with enthusiasm. "I'm so proud of her. She was such a trouper in the delivery and seeing her with Keegan—even Brady is getting the hang of things. I think they'll be okay."

"How was supper at Cat's?"

Maggie's face fell as she told Ben about Dory, how they had decided she was to stay with Maggie during her upcoming chemotherapy treatments and the recovery. "But I don't want to talk about that right now," she finished. "Tell me about your day."

They sat on the steps and talked. Eventually, the dogs returned and lay panting at their feet, and soon Ben reached over for Maggie's hand as he told her about the plans for his new house.

Maggie smiled and laughed and her heart lifted like a balloon floating into the sky. She liked the warmth of Ben's hand, the solid length of his thigh pressed against hers.

Did that mean she was moving on? Mike had been her life, her love, and she would never get over him. Ben—

Maggie didn't know what Ben was, or what he would be, but she thought Mike would approve.

"It's going to be okay," Ben said in a soft voice as if he could read her thoughts.

"It's going to be just fine," she agreed.

And then, sitting on the steps, enjoying the warm June night, Maggie kissed him.

Next up is Kayleigh and Dory in Stepping Up

Acknowledgments

I love the idea of having a big family.

I grew up with a sister, and our relationship wasn't the best one. (See Coming Home) I loved creating the Skatt/Ebans family because it was something I would have loved to be a part of.

My father grew up in a big family. There were ten of them.

I have five aunts (we lost my Aunt Lois a few years ago.) They are all lovely, caring women, and each one of them has read my book, Coming Home.

It's the only one of my books they all have read.

It was my aunts who gave me the idea to write a sequel, and now a series. Their relationship has inspired me to write Hanging On, as much as my relationship with my sister inspired Coming Home.

I think it was my Aunt Joan who wanted me to tell readers that my aunts are NOTHING like Maggie and her sisters! Deep down, I think they had even better adventures!

So I need to thank my aunts—Aunt Donna, Aunt Della, Aunt Joan, Aunt Jane, and Aunt Lorna. I think you're awesome!

I need to thank my mother because it's our mother and daughter relationship that is the basis for Maggie's relationship with her daughters. I hope no reader thinks Carly was inspired by my mother, because nothing is farther from the truth. Thank you, Mom, for being so great!

Thank you to the girls of Team Kerrazy in the Leaside Girls Softball League, for unknowingly becoming characters in my book. Team Kerrazy, with Coach Holly Kerr, was the Peewee Champions for the second year in 2018. Let's go Team Kerrazy for the Three-peat!

Thank you to my critique partners – Lisa and Estee and Glynn, but especially Nita. I've said it before, and I'll say it again. You make me a better writer.

Thank you to Paula for always fitting me in at the last minute!

Thank you to my Street Team, the amazing bunch of readers who support and want to read what I write! I appreciate you so much!

Thank you to my readers, who follow me from book to book. I write because you read, as simple as that.

And finally, thank you to my family. Being Holly Kerr, Author is a dream come true, but it's nothing compared to being Kaitie, Sam, and Sarah's Mom.

Thanks for reading

Holly xo

Suitor Science

Hating the Chemistry Teacher
Falling for The Suitor
Fraternizing with the Ex
Marrying the Billionaire Best Friend
Loving the Wrong Guy
Finding the One

Love & Alliteration

Perfectly Played
Beautifully Baked
Pleasantly Popped

Don't

Don't Tell Me You Love Me
Don't Want to Be Friends
Don't Stop Me Now
Don't They Know It's Christmas

Sisters in a Small Town

Coming Home
Hanging On
Stepping Up

Charlotte Dodd

The Secret Life of Charlotte Dodd
The Missing Files of Charlotte Dodd
The Best Worst First Date Ever
The Hidden Past of Pippa McGovern
The Last Stand of Charlotte Dodd

Love in Laandia

Royal Rumble
Royal Retelling
Royal Rising
Royal Reluctance

Unexpecting
Unexpectingly Happily Ever After

Absinthe Doesn't Make the Heart Grow Fonder

Oceanic Dreams – I Saw Him Standing There

Cinnamon Rolls and Pumpkin Spice – Coffee Break with the Billionaire

Kid Lit

The Dragon Under the Mountain
The Dragon Under the Dome

www.ingramcontent.com/pod-product-compliance
Lightning Source LLC
Chambersburg PA
CBHW070413310726

48977CB00003B/672